THE STRANGER IN MY BED

AMANDA MCKINNEY

Storm
PUBLISHING

Ebook ISBN: 978-1-83700-227-6
Paperback ISBN: 978-1-83700-229-0

Cover design: Lisa Horton
Cover images: Arcangel, Shutterstock

Published by Storm Publishing.
For further information, visit:
www.stormpublishing.co

Buried Deception

Trail of Deception

Broken Ridge

The Viper

Mad Women

The Raven's Wife

The Widow of Weeping Pines

Berry Springs

The Woods

The Lake

The Storm

The Fog

The Creek

The Shadow

The Cave

Black Rose Mystery

Devil's Gold

Hatchet Hollow

Tomb's Tale

Evil Eye

Sinister Secrets

Standalones

Lethal Legacy

For Henry and Mama

PART ONE

A LITTLE OVER A YEAR AGO

ONE

OLIVIA

"Unidentified male found along riverbank..." The headline ricochets through my head as my Porsche slices through the cold, dark night.

I take a corner too quickly, skidding on the wet pavement. My Saint Laurent handbag tips over in the passenger seat, the contents spilling across the black leather. I glance down at my phone now sitting crookedly on the seat, still lit up with the tail end of the latest headline from only minutes earlier:

Suspected Suicide

My fingers clamp the wheel.

I need to slow down. But I can't. I have to get there—I have to see it for myself.

The Porsche crests a hill, nearly going airborne. I glance in the rearview, then at the moon, pale and swollen, casting a silver glow over the wrought-iron gates and manicured lawns of Potomac Crossing. Every mansion I pass is lit with security lights, a thin veil of safety for the elite tucked behind their fortress-like doors.

If they only knew what happened behind our closed doors.

I grab my phone. Redial.

Still no answer.

"Dammit," I hiss between clenched teeth.

My foot presses harder on the gas.

I fly around a bend and nearly miss the turn for Ridgeview Bridge.

As soon as I hit the span, my stomach drops.

Below, the lake stretches out like a sheet of black glass.

The shoreline is chaos.

I slam on the brakes. The Porsche fishtails, tires shrieking on the pavement before jerking to a stop just off the shoulder, a few feet from the beginning of the bridge.

For a long moment, I can't move. I just stare.

Along the bank, floodlights on tripods cast hard, angular shadows over the rocks and into the bare, skeletal trees that backup to the river. Red-and-blue strobes pulse across the water. Police cruisers are parked at crooked angles. People move in synchronized urgency, ducking under yellow do-not-enter tape. Some wear uniforms, others reflective vests.

Suspected suicide...

It's a hundred-foot fall from the bridge to the water. Unfortunately Ridgeview Bridge is not an uncommon location for people to go when they've decided to end their lives. The sharp, jagged rocks below the surface ensure no room for error.

A masked diver kneels near the edge of the water, his black wetsuit glossy and alien under the lights. Another rises from the depths, water sloughing off his suit like oil. He says something to a man in a long coat, who immediately starts scribbling on a clipboard.

This isn't a search. This is a potential crime scene.

Unidentified male body...

My stomach twists.

I grab my phone and redial Matthew's number for the hundredth time.

Voicemail.

Again.

It's not him. It can't be.

A dark silhouette steps into view a few yards in front of my car, breeching the small slope of land that slides into the river below. I quickly turn off my lights. He is tall and uniformed, holding a flashlight with one hand and speaking into a radio with the other. Another follows, holding a clipboard. They don't notice me parked.

I watch them, forcing myself to breathe, forcing the thought again: *It's not him. It can't be.*

Matthew wouldn't end his life. Hell, there was nothing more important to my husband than himself.

The officers shift toward my direction, and I realize then that I don't have a plan. I'm in my pajamas. I'm half drunk. I don't know what I'm doing. Just that I've been up all night, and the second I saw the breaking news headline, I grabbed my keys and lunged for the door.

I slump against the wheel, the cold leather pressing into my forehead. I close my eyes, inhale.

A memory flashes:

Just three days ago, Matthew leaning in, brushing his lips across my temple as I made coffee. "You're so beautiful," he said. "I never said it enough. And you're mine. How lucky am I? I'm going to make this right, Liv. We're *us* and we're always going to be *us.* The fabulous Mr. and Mrs. Grayson."

I had smiled. Nodded.

Because of course I knew. Everyone did. I was the wife of Matthew Grayson—CEO of Grayson Investments, one of the wealthiest and most influential men in the industry. I was the polished other half of the power couple, the woman who said the right things, smiled on cue, attended the right events, and posed for the cameras from all the right angles.

Now I'm sitting in a parked car at 3:24 a.m., wearing silk pajamas beneath a belted Burberry trench, my hands shaking so violently I can barely keep hold of my phone.

"Matthew," I whisper. "What have you done? What have you done?"

A sudden knock at the window startles me so badly I scream.

It's one of the uniformed officers. Mid-forties, buzz cut, calm eyes. I roll down the window. A blast of sharp winter air cuts through my hair.

He shines a flashlight in my face, nearly blinding me.

"Ma'am, are you alright?"

I nod, blinking, even though I'm clearly not.

He squints, scanning the interior with the light. "We just noticed your car and wanted to make sure..."

I glance past him, down the hill. "What—what happened down there?"

"It appears someone jumped."

"Why all the people, then? It looks like a crime scene."

"It's..." He catches the slip, then corrects. "We *believe* it's someone who is very high profile. Therefore, we're taking extra precaution, per protocol."

My stomach rolls.

"Who found the body?" I ask.

"I'm afraid I can't give details. It's an active scene." He studies me for a moment. "Can I see your identification, please, ma'am?"

I almost drop my driver's license while handing it through the window.

"Mrs. Grayson?"

"Yes."

"Wife of Matthew Grayson?"

"Yes."

"Is..." He pauses in a way that makes me think he's choosing his next words carefully. "Is your husband home this evening?"

"No," I croak.

The officer blinks, straightens, then looks over his shoulder, motioning to his partner, still standing on the slope.

I watch as he steps away, speaks in a low voice to the officer. Their gazes flicker to me.

My heart is pounding so hard it feels like it could burst out of my chest.

The officer returns.

"Ma'am, we'd like you to come to the coroner's office, where they're processing the body right now, if you don't mind."

The *coroner's* office? He means the morgue.

I suddenly can't breathe. Though I feel like I'm falling, I nod anyway.

My hand trembles as I reach for the ignition.

"Oh, no, ma'am," the officer says quickly. "You can leave your car here. We'll drive you."

TWO

OLIVIA

The county morgue sits at the edge of an old industrial corridor. A gray, windowless slab of concrete flanked by scrub grass and chain-link fence. The parking lot is cracked and empty, save for a single dented Corolla parked near the side entrance. A security light buzzes overhead, casting a flickering yellow glow that makes the whole building look like a scene from a crime documentary.

We pull in beside the Corolla and kill the engine.

The officer explained on the ride over that I'd be asked to look at the body—to confirm whether it is, or isn't, Matthew Grayson, my very high-profile husband. But based on the way he looked at me when he said it, I think he already knows the answer.

I think I do, too.

The wind claws at my coat as I step outside.

Our shoes crunch across the gravel shoulder. I catch the officer glancing down at my silk pajama bottoms, and the cartoon red chili peppers that grin up at him. Each pepper has large, googly eyes and manic smiles. Of course, out of all the elegant pajama sets I own, I had to pick the one with grinning chili peppers for this blessed evening.

There's a faded metal plaque by the door that reads: *Montgomery County Medical Examiner's Office.* Below it, a doorbell.

The officer presses it.

The speaker crackles. "Yeah?"

"Officer Alex Martin here. I believe my colleague already called you."

"Yes, be right there."

The door opens with a mechanical click, and a man wearing a white lab coat peers out. Tall, lanky, and somehow looking both exhausted and caffeinated. His hair is unkempt, flecked with gray. Round glasses sit low on a long, crooked nose.

After checking our IDs he introduces himself as Dan Pittman —county coroner—then ushers us inside. The door closes behind us with a heavy *thunk*.

The front of the coroner's office is unremarkable. A scuffed reception desk sits to one side, papers stacked in uneven piles. Two plastic chairs line the opposite wall, their vinyl cushions cracked with age. A heavy metal door at the back of the room leads into the main lab, windowless, separating the living from whatever waits beyond.

Dr. Pittman and Officer Martin exchange glances.

I shift my weight.

"I was going to chill him overnight and start paperwork in the morning," the doctor begins. "Are you sure you want to do this tonight, Mrs. Grayson? You can come back in daylight, when you've had a moment to process."

"No. I won't sleep until I know."

He nods like he understands.

"This way."

We follow Pittman through the metal door and into the coroner's lab. The smell hits me first—an acrid wave of bleach and formaldehyde, barely masking the deeper scent beneath: something sickly-sweet, like meat that's just begun to turn. The center of the room is dominated by two autopsy tables, gleaming under fluorescent lights, surrounded by metal carts lined with bone saws, rib spreaders, scalpels, and shears. The far wall is made up of a row of stainless-steel coolers, with numbered tags. I shudder to think how many are filled with dead bodies.

A black body bag lies on the nearest autopsy table, zipped tight, the shape beneath it unmistakable. My stomach lurches.

Everything in me wants to run.

Officer Martin lingers behind, as if to give me space, as Pittman pulls on a pair of latex gloves with a loud snap. He picks up a clipboard, scans it, then glances back at me.

"The body was recovered around 2 a.m., pronounced dead at the scene. Found near the east shoreline of Ridgeview Lake. No ID on him. Clothes were waterlogged, face and body bruised but mostly intact."

My knees nearly buckle.

"You can stand back if you need to."

I don't move. I can't.

He unzips the bag halfway, slow and deliberate, like he's peeling back something radioactive. The teeth of the zipper screech against the plastic in a sound that makes my skin crawl. A scent wafts out, damp and metallic, tinged with the musty stench of river water.

The face reveals itself to me in slow motion.

Pale, almost translucent skin. Wet hair plastered to his forehead in limp, dark strands. His eyes are closed, swollen, and marred by black bruises. His lips are bluish-gray and slightly parted, as if he meant to say something and never got the chance. The zipper stops at the collarbone, at the blue dress shirt I've ironed a hundred times. I recognize the threading, the faint monogram. It's torn now, dark with mud and blood, stuck to his skin like tissue.

My husband died wearing a suit.

Of course he did.

The sound that escapes me is somewhere between a gasp and a sob.

It's him.

"Can you confirm?" Pittman asks gently.

I nod, tears building behind my eyes. "Yes. That's my husband. That's Matthew Grayson."

I'm faintly aware of Officer Martin behind me, moving closer.

The coroner writes something down. "Does your husband have identifying marks? Scars, tattoos, piercings?"

I swallow hard. Step closer.

"He has a scar," I say. "On his collarbone. From a skiing accident in Zermatt."

Pittman lifts the sheet lower, unbuttons the shirt. There it is. Pale and jagged.

"And a birthmark," I add, "just under the ribs on the left side. It's shaped like a seahorse."

He nods. Pulls the sheet down another few inches. The mark stares up at me.

"That confirms it," he says, voice soft. "You can step out if you need."

And just like that, Matthew is gone.

And I am a widow.

THREE
RACHEL

The week before…

It's barely 7 a.m., and the house is already spinning with activity. Toast pops, the dryer buzzes, the twins, Ashley and Levi, fight over a Lego head that doesn't belong to either of them. I stand in the kitchen, one hand wrapped around a chipped coffee mug, the other pressing into my temple.

The kitchen is small—more like a nook off the living room. Scuffed linoleum floors, cabinets that don't quite shut. The fridge buzzes with effort, covered in crayon drawings and oil change reminders. Paul replaced the sink last spring, said it would stop the leaking. It didn't. But he tried.

Paul walks past me, red hair still damp from the shower, work boots half-laced. He doesn't look at me, just mutters something about being late for the lumberyard. He's been there since high school.

I nod, sip my coffee.

We haven't touched in months.

A year, maybe?

I glance at the window above the sink. The world outside is a blanket of snow and salt and gray skies. There's a factory down the road, and a plow goes by every twenty minutes, like clockwork. Across the street, Mrs. Levine's dog barks at nothing again.

My phone vibrates on the counter. I lift it, reading the message from the school:

> Due to snow, school will be delayed by one hour.
> Please plan accordingly.

Another hour with the kids underfoot.

I force a smile, tuck a wayward strand of blonde hair away from my face, and turn toward the hallway. "Levi, Ashley! Good news! You've got one more hour of cartoons before we have to leave. But if either of you don't stop arguing about the Legos, I'm feeding you frozen broccoli for breakfast tomorrow."

Squeals erupt from the living room. Levi yells something about *Peppa Pig*. Ashley asks if she can wear her Halloween costume to school.

I return to the kitchen and run my fingers along the frayed edge of the red scarf I wear every minute of every day. It doesn't matter that it's threadbare and unraveling, or that it's never been washed. I won't wash it—not ever—because it smells like him.

Paul returns briefly to grab his thermos.

The garage door closes behind him with a soft thud.

I stand there a while, staring out the window, watching the snow fall, knowing that this time next year, I won't be here anymore.

Not in this house.

Not in this life.

The thought used to terrify me. Now it feels like the only way I'll survive.

I haven't said the word *divorce* out loud. Not to Paul. Not even to myself, not fully. But it's there, thick and heavy, pressed between us like all the other things we no longer say.

We got married too young. And now we're just two people orbiting the same tired routine.

He doesn't ask why I go to the park so much. And I don't ask what he's thinking when he stares out at the back yard, jaw tight, eyes dull. We don't fight. We don't touch. We just... exist. Barely.

The truth is, I don't hate my husband. I wish I did—it would be easier that way. But I don't. I think we're both just too tired to fix it.

I clutch the red scarf, memories tugging at me. He gave it to me two winters ago on a walk in the park. I had three unread texts from Paul on my phone that afternoon—texts I didn't even bother to answer.

It had started snowing hard, just like today. The flakes caught in his inky black hair, his eyelashes. We were sitting on a bench, boots buried in white, watching children throw snowballs and lovers pass by arm in arm. I'd made some joke about not being built for winters like this, and he pulled the red scarf from his pocket and wrapped it gently around mine.

"I bought this for you last week," he said.

"You *bought* me something?" I responded, my heart fluttering.

"I did."

"Why?"

"So you always have a piece of me with you," he said, his voice quiet.

It was the first time he touched me like that, and I thought— just for a second—that he might kiss me.

He didn't.

Later, I sat in the driver's seat of my car, the scarf still warm against my skin, and cried without knowing exactly why.

FOUR
OLIVIA

After leaving the morgue, Officer Martin drove me home, promising to bring my car shortly after, which he did.

It's now eight in the morning—only four hours later—when I walk into the police station. Martin said this could wait until the afternoon, but I couldn't sleep.

"We just have a few questions for you," he'd said. "Also, there might be a few additional people who want to interview you, because, you know, your husband's company was being investigated by the SEC."

The station is buzzing with the latest local headline: *CEO Found Dead in River*. The lobby, usually quiet, now brims with tension. Phones ring. Conversation hums in the air. Footsteps echo down tile floors. A television mounted on the wall flickers muted footage—stock photos of Matthew, red banners pulsing across the screen.

Heads turn as I enter. Matthew Grayson's wife.

Even though I'd changed out of my chili pepper pajamas before coming, I feel myself shrinking under the weight of their stares. My suit is dark, my blouse silk, my heels polished, every strand of hair pinned into place. Yet my legs are unsteady. My heart, pounding.

I lift my chin and hold my shoulders back, forcing the brave face I wore through every state banquet, every charity gala, every lie of our marriage. A mask that never once cracked in public—and I sure don't plan on breaking that streak anytime soon.

A young officer meets me at the door and gestures for me to follow. I move without thinking, still half-frozen from the shock of it all.

The shock that my husband ended his life.

They bring me to a windowless room with a table bolted to the floor and two metal chairs that screech when you move them. A pitcher of water sweats in the middle of the table, flanked by two Styrofoam cups.

Two men stand in the room, talking quietly. One is tall—mid-fifties, broad-shouldered, silver hair cropped close—his dark blue suit pressed to perfection. A faint scent of peppermint hangs in the air as he sucks on a red-and-white Starlight mint, the candy clicking softly against his teeth. The other man is shorter, rumpled in a tweed jacket and wrinkled pants.

The tall one steps forward and extends his hand. "Special Agent Ryland," he says.

Special agent? Like the FBI? My stomach rolls.

His grip is firm but not intimidating, his blue eyes steady. Then, as if sensing my nerves, he offers me a mint and a small, genuine smile. I take it, gripping it in my hand, as he excuses himself from the room.

Then, Detective Gibson introduces himself, his voice like gravel. He doesn't look like a man easily surprised—yet something in the way he studies me makes my pulse kick.

"Mrs. Grayson, I appreciate you coming in," he says, settling in across from me. "I know it's been a rough few hours. I just have a few questions, and then we'll get you out of here. Standard procedure."

I clasp my hands in my lap to keep them from shaking, the mint tucked between my palms.

"Of course."

He clicks a pen and starts with the basics. When did I last see Matthew? What was he wearing? Did he seem agitated? Unusual texts? Phone calls?

I answer as best I can. "We had an argument a few days ago, and I left, and stayed in a hotel. We didn't speak or communicate at all during that time. Eventually, I cooled off, came home, and that's when I realized he wasn't there, and it appeared he hadn't been there in a while. And later I saw the headline."

"And this argument—what was it about?"

I swallow deeply. "He confessed to me that his business was under investigation."

"You didn't know?"

"No."

He stares at me for a moment.

I shift in my seat.

"So, he told you... what exactly?"

"That, exactly—that his company was under investigation."

"And you got mad?"

"Of course I did. I had no idea."

The detective tilts his head, studying me.

"And then what?" he asks.

"I told him to leave. He said he wouldn't, said it was his house and reminded me his money paid for the house, and so I packed a bag, grabbed my keys, and I left."

"Where did you go?"

"I drove for eleven hours straight."

His brows pop. "Where did you go?"

"To a small town in Georgia."

"Why?"

"The location wasn't intentional, I just wanted to get as far away from him as possible. I was very, very angry. I didn't have a plan, so I just drove south and ended up in Georgia."

"Where did you stay?"

"I can't remember the name. It was a motel off the interstate. I can get it for you."

"Please do. Thank you." He writes something in his notebook. "Did you use your credit card to check in?"

"Yes."

"Did anyone see you arrive?"

"Aside from the woman at the front desk, I don't think so."

"Do you still have the receipt?"

"I think so."

He scribbles a note. "We'll need that."

"Okay."

"When you left, what was Mr. Grayson's disposition? Angry or depressed? Sad? Pleading?"

"He was angry. Like I said, we'd just gotten into an intense argument."

"Did he touch you?"

"How so?"

"Was he physical with you during this argument?"

"No."

"Never?"

"No."

He jots something down, pauses. "Any history of mental illness? Threats of self-harm?"

I shake my head.

A long silence stretches between us.

Then he says, "From the outside looking in, you and your husband have it all. You have lavish homes on both coasts, one in Hawaii, a co-op in Greece. The media loves you both. You donate to charity. You smile in all the photos. It would appear you have a life that most dream about. I mean, all businesses have issues, right? I imagine your husband could have gotten a hell of a lawyer to handle them, pro bono."

"I don't know where you're going with this."

He squints at his pen, tapping it on the table. "Ending it all feels like a very drastic action considering he hadn't been convicted or arrested for anything. As I understand it, he'd told the SEC investigators that his company was clean."

When I don't respond, he asks, "Do you believe your husband took his own life, Mrs. Grayson?"

I don't answer right away. The word *suicide* still feels foreign, like it belongs to another story.

"I don't know what to believe." My shoulders drop, but I quickly correct, straightening my spine.

"That's fair." Gibson sets his pen down.

"Do *you* think it was a suicide?" I ask.

"That's what the initial report reads, yes. But the autopsy will confirm if there were any defensive wounds or anything to lead us to believe it was something nefarious."

He studies me for a moment, the tip of his pen hovering above the page. The silence stretches. My pulse ticks in my throat.

"Mrs. Grayson... aside from the recent argument, were you and your husband having ongoing problems?"

"I don't—I mean, normal marriage issues. Certainly nothing that would make him do something like this."

I shift again in my seat. It's the first time I wonder if I should've called a lawyer.

"We were fine," I add, too quickly. "We had our issues, like anyone."

"Affairs?"

"No."

A pause. Then: "Was there a prenuptial agreement?"

My mouth is suddenly dry. "Yes."

"May I ask what you stood to gain in the event of your husband's death?"

"I—I don't know the specifics. Matthew handled all the legal paperwork."

"But you have no children, correct?"

"Correct."

"And you're his sole beneficiary, correct?"

"I suppose so. Yes."

"And his life insurance policy? Any idea of its value?"

"I don't know. I mean—he always said it was significant. For tax reasons. But I never looked at the numbers."

The detective watches me for a long moment, then slides his card across the table.

"If you remember anything else—no matter how small—call me."

As he gathers his clipboard, he pauses.

"One more thing, Mrs. Grayson."

I brace myself.

"Some local reporters have already picked up the story. When the regional and national press gets ahold of this, it's going to be chaos. Your husband wasn't just anyone. He was money, power, scandal."

"What are you saying?"

"I'm saying if you have secrets, now's the time to prepare for them to come out. Reporters will be camped outside your house by this afternoon, probably. They'll talk to neighbors. Friends. Anyone who ever shook his hand. And they'll come after you, too."

I swallow deeply. "But I didn't do anything."

"Okay. But they won't care," he says. "You were married to a man who appeared to have it all, then jumped off a bridge in the middle of the night. That makes you the next story."

"I'm not hiding anything."

"I didn't say you were."

We stare at each other for so long sweat begins to bead on my forehead.

"Are you okay to drive, Mrs. Grayson?"

"Of course," I say, forcing my legs to stand.

"I'll call you as soon as the autopsy is complete or if anything new comes up," Gibson says as we walk to the door. "In the meantime, I'll have a local grief counselor reach out—someone to help you process the loss."

Grief.

I have a sick feeling that grief might be the least traumatic thing I'm about to face.

FIVE

RACHEL

The week before...

The fluorescent lights overhead are enough to drive a person mad. They buzz and flicker in uneven rhythm, casting a sickly yellow glow over the small room filled with beige cubicles. Mine is decorated with crayon drawings and a ceramic mug that reads _Best Mom Eve_ in faded rainbow lettering. (The _r_ has faded away completely.)

Invoices are piled in half-finished stacks around me, some rubber-banded, most not. My monitor displays a spreadsheet I haven't touched in twenty minutes. Under my desk, next to my worn black flats, rests a crooked diorama of the solar system made from a pizza box and foam balls—Levi's third-grade science project. He told me last night he wanted the Earth to spin, so I brought it to work, along with a glue gun and a bendy straw to see if I could make it happen during lunch.

Sighing, I glance up at the wall of my cubicle. My name tag—Rachel Sinclair—hangs slightly crooked, the cheap paper curling at one corner. I've worked here for nearly seven years, plugging away in accounts receivable for a company that sells industrial pipe fittings and water control valves. I spend most of my day on hold, chasing overdue invoices and typing numbers into boxes that never end. I don't hate it, but I don't love it either. It's just... what I do.

I stare at my name tag, imagining the day I'll finally peel it off the wall. I imagine the words I'll say to my boss when I quit, and the life I'll be living this time next year. The thought sends a strange, giddy warmth through me, and before I can stop it, a smile spreads across my face.

"Um, can I get a little of whatever you took this morning?"

The voice belongs to Tanya, who's already on her second Diet Coke of the day. It's only ten in the morning.

Grinning, she plops into the chair across from me, breasts barely contained by a fuchsia top. Her glasses are too big for her face, her lipstick is always smudged, and she smells faintly of feminine deodorant spray and dry shampoo.

Tanya handles customer service—mostly returns and complaints—which means she spends her days apologizing for things that aren't her fault and forwarding emails she never actually reads.

I love the woman.

"Sorry." The smile drops from my face. "Was just thinking about something Ashley said yesterday."

"Liar. That was a *genuine* smile."

I snort.

"You okay?" she asks.

"Yeah. Late night. Levi had a nightmare."

"Uh-huh," she says, taking a long sip through a white straw stained red at the tip. Then she tilts her head to the side, studying me in that way that sometimes makes me think she sees too much. "You've been off lately. Not in a bad way. Just... somewhere else."

My hand moves to the red scarf poking out of my purse.

"Want to talk about it?" she asks, softer now.

I sigh, swivel my chair to fully face her. "Do you ever just feel like you were meant for something more?"

Tanya leans back in her chair, crossing one leg over the other with a squeak of her leather skirt. "Girl, I work in a warehouse and get yelled at by men named *Dick* who think free shipping entitles them to scream at me. Meanwhile, every man in this building talks *only* to my boobs. Not that I mind—I paid good money for them—but it'd be nice if just once someone made eye contact long enough to realize I have a degree in communications and a blue ribbon in competitive knitting from the county fair. So yes, of course I feel like I'm meant for something more."

"It's like we're all here on this earth, just doing the best we can every day in this," I gesture around the room, "boring—yet somehow *always* problem-filled—mediocre life. And it's like, you just kind of get stuck on this ride that goes around and around in the same circle—but it's never an exciting ride. You know what I mean? And... it sucks, ya know?"

She lets out a short laugh, but there's no humor in it.

"I hear you, sister. I've spent a decade in this industry smiling through comments I should've reported and training men who now outrank me. And I still bring donuts on Fridays. I still get asked if I'm someone's assistant in meetings I'm running."

She pauses. "But you know what keeps me showing up? Women like you. Women who, despite all the mediocrity show up with a true desire to help others. Women who would give you the shirt off their back all while figuring out how to make the earth spin for their kid's science project."

I smile but, honestly, the words don't land like she intended.

Tanya shifts forward. "You know what I think?"

"What?"

"I think you've been carrying something heavy for a long time. And maybe you've gotten real good at pretending it's not there. But I see it, Rach. Even if nobody else does."

My throat tightens. I look away.

I have a good a life—a fine life.

I've got Paul, who works hard and remembers to fill my car up with gas.

I've got Levi, who still calls me Mama when he's sick.

I've got Ashley, who asks big questions and tells bigger stories.

I've got dinners at five, and PTO forms in the backpack, and Friday night cartoons.

I've got a name tag on a stained cubicle wall, and coffee that tastes like dirt.

I've got regret. And dishes in the sink. And tired bones.

"I just wonder," I whisper, "if this is it. If I already made all my big choices and now I'm just... living the consequences."

Tanya leans forward. "You are not defined by your past decisions, Rachel. Period."

Her phone rings. She stands, smoothing down her skirt with one hand and grabbing her Diet Coke with the other. "Speaking of consequences, I've gotta go deal with a customer who thinks a leaky pipe fitting ruined his marriage and he wants us to pay for it. Pray for me."

Tanya steps out of my cubicle, then turns back, leans in. "I'm here for you when you're ready to talk."

I nod, but don't say anything.

When she's gone, I swivel back toward my screen, my fingers drifting again to the edge of the red scarf peeking out of my bag.

SIX

OLIVIA

The iron gate swings open without a sound, just as it always does. It's programmed to respond to my car the moment it turns onto the private drive. Everything about our home is designed to look elegant and make life easier.

If only.

The estate rises out of the trees—three stories of glass and stone, flanked by manicured hedges and sentinel pines. A long circular drive curves past a fountain, the statue at its center looking almost mournful under the gray, bleak early morning.

I pull into the porte cochere and shift the car into park.

My heels click loudly on the slate walkway, reminding me of how totally alone I am.

Inside, the house is silent.

I drop my keys on the console table in the foyer and for a moment I just stand there in a dazed stupor. It feels like I am suddenly living in some crazy alternate universe.

My gaze sweeps the interior of my home. It feels different. Almost like I'm seeing it for the first time. In a way, I guess I am.

Yesterday my husband was alive.

This morning, he is not.

Yesterday, I was a wife.

Today I am a widow.

I step into the living room, shadowed beneath the dreary morning. I flick on a lamp.

Again, I just stand there.

Then I sit. Back rigid, breath short, head aching.

The silence presses all around me.

My focus lingers on the photographs on the mantel. Me in red couture, Matthew in a tuxedo. Galas. Ceremonies. Ribbon cuttings. I barely recognize the woman in the pictures. That version of me was polished to a high shine. Knew how to smile just enough to be charming, never enough to look desperate.

I stare at her, wondering if she had acted on all the red flags, would her husband still be here today? Because she saw the cracks. She heard Matthew's whispers behind closed doors. She noticed the missing pieces in his stories, the flicker in his eyes when she asked about certain trips or unfamiliar names. And she smiled anyway. Hosted another dinner party. Put on another eight-thousand-dollar dress.

Because if I didn't look too hard, I didn't have to see it. And if I didn't see it, life continued as normal.

Avoidance is a kind of survival. At least, that's what I told myself. The ugly, unlikeable truth is that I was too scared to walk away from a glamorous, easy lifestyle that I knew I couldn't recreate on my own. I constantly reminded myself how lucky I was to have a life where I didn't have to worry about money. Many, many people don't have that luxury. I reminded myself to be grateful and not wish for more. Add to that, I'd made a commitment to my husband—through thick or thin.

And now...

Now what?

My phone buzzes from my suit pocket. It's a text from one of Matthew's business associates.

Have you heard from him yet? I still haven't.

I put the phone face-down, the detective's words echoing in my head: *When the press gets ahold of this it's going to be chaos...*

I don't know what I'm supposed to do now. I don't know if I'm meant to cry, or collapse, or begin making calls.

How long are you supposed to wait before telling people your husband is dead? I have no relatives to call. Matthew's mother and father are dead and he was an only child. Same for me.

I slide my elbows onto my knees and bury my head in my hands. But the moment I close my eyes, I see his face being slowly revealed from the body bag.

I surge to a stance and stride to the kitchen. I pour a glass of vodka, take a deep sip, and press the cool glass to my forehead.

I strip out of the jacket, kick off my heels, unbutton the top button of my pants, and step onto the patio, drink in hand. I sink into the chaise longue, pulling a blanket over my legs.

As I watch the sun rise farther into the sky, my fingers drift to the diamond necklace around my neck. I find myself reflecting on my marriage. On Matthew.

The first time Matthew scared me, he was wearing a tuxedo and holding a diamond necklace.

We were late for a gala in Manhattan—some fundraiser for a politician he loathed but publicly supported. I was standing by the mirror in our dressing suite, my fingers slipping as I tried to clasp the delicate necklace around my neck. He'd walked in behind me, silent as always, the low click of his polished shoes muffled by the carpet. Then he reached forward, took the necklace from my hands, and fastened it for me without a word.

I remember the way he looked at me in the mirror—not at my dress, or my hair, but my neck. Like he was measuring how deep to drag a knife across it.

Earlier that day, I'd told him I planned to stop by a new gallery opening later that week—a local art space downtown that restores old relics, small but promising. I'd met the owner at one of our charity galas and offered to volunteer. He hadn't liked that. Not because of the gallery itself, but because I'd made the decision without him.

"You want to restore other people's trash now?" he'd said, glancing at the postcard invite. "That's cute."

It wasn't cute. It was my way of trying to find something of my own.

He smoothed a hand over my shoulder. "You really should smile more when we're out. It makes people feel more comfortable."

"I didn't realize I wasn't smiling." I looked down, began closing the side of my dress.

"Here. Let me," he said, reaching for the zipper.

"It's fine, I almost—"

His fingernails bit into my skin as he gripped the fabric with a hard yank, jostling my body. He tugged the zipper up, fast and hard. I gasped as my skin caught in the metal teeth.

"Wait!" I squeaked as white hot pain bloomed along my ribcage. "Matthew. It's caught—"

Instead of stopping, he tugged again, violently, slicing into my skin and sending me stumbling back into him.

He didn't let go.

My heart lodged in my throat. It felt like fire had been dragged across my skin.

"Smile more," he reminded me, leaning in, inches from my ear. "But don't ever—*ever*—look at the gardener like that again."

In one final brutal motion, he zipped the dress the rest of the way, sending a burst of nausea through my body.

Finally, my husband released me, stepped back, and smoothed the lapels of his tuxedo like nothing had happened.

While my face was flushed and wild with expression, his was stoic and completely calm.

I watched in shock as he reached into his pocket and withdrew a black velvet box.

My blood speckled the tips of his fingers.

He opened it, revealing a diamond bracelet.

"For you, darling," he said, before draping it around my wrist, his touch featherlight.

I stared at the shimmering line of stones, pulse pounding in my ears, pain like acid running down the side of my torso.

Then he did something that still makes my skin crawl: Eyes locked on mine, he licked my blood from his fingertips. Then, like he was switching characters, his face fell with something that resembled concern.

"Oh no, you're bleeding, sweetheart? Here. Let me see."

I couldn't speak.

He retrieved a tissue from the vanity, knelt at my side, and began unzipping the zipper.

I literally had to bite my cheek to keep from screaming.

He began gently dabbing at the raw slice beneath my arm.

"There, there," he said softly. "Darn it, that looks like that's going to hurt awhile. I'm so, so sorry, sweetheart."

His tone was so casual, so tender, that I almost forgot what had just happened.

"We need to be careful, you and I," he murmured. "You looked at the driver in a way that people could misinterpret. We can't afford that kind of gossip. Not in our position. Not with everything we've built. We must always be united. That's how strong couples survive scrutiny. Because that's what we are, right?"

He pressed the tissue more firmly now, and met my gaze, still kneeling. For a moment I considered slamming my knee into him—his gasp, his face twisting, the release I would feel—but why would I do that while he was being so... calm?

"Liv... your lifestyle—the house, the staff, the travel, the clothes—it all comes from my company. From the choices I make. And I can only keep making those choices, keep running an empire, when my head is clear."

Then, he shifted in front of me, still kneeling, reminding me of when he asked me to marry him. He grabbed my hands, his thumb brushing the sides of my wrists.

"You give me that peace, Olivia. That stability. You help me show the world I have it all under control. And in return... I give you the world."

I nodded before I even realized I was doing it.

"And I love you so, so much, my beautiful bride."

It was like emotional whiplash. One minute, he was hurting me —deliberately, carelessly—and the next, he was nursing the very wound he caused. Calling me his peace, and reminding me what a beautiful life we had together.

"I was thinking," he continued, smiling up at me. "We should go away soon, you and I. Tahiti, maybe?"

And just like that I was thinking of the beach, of being his bride, and how lucky I was because of all the things he provided me.

Maybe he didn't mean to hurt me. Maybe it *was* the stress. Maybe I shouldn't have smiled at the driver. Maybe I just needed to be more careful.

Maybe *I* was the one who needed to apologize.

I stared at the bracelet glittering on my wrist, my skin still throbbing beneath the dress.

"It's us, Olivia," he said, squeezing my hands. "You and me. Forever."

Then he stood, turned, and walked out of the room, whistling.

SEVEN

RACHEL

The week before...

The parking lot is empty except for his truck and my car.

We're tucked behind the old truck stop on the edge of town, where the pavement turns to gravel. It's our spot, has been for a while now. Just far enough off the main drag that no one bothers to look twice, especially at night.

In the distance, we watch the haul trucks come and go beneath the harsh fluorescents, their exhaust swirling in the headlight beams. The lot is lit like a crime scene, smells like diesel, and the pavement is stained with oil. Unromantic by anyone else's standards. But with him, it feels like the most romantic place on earth.

We sit in his cab, the heater humming softly.

Matt is smiling at me like I just said the cutest thing in the world. One arm is slung casually over the steering wheel, the other resting near my leg—close, but not quite touching. Like he's waiting for me to make the move I never quite make.

"You're staring," I say softly.

"I know."

I try not to smile, but it's useless. I look away, out the windshield, where snow has begun to collect on the glass. Just flurries, but enough to make the moment feel like something out of a dream.

"Stop," I whisper, blushing.

"Can't," he says, grinning. "You're kinda hard to look away from."

I roll my eyes, but my stomach tickles anyway.

"You look good in red," he says. "Have I ever told you that?"

I touch the scarf around my neck. "You say I look good in everything."

Matt leans in slightly, fingers catching the edge of it. "I picked that out in a snowstorm, you know. Drove all the way to the next town just to find a red scarf."

"You did?"

"Yep."

"Why red?"

"It's a Rachel color. Bold. Brave. Strong. And my favorite thing about you: a little messy."

I laugh under my breath. "I didn't know red was considered a messy color."

"Don't take this moment from me."

I laugh. Then, "I think about that moment all the time, you know. We were walking through the park. It was snowing, like this. You wrapped it around me and said, 'So you always have a piece of me with you.'"

"And you always wear it."

"I do. It's never far from me."

"That makes me very, very happy." He shifts a little closer now, closing the gap between us. "You know what I keep thinking about?"

"What?"

"How we've never had sex."

I nearly choke on a laugh. "Matt."

"I'm serious." He's grinning ear to ear now, totally unbothered. "It's insane."

"Are you disappointed?" I ask.

"About what?"

I roll my eyes and slap his arm. "That we haven't slept together yet."

He shrugs. "A little. I mean, have you seen you?"

That makes me laugh, and his grin widens.

"But no," he says. "I'm not. Because it means we've done this the right way. With respect and patience. It means we didn't just... fall into something. I mean, we've been in love for *how long* now?"

"Don't say it like that," I whisper, glancing out the windshield like someone might be watching, even though I know we're alone. "It's complicated."

"No, it's not," he says, and this time his voice is different—confident. "You're married to someone who doesn't see you. Doesn't hear you. Doesn't care anymore. I'm just a guy who does. This," he gestures between us, "is the purest, most uncomplicated thing on earth."

"It's everything *else* that's complicated," I mutter. My fingers curl around the scarf again, twisting the edge in my lap.

"Hey." Matt tucks a strand of hair behind my ear, dipping his face into my line of sight. "I can't wait until we finally can be us," he says. "Until everything's out in the open. Until it's you and me, for real."

"I made the appointment with the lawyer today," I blurt.

His eyes widen with surprise. "You did?"

I nod, biting my lip. "Yep. The first consult will be over the phone. Sixty minutes. I'll take it in my car at work. Guess how much I had to pay just to book the call?"

"Oh no..."

"Three *hundred* dollars."

He groans and drops his forehead to the steering wheel. "That's criminal."

"Right? I couldn't believe it—just for a consult?! But it will go toward the final fees, so you know, it's not really that bad."

He straightens and grabs my hand with both of his. "I'll give it to you tomorrow. I'll pay for it."

"No—*no*. You don't have to."

"I know I don't," he says. "But I want to. We're in this together, remember? You and me."

God, I love this man.

I look at him, *really* look at him. His dark hair is a little messy, his jaw sharp under the glow of the streetlamp filtering in through the glass. There's something about him—always—that makes me feel young and brave and reckless and safe, all at once.

I intertwine our fingers, holding on like he's the only solid thing in my life. Because most days, he is.

"Are we *really* doing this?" I whisper.

"Yes!" His eyes glisten. "Rachel, you are the one for me. There is no one else. I've known it since that night at Miller's when you were sitting at the bar, pretending you didn't know I was watching you."

I smile through my tears. "You were terrible at pretending."

"You were terrible at hiding how sad you were."

The words hit deeper than I expect.

Tanya and I had met for happy hour—a rare outing for me. The twins had both been sick that week, clingy and feverish, and Paul had barely looked up from the TV long enough to notice. I was exhausted in that bone-deep, no-one's-taking-care-of-me kind of way.

When Tanya left, I stayed behind, telling myself I was just finishing my drink. But the truth was that I just didn't want to go home.

"Rachel, I want to be with you forever," he says, a hint of desperation in his voice. "And I'll wait forever if I have to."

"I'm done waiting."

"Me too."

He squeezes my hand. "I was going to wait to tell you but... I want to buy the bar."

I blink. "Are you serious?"

He grins. "Yep. I've been saving. Talking to the owner. He's thinking about retiring next year."

I shake my head, stunned. "Matt, that's incredible!"

"I want to turn it into something better." His eyes light up. "A real tap room. With beers from all over—Belgium, Germany, Japan. Not just bottled stuff. I'm thinking flights, tastings, maybe even a private room for events. I want it to be a place people *drive* to, not just stumble into."

I beam at his excitement. "That sounds amazing."

"And I want you to run it with me."

"Me?"

"You're so good with people, Rach. You're smart, and you've got this heart—this instinct—for showing up for people. It's in your bones. You love to help people. You are the kindest person, Rachel. You make people feel seen. And that? That's everything."

He wipes a tear from my cheek. It's not tears of sadness, it's tears of being so overwhelmlingly in love with another human being.

"The number one thing people are looking for at a bar top isn't a drink—it's connection," he continues, the passion evident. "They're escaping something—like you were that night. And more often than not, they just want to talk about it. They want to feel like they matter, even if it's just for one night. You could give them that. *We* could. We'd make a damn good team."

Something in my chest cracks wide open. "I want that too," I whisper. "God, I want that so much."

"Then let's do it," he says. "Let's start building the life we actually want."

I don't know what comes over me, but I lean forward and kiss him.

Actually *kiss* him!

There is no hesitation. No second-guessing. No pretending we're anything but two people who've been aching for this—for *each other*—for far too long.

The moment our lips meet, everything else falls away. The cold, the noise, the rules. It starts soft and hesitant, like we're still checking to see if this is real. Then his hand slides to my cheek—hello, most romantic thing ever—and I *melt*.

I reach for him instinctively, fingers curling around the collar of his flannel, pulling him closer. He groans softly, one hand sliding into my hair, the other gripping my waist like he's afraid I'll disappear. His kiss deepens, urgent and full of everything we've been trying so hard not to say. It's not just longing. It's *need*.

I climb halfway into his lap before I realize what I'm doing. He's hard beneath me, his chest rising fast under my palms, and suddenly we're breathless and tangled and trembling in the dark. My body is humming, aching for more. Every part of me wants him. *Every single part.*

Suddenly he pulls back, forehead resting against mine, both of us gasping. "Rachel... are you sure you want..."

"Don't take this moment from me," I whisper, grinning against his lips.

He grins back, and we kiss again, and I realize I've never wanted anything this badly in my life. And, based on the way Matt is now literally sitting on his hands to keep from undressing me, he feels the same.

We sit in silence after that, holding each other, but it's not awkward. It's full of hope.

"Thank you," I say. I don't need to say why.

He nods, gently running his thumb down my shoulder.

"I love you," I whisper.

Matt's eyes are dark and steady. He touches my cheek.

"I know."

EIGHT

OLIVIA

Matthew's entire life is in his office—and I'm going snooping.

I knock back the last of the vodka. It's done the trick. My body is languid, but now, my mind is racing.

I push out of the lounge, step back into the house, and pad down the hallway.

I feel buzzed and lightheaded—a little too heady. Especially considering it's not even noon. I haven't slept in over twenty-four hours. I haven't showered. I've barely eaten.

Matthew's office is at the far end of the east wing. Two glass-paneled doors that lead into a space I was never explicitly banned from, but knew never to enter. Like everything else in our marriage, the boundaries were unspoken but implied.

The detective was right. Outside looking in, we had the perfect life. But the truth is, I had everything *he* wanted me to have, accompanied by a long list of rules. Always answer his calls. Don't question his business. Wear the necklace on Tuesdays. Smile more, smile less. Be polite. Be his.

And yet I loved him.

God help me, I did. In the beginning, at least. Before Matthew, I was just trying to keep up—new city, new job, tiny apartment that always smelled faintly of someone else's cooking. I worked long hours, spent weekends doing laundry and worrying about bills and paying off my mountain of student loans. Life wasn't glamorous, but it was mine. Then he appeared—confident, magnetic, the kind of man who made you believe the ground beneath your feet had shifted. Matthew was endlessly charming, handsome, and gave me an exceptional life. I'd never met someone with so much charisma. He could make anyone fall in love with him. He was the kind of man other men envied, and women melted for.

It started with a bounced payment. I'll never forget the look on the assistant's face when she handed me the declined card at Neiman Marcus. Pity despised as politeness. "Try this one," I'd said, offering another card. It worked. But the moment lodged itself in my mind.

Later that night, Matthew had laughed it off. "Oversight," he'd said. "One of the accounts is being restructured. Don't worry your pretty head."

So I didn't.

Until it happened again. And again. And again. And then a man came to our door. He said he was a client and Matthew owed him money. I refused to let him in and just then, Matthew pulled up. Breezed out of his Range Rover with a smooth, confident smile, and invited the man into his home office.

I didn't sleep that night.

Now, with Matthew gone, I need to know exactly how bad it was because I need to protect myself. I don't know much about my husband's business, but my gut tells me our current accounts will not cover whatever debts he owes... and then what?

My pulse starts to race.

Will they come for me?

Can they?

Can I be arrested for anything illegal *he* did?

I never signed anything—not knowingly. But I went to the galas. I shook the hands. I posed beside him while he toasted billionaires and promised the world.

I think about the house. The cars. The art on the walls. If his company is underwater—will I lose all of this? Will they seize it?

No. That can't happen. I won't allow it. If they—the feds, the SEC, the bad people, whoever—decide to look too closely, I need them to see what I see: a man spiraling, desperate, and dangerous. A man who would jump off a bridge in the middle of the night.

Not a woman who knew.

I reach for the doorknob, my heart racing far too fast.

His office is as pristine as it was last time I saw it. Everything in its place. The leather chairs. The bar cart stocked with untouched scotch. The abstract art on the wall that cost more than my first car. It smells faintly of cedar and the spicy cologne he wore that cost 600 dollars a bottle. I hated it.

The desk drawers are locked. Because of course they are.

I turn his office upside down looking for a key. Finally, I find it under a bust of Caesar on the bookshelf—a gift from a senator he despised but pretended to admire.

The desk yields with a soft *click*. I open the drawers slowly, careful not to disturb anything too much.

I find bank statements. Investment portfolios. Folders marked with names I don't recognize. Some of them are coded—aliases, maybe? Projects?

I open the next drawer. More documents, neatly stacked. Receipts. A single photograph of us at a gala—his hand gripping my waist, smile perfect. I shove it aside. When I do, the picture catches on something deep inside the desk.

I push back the folders and run my hand along the wood. My fingertips snag on a thin ridge. A hidden panel.

"Matthew..." The whisper escapes before I can stop it.

I press. The panel clicks open, releasing a shallow compartment lined in felt.

I find *two* burner phones, both tucked behind a sheaf of invoices, wrapped in a rubber band. No charger. No power. Just dead weight.

There's a manila envelope, too. Inside are photographs, grainy surveillance-style images. One is of a man getting into a black SUV. One of a woman walking through an airport terminal. Another of someone's front door.

No names. No notes.

The room spins. I grip the edge of the desk to steady myself. Every instinct screams to stop, to close everything and pretend I saw nothing. But I can't. If I don't get ahead of this, someone else will—and they won't be looking to protect me. They'll be looking to bury me.

I take the burner phones and the envelope. I close everything else the way I found it.

Then I turn to the window just as the sun breaks through the clouds.

Let them come, I think.

Let them try to figure out who Matthew Grayson really was.

Let them see the man I saw behind closed doors.

NINE

RACHEL

The week before...

I'm elbow-deep in pancake batter when the door flies open and the kids come barreling inside, breathless and pink-cheeked from the cold.

"Mom! Mom!"

"Mommy, look!"

Their boots thud against the tile as they scramble out of them, tracking snow and muddy slush halfway into the kitchen. Ashley bursts forward first, her coat unzipped and hair wild with static, proudly holding a toy dinosaur above her head like it's a trophy. Behind her, Levi trips over his untied sneakers and goes down with a dramatic shriek, limbs flailing, jacket half off.

I rush across the kitchen, swatting cream from my apron, and scoop him into my arms. "Oh, my little gymnast," I coo, leading him to the table. "Let me help you—where does it hurt?"

He points to his knee. I grab a container of Band-Aids from the drawer (that the scrape doesn't need), and patch him up, singing the "Baby's got a boo-boo" song I made up years ago:

"Oh no, baby's got a boo-boo,
But don't you fret, we know what to do!

A little kiss, a bandage too,
And soon you'll roar like tigers do!"
Levi giggles and nudges Ashley, who's already helping us with extra pats and kisses.

"Guess what?"

"What?" They say in unison.

"It's breakfast for dinner tonight."

Both of them cheer like I've just announced Christmas. No more boo-boo.

Paul wanders in—steel-toed boots heavy on the linoleum, hands smudged with grease from the forklift—just in time to drop a damp jacket over the back of a chair and check his phone.

He looks up, one eyebrow slightly raised, but says nothing. The kids climb onto him for hugs and tickles, then they grin and disappear to their upstairs fortress. I watch him slump into his chair, absorbed in his phone's glow. Paul is incapable of dealing with anything in the home—conversation, help, whatever—until he has scrolled social media for at least thirty minutes. It's his decompress time, I get it, but it drives me absolutely mad.

My phone buzzes, and I nearly drop the spatula. The text ID reads *A. Smith*. It's the fake name I assigned Matt's cell phone number after we exchanged them long ago—only to be used in extreme emergencies.

My pulse spikes.

I slip out onto the covered porch and slide the door closed behind me.

After glancing over my shoulder, I open it:

> Had something come up. Leaving town for a bit,
> will message when I get back.

That's it. No details. No emojis. No goodbye.

Goosebumps rise on my arms.

Matt has never texted me like this. Not in all the time we've known each other. Not even when his truck got stuck in a snowstorm last winter or when he was rushed to the hospital for appendicitis. This... is different. It feels off. Especially right after we shared our first kiss.

I press the phone to my heart and grip the porch railing. The snow spins beneath the orange orb of the streetlight in the distance.

I look at the message again. My thumb hovers over the keyboard.

Do I text him back?

No. That's the rule. No unnecessary messages. No digital trail.

But where is he going? Matt has no wife. No kids. No reason to just vanish in the night.

Had something come up...

What? Matt lives a relatively uneventful life. He works full-time at the bar, and crashes when he gets home. Gym in the morning, then back at the bar. What could be an emergency?

Does he regret the kiss and is ghosting me?

Is he meeting someone?

A *woman?*

The thought hits like a punch to the gut.

I shove the phone into my pocket and swallow the ache rising in my throat. Inside, Paul yells something about pancakes burning.

I swallow deeply and step back to my totally normal, boring, mundane life.

TEN

OLIVIA

I startle at what sounds like a million bees swarming overhead.

My eyes fly open.

I must have fallen asleep.

The house is flooded with soft, late-afternoon light. I bolt upright on the sofa, still dressed in my suit pants and silk blouse, both horribly wrinkled now. My neck aches from the angle I passed out in and my body feels like it was poured full of concrete.

It takes me a moment to realize the buzzing sound is from my phone which is sitting on the glass end table.

I reach forward and grab it, sending a decorative pillow tumbling to the floor. A number I don't recognize flashes on the screen.

"Hello?" I immediately curse myself. I have no freaking idea why I just answered my phone.

"Mrs. Grayson, this is Alan from Ridgeview Security." His voice is tight.

Alan is the head of security at the gated community where we live.

"What is it?" I ask, my body already spiking with adrenaline.

"I wanted to give you a heads-up, ma'am. There's a crowd outside the gates. New vans and reporters, mostly. A few look like they're trying to come up the hill on foot. We've already contacted the police for support—they're on their way. In the meantime, we advise you to stay inside. Do not engage."

"Wait—what?" I stagger to a stance, the blood draining from my face. "So it's out? They know?"

"It's all over the local news, ma'am. I—you might want to turn it on. And also, I'm very sorry for your—"

I hang up before I can hear anything else.

The remote is already in my hand before I realize I've moved. I switch on the TV. The screen flares to life, and there it is:

BREAKING NEWS: FAMED INVESTOR MATTHEW GRAYSON FOUND DEAD IN APPARENT SUICIDE

Below it, a bold subhead scrolls:

What's to blame: Financial Ruin or His Socialite Wife?

Socialite wife?

The footage cuts to aerial shots of Ridgeview Lake, gleaming silver under the sun, then zooms in on the front gates of our neighborhood.

A sea of reporters crowds the entrance, spilling onto the manicured sidewalks and swarming the decorative stone. Cameras are mounted on tripods and shoulders, lenses aimed like weapons. Reporters with microphones peeking through the wrought-iron bars. White news vans line the curb in both directions, their satellite dishes extended toward the sky like skeletal fingers.

It looks like one of those scenes that plays on TV after a celebrity scandal breaks. A political implosion, maybe. A starlet arrested. Except this is not a celebrity scandal—it's my scandal. *My* front gate. *My* name on everyone's lips.

The camera zooms in on the guardhouse where I usually hand off a wave and a tired smile. Now it's surrounded by flashing lights and security guards who look completely overwhelmed. One of them is on the phone. Another is holding his arms out to push back a reporter who's practically climbing the windshield of an idling sedan.

They're desperate for a soundbite. A scandalous detail. A glimpse of the woman at the center of it all.

Me.

I stagger back from the TV.

My phone starts ringing again, but I don't answer. I can't.

Instead I silence the call and open my news app, praying it hasn't hit the national news.

It has.

His name. His picture—*my* picture.

I scan the short article, the words jumping out at me like an ambush: Forged contracts. Shell companies. Wire transfers to fake locations.

The phone drops from my hand. Panic mixed with humiliation washes over me.

How do they know—and I didn't?

My chest heaves for air that it can't seem to take in. My stomach turns violently with shame. *Public* shame.

I squeeze my eyes shut, but my mind spins.

You should've asked more questions, Olivia.

You should've seen the signs.

You should've known who you married.

You should have left long ago.

The walls around me suddenly feel like they're closing in, warping with every pulse of humiliation.

A car passes slowly outside, stopping at the bottom of our driveway.

I run to the front window and peek between the drapes. A car —that I don't recognize—speeds off, then, in the corner of my eye, I notice two women walking briskly up the sidewalk.

Beverly and Elaine.

"Oh you've got to be *kidding* me," I grumble.

They're my neighbors. Surface friends. The kind of women I

meet for lunch at the clubhouse twice a month and play pickleball with every other Saturday.

And now they're here, circling like vultures who've smelled blood.

Beverly is dressed in head-to-toe Tory Burch—a floral midi dress under a tailored cream blazer, oversized sunglasses perched on her head like a crown. Her ponytail bounces as she walks, immaculate and effortless. She clutches a white bakery box with a gold ribbon, the kind they sell at the French patisserie in town.

Elaine is in full Lululemon leisure armor—a fitted zip-up, buttery-soft leggings, and a monogrammed tennis tote slung over one shoulder. A Cartier watch glints on her wrist. Her phone is already in hand, her thumb hovering near the record button, no doubt.

They walk with purpose. With barely restrained glee. Because they are here for nothing but the story.

Gossip disguised as sympathy.

My hands begin to shake.

I move quickly from the window and ensure the front door is locked. I flip the second deadbolt for good measure.

I can hear their footsteps closer now, so I press my back against the front door, freeze, and hold my breath.

The doorbell rings.

Again.

My phone keeps buzzing in my hands. Emails. Texts. Unknown numbers. Our lawyer—who I will *not* call back. Why? I don't trust him. Why? Because he was *Matthew's* lawyer, and likely assisted him in making very, very poor decisions. I have already made the decision to find a new lawyer to handle this.

Tiny black dots pop in my vision and for a moment I think I am about to have a full-blown panic attack. I sink down to the floor, pull my knees to chest.

I can smell their Chanel perfume through the crack in the door.

Knocks, more dings. Chatter as the women impatiently wait.

"Do you think she's even home?"

"Maybe she's with her lawyers already. Or hiding somewhere."

"Oh my gosh, you think she ran? Wouldn't surprise me. Honestly, none of this does. She was always too perfect, ya know?"

I put my head between my legs.

Breathe, breathe, breathe.

Knock, knock, knock.

A new email alert pings onto my screen. It's from Andy, our publicist, marked URGENT. The subject line is all caps:

CALL ME. CONTROL THE NARRATIVE BEFORE SOMEONE ELSE DOES.

There's a draft statement attached. I click into it. It's hollow, polished, and not remotely true. A paragraph about Matthew's brilliance, his legacy, our heartbreak. It doesn't mention the lies, the debts, the slow implosion of everything beneath our perfect facade.

I close it without reading the rest.

Nails tap on the window next to the front door.

I drop to the floor like I've been shot, flattening myself against the cold marble. My cheek presses into the stone, my breath fogging the surface. I don't know if they can see me through the slit in the curtain, but I don't dare move.

Tears sting my eyes as I picture myself from above—sprawled on the floor in a wrinkled and now-stained Alexander McQueen suit, shaking, hiding from the women who once envied me.

Me. The polished wife who could sip champagne while reciting stock forecasts and guest lists. The woman who smiled from magazine spreads beside a man with perfect teeth and perfectly timed charm.

And now I'm nothing more than a breathless silhouette on the floor, drowning in panic while strangers circle like vultures— reducing everything I was before yesterday to nothing more than a salacious headline.

Finally—*mercifully*—the voices fade.

Once I'm certain they're gone, I peel myself off the floor and wipe the tears from my cheeks.

I'm so *scared*.

Scared of the media outside, of my neighbors, of what the next hour will bring, of what the headlines will say tomorrow.

I'm scared that the truth is slipping out of my control.

Scared that I am utterly, completely alone—and that this is only the beginning.

I step away from the front door and head straight for the only place I've ever been able to completely unravel: my closet. It sounds absurd, I know. But it's always been my safe place. When I was a teenager, I used to sneak into my childhood closet with a flashlight and a bag of pretzels to escape the sound of my parents fighting. In college, it doubled as a panic room and makeshift wine bar during finals. And now? It's still my sanctuary. A linen-scented bunker of emotional damage.

I duck behind the dresses and pull my knees to my chest.

A grown woman. Hiding in a closet. From her own life.

My phone buzzes again.

This time it's a voicemail.

I listen.

"Olivia, it's Beverly—I was just there. You poor thing. I saw the news. I'm so sorry. If you need anything—truly, anything—don't hesitate. I'm just around the corner. I could drop by? I made that lemon shortbread you love..."

I delete it before she finishes.

What I need is for everyone to go away.

I bury my face in my hands and begin sobbing.

Last night, I was grieving.

Today, I am a headline.

ELEVEN

OLIVIA

I'm standing in the kitchen—finally out of the wrinkled suit and into an oversized sweatshirt and leggings—holding a coffee cup I haven't sipped from when the phone rings. It's at least the hundredth ring today.

I look at the clock—3:07 p.m.

When the screen lights up with Detective Gibson's name, my heart drops.

I answer immediately.

"Mrs. Grayson," he says, sounding tired.

Me too, I think.

"I wanted to follow up. The autopsy's complete."

My stomach drops so hard it's like the floor vanished beneath me.

"Already?" I manage to say.

"Yes. Because of your husband's notoriety, they pushed it through first thing this morning. We wanted something concrete to feed the media—to get them off your back."

I glance at the television that I'd turned off long ago.

"And?" I ask. "What were the results?"

"There were no signs of foul play. No defensive wounds. No

trauma consistent with a struggle. No ligature marks. No hesitation injuries. His body shows a clean fall."

"So... he jumped," I whisper.

"Yes. Suicide. That's our finding," he says gently. "There's no evidence suggesting he was pushed, or coerced. From everything we have, this was voluntary."

Voluntary.

He continues, "Cause of death was massive blunt-force trauma. He struck the rock shelf just below the bridge."

My throat closes. I can't tell if I'm going to cry or throw up.

"We believe he died on impact," he adds, as if that's meant to comfort me.

My mind conjures the image against my will—Matthew dropping through the air, suit jack flapping, wind howling, then the sickening finality of flesh and bone against stone. His perfect profile split open.

"Thank you," I say, though I'm not sure what I'm thanking him for.

The detective clears his throat. "If you need anything—help navigating the press, a contact for a grief counselor, estate logistics —my office can assist."

"Estate logistics... yes... I do have a question. Lots actually."

"I'll answer best I can, and for the ones I can't, I'll find someone who can."

"Thank you. What happens to my husband's business debt?"

"Great question," he says it quickly—too quickly—like he's been wanting me to ask. "The way I understand it, the business becomes part of the deceased's estate. Creditors can then file a claim against the estate to recover what they are owed. If the estate —your estate—has enough assets, those can be sold or liquidated to pay off the debts."

My stomach drops.

"What about me? How does that affect me?" I ask, hating the quiver in my voice. The desperation.

"As long as you didn't co-sign anything, and weren't a business partner, you're not liable for the business debts."

"But the house, the cars, the art, everything is in his name, I think. So you're saying they can take my house and everything I own?"

"That's just my understanding... but..." He pauses. "When you and I met, we briefly spoke about the financial issues your husband's business was having... issues that might not have been on the right side of the law—"

"Yes. I have proof," I blurt. "Records, photographs, a burner phone. Evidence. I'll give it all to the authorities, all of it. Do you want it now?"

"Ms. Grayson, if your husband was involved in fraud, money laundering, or embezzlement, the proper authorities—the SEC or FBI—will likely take over and, it becomes a bigger, much more complicated deal."

I cover my heart with my hands, fearful that it could burst right out of my chest. "Could *I* be charged?"

"I don't know all your business ma'am, but honestly, I don't *think* so. Only if investigators find evidence that you were actively involved or that you willfully turned a blind eye. But remember, even without charges, your assets and lifestyle might be scrutinized or frozen, especially if they're believed to have been funded by illicit activity."

The breath whooshes out of my lungs.

...willfully turned a blind eye.

"I'm sure you've got good lawyers," he continues. "I'm assuming you've already contacted them. They've probably already told you all this."

"Yes," I lie.

"Good. Anything else?"

"Honestly, I can't even form a coherent sentence now."

"I understand, it's a lot. You've got my number. If the feds want to interview you, I'm assuming it will happen very quickly. If I were you, I'd be ready." He hesitates like he wants to say something else, but then just says, "Take care, Mrs. Grayson."

The line goes dead.

I set the phone down. The ceramic coffee cup trembles in my hand. For a long time, I just stand there, staring into the marble counter.

It's official now.

He did it.

Matthew killed himself. My husband got in over his head, and instead of facing it, he jumped—and he left *me* to pick up the fucking pieces.

Rage shoots through my veins.

I hurl the cup against the wall and release a guttural scream as it shatters into a million pieces.

Just like my life.

TWELVE

RACHEL

Two days.

That's how long it's been since Matt's message. The vague, eerie text that felt like someone else wrote it.

Had something come up. Leaving town for a bit, will message when I get back.

I haven't heard from him since.

I've driven by his house twice. Fine. Six.

Six times.

The lights remain off. No movement in or out. Two unopened delivery boxes sit on his front stoop. His mail is piling up.

I went to his bar, causally asked the owner where he was. He said he didn't show up for work and he hasn't seen him since. I've even considered trying to locate his mother, whom he's only ever spoken of briefly, but I wouldn't even know how to explain who I am to her, or why I'm so desperate to find her son.

There's *no way* Matt just disappeared. We were planning a life together. A *future*. We were going to buy the bar. Build something. Be *us*.

Now, I sit hunched in my cubicle, buried in spreadsheets and emails I can't focus on. The sound of clacking keyboards fills the office like a woodpecker pecking at my brain. A half-eaten protein bar sits by my keyboard, stale and forgotten. My phone is beside my mousepad.

Tanya's across from me, biting a hangnail and typing with one finger. She glances up every few minutes like she's expecting me to say something.

I know she knows something's up. She always does.

I mindlessly rest my hand on my stomach—upset since the moment that message landed.

In the last forty-eight hours, I've crafted no less than a million possible scenarios. Some logical. Some totally unhinged.

He's in the hospital.

He lost his phone.

He got mugged.

He joined a cult.

He saw my Costco receipt and ran.

He hated the kiss.

He regrets everything, and instead of facing me, he ran away.

I picture him somewhere warm, somewhere far away, sipping a craft beer from Belgium—one of the fancy ones he swore he'd serve in our taproom—and laughing with a new woman who doesn't ask complicated questions or come with kids and a mortgage and emotional baggage disguised as sarcasm.

I stare at my monitor.

No.

He wouldn't just run away. Not Matt. Not the man who picked out a red scarf in a snowstorm because he thought it matched my soul. Not the guy who looked at me like I was worth waiting forever for.

I swallow hard, staring at my phone, willing it to light up with a text from him.

When it doesn't, I open my local news app for what feels like the millionth time since he disappeared. I'm searching for a head-line that might explain it all. A car crash. A fire. A missing person. Something wild enough to make his silence make sense.

Nothing there, so I check the mainstream news apps.

I scroll, scroll—
And freeze.
There's a photo of him. Of *Matt*.
Beneath it, a headline:

*Wealthy businessman Matthew Grayson jumps to his death
following SEC investigation.*

My heart stutters. My eyes scan the words, disbelieving.
Matthew Grayson.
Matt—*my* Matt.
Wealthy businessman?
SEC Investigation?
What?
I lurch upright, my chair screeching and slamming into the cabinet behind me. Tanya startles, Diet Coke halfway to her lips. "Rach?"
But I can't answer. I'm too confused.
I check the top off the feed to make sure I'm not on some bogus fake news app.
I'm not.
What is this? Matt—*my* Matt—is not some "wealthy business-man." He's a bartender who never went to college. He drives a rusty truck with duct tape on the taillight and dreams of Belgian beer on tap. He says *ain't* and sings old George Strait songs when he thinks no one's listening. He smells like spice and leather and dish soap.
Matt doesn't live in the United States. He lives in Canada.
He lives *here*. With *me*.
He didn't jump to his death. I just saw him. We were just together.
My stomach turns to water.
He's not dead.
He can't be.
Then, another photo pops up. This one of an elegant, stunning

woman in a tailored suit and high heels. Her posture perfect. Her eyes sharp.

Caption:

Matthew Grayson and his wife, Olivia.

Wife.

Wife?!

Tanya rushes over. "Hey. You're as pale as a ghost. What's going on?"

I can't speak. I can't even move to click out of the app before she sees.

Matt—Matthew—whatever his name is—is *married?* Has a whole other life in the States?

No. It's insane. It's not possible.

But there it is, his picture. I'm *staring* at it. His face. The headline. The wife.

...jumps to his death following SEC investigation.

Jumps to his death?

No. Matt would never. He's scared of heights. And even if he weren't, we were planning our life together.

No—*no, no, no, no.*

Tanya's voice cuts through the buzzing in my ears, and I'm faintly aware of her hand suddenly gripping my arm. She's saying something—I don't know what—but her face is blurry, and the floor doesn't feel like it's where it's supposed to be.

Then everything goes soft and gray.

And I pass out.

THIRTEEN

OLIVIA

It's well past midnight when I wake with a jolt. The lamp is still on, casting a low amber glow across the living room. An untouched glass of wine sits on the coffee table. My head throbs from the half-bottle I drank earlier, my limbs heavy and unresponsive.

The doorbell rings.

My eyes pop with both surprise and fear. Who would be visiting me at midnight? The media? Did they get through the gate? Or is it Beverly and Eliane again?

I stare at the ceiling, frozen still, wrapped in a wool blanket that does nothing to block the chill seeping through the house.

Don't move. Just don't move.

My eyes burn. My mouth tastes like metal.

It rings again, followed by a knock.

Go. Away.

God, I want to die.

I close my eyes and sink deeper into the couch cushions.

The knocking finally stops.

I let out a slow breath, but don't dare to move.

I stare at the ceiling listening to the grandfather clock in the dining room.

Tick... tick... tick...

One minutes passes, five, then I feel it—the air shifts. The unmistakable sensation of someone standing behind me.

Before I can sit up, a forearm slides into my vision and something cold and thin presses against my throat.

A blade.

The black shirt that covers the forearm—now in front of my face—smells like cologne and cigars.

"Where's your safe?" the man says above me in a terrifying voice.

My pulse spikes.

"I—I don't..." I croak, eyes locked on the forearm.

"I'm not going to repeat the question. Where is your safe?"

"I don't *know.*" My voice cracks in the last word.

In a sudden surge of adrenaline, instinct takes over. My body remembers the self-defense moves I learned years ago when a personal trainer offered free classes at the clubhouse.

I grab the man's wrist and twist hard, yanking his arm away from my throat. At the same time, I shift my weight, rolling on the couch and wrenching his elbow in a direction it's not meant to go.

The knife clatters to the floor.

I surge off the couch, breath ragged, heart pounding. I spin around, fists clenched, ready to run or fight—whichever comes first.

Three men stand in my living room, all dressed in black, all staring at me.

Three.

One is pointing a gun at my forehead, the other hovers under the doorway, as if to ensure the coast is clear. Their faces are covered in black ski masks, their hands covered in black gloves.

The one who held the knife to my throat—massive, towering, unmistakably in charge—stares at me with one good eye. The other socket is a bumpy scar tissue.

My voice shakes. "What do you want?"

"I think you know exactly what we want."

My gaze flickers to the security keypad on the wall, close to where the other man is standing. We have several throughout the house. Each has a panic button.

"Don't even think about it," the man growls from the doorway.

I return my focus to the one-eyed man. "I—I don't have anything to do with my husband's business stuff."

"My client doesn't care, he just wants his money."

His *client*. This man is a bounty hunter and his "client" must be one of Matthew's.

I take a slow breath, trying to keep my legs from trembling. "How bad is it?"

"Bad."

My throat tightens. "What happened to my husband's money?"

The man considers me, squinting. Perhaps realizing that I truly don't know the magnitude of trouble I'm in. Finally, he says, "He spent it. All of it. And not just my client's. Dozens of others. You've heard of Bernie Madoff?"

I nod, swallowing the knot in my throat.

"Just like that. And he got into debt with some very, very powerful people."

"I don't have any money to give you."

He makes a show of glancing around at the opulence of our home.

"You want things?" I say with a spark of hope. I'll give this man whatever he wants to spare myself.

"Jewelry," he says. "I know you have a lot of it."

"I will give you all of it, just please, don't hurt me."

He dips his chin.

The rest happens in a blur.

I nod once, tightly, then turn and walk.

They follow.

Their boots are heavy against the polished floors. My bare feet make no sound.

I lead them through the halls. Up the stairs. Down the east

corridor. Into the dressing room where the safe is hidden behind a sliding panel of my husband's closet.

My fingers shake as I punch in the code.

I open the velvet-lined drawers one by one, pulling out the pieces.

The first is a necklace from St. Petersburg. Rose gold with white sapphires, bought after Matthew closed a deal he wasn't supposed to win.

I hand it over.

Next, a pair of emerald earrings from Dubai. I wore them to a fundraiser where a senator kissed both my cheeks and called me radiant. I place them in the pouch without a word.

A ring from Paris. Platinum. Custom-designed. Matthew gave it to me on our fifth wedding anniversary. My throat tightens as I set it down.

Cartier bangles.

A diamond tennis bracelet from our anniversary trip to Bali.

A set of chandelier earrings from Vienna I'd only worn once because they were too heavy.

I keep going.

Pearls from Tokyo. A brooch. A vintage watch I'd never liked but always kept wound.

Two million dollars, at least.

All in one pouch.

I hand it to the man with one eye.

He doesn't thank me.

He weighs it in his palm. Satisfied.

He turns to leave, the others trailing behind him like shadows.

Then he stops at the threshold and turns back.

"You really didn't know?"

"No," I say between gritted teeth. "I guess I'm the cliché: a dumb, stupid trophy wife."

He studies me like he trying to figure out if he believes me or not.

"In that case…"

I wait, my heart pounding.
"A little piece of advice…"
His eye narrows.
"Run."

PART TWO
ONE YEAR LATER

FOURTEEN

OLIVIA

The sun is just beginning to peek over the horizon when I step outside, robe cinched at the waist, slippers snug, coffee cradled in both hands. From this spot on the porch, I can just see the ocean in the distance.

A mild breeze sweeps over my bare legs, scented with morning dew, pine, and sea salt. Spring is quickly fading into summer here in the Pacific Northwest, though you wouldn't know it. Most mornings are still wrapped in fog, and the sky remains a permanent gray.

I've never experienced so much mist. Or so much rain. It sinks into everything—the ground, the siding, your bones. But somehow, I don't mind. There's something about the way the gray softens the edges of the world. It makes things easier to disappear into—which is, after all, the whole point of this new life I've built, the one I began after running from my old one, after the acquittal in my husband's scandal.

I pad down the three creaking, crooked steps and onto the barely-there flagstone path, winding through the unruly garden I've revived from the ground up. Nothing here is manicured. Just wild color and stubborn resilience. Perennials elbowing their way through rocky soil. Climbing vines threading themselves into everything. It's chaotic and overgrown.

But it's mine.

"Morning, Beatrice," I murmur to the plump hydrangea bush I brought back to life when I first moved here. Despite that, she never blooms. "Summer's almost here. Think you'll give me some blooms this season?"

I spend a few minutes tending to the others—trimming back the sword ferns, checking the damp soil around the camas lilies and red columbine.

Behind me, the creaky cottage glitters under the morning light. Weathered gray shingles, white trim flaking in places, the porch sagging just slightly on the eastern side. It was all I could afford after I disappeared, after the SEC and FBI finished investigating me, after the media storm nearly swallowed me whole.

I crouch down and address the pair of roses. One pale peach, the other deep crimson. The peach one is Nora. The red, Maurice. Technically, they're climbing roses. In theory, they're supposed to wind together and fill the trellis with tangled color and harmony. But these two? They refuse to grow together, no matter how much twine and blood I've sacrificed trying to make them. They're spiteful. Dramatic. Absolutely opposed to the idea of partnership.

Despite my best efforts last night, they're turned away from each other again this morning, their stems pulling in opposite directions like lovers in mid-silent treatment.

I sigh, tilting my head as I study them. "Nora, I've told you too many times—I need you to lean into your husband."

The words come out lightly, but they land somewhere harder. Maybe Nora is trying to get away because Maurice has secrets. Maybe he's a possessive asshole who pricks her with his thorns the moment I turn away. Maybe he's a selfish conman who's willing to burn down everything in his path to protect himself.

Stop, Olivia. Not healthy thinking.

I clear my throat and address Maurice. "And you—maybe if you'd stick around long enough, Nora wouldn't keep turning away. Remember, relationships are a two-way street, sweetheart."

I can't remember when I started naming my plants. It just sort of happened. A slow creep of loneliness, like ivy up the side of a house.

I carefully maneuver between the thorns and start adjusting the twine again. "I need you both to work on this. I'm not giving up on you."

The garden is the only place I speak freely, the only place I can be the real me.

No trace of Olivia Grayson remains. Not here, anyway. Not in the deed to this cottage, or in the hardware store where I fumble through aisle three pretending I know what I'm doing, or the coffee shop where I sit and pretend I'm someone who was born here.

Here I am known as Marie. Just Marie. I never give them more.

Marie is my middle name, otherwise known as *new* name.

I pretend that Olivia no longer exists.

After finishing my morning walk-through of the gardens, I return inside, silence greeting me... as it always does.

I shut the door behind me and hang my robe on the hook by the window. On the wall beside the kitchen table hangs a calendar from the local hardware store. A dog-eared business card is tucked behind one corner, the FBI seal still visible through the curl of paper. It falls when I brush past, landing face-down on the counter. I stare at it for a moment, then leave it there.

A stack of legal documents sits in a shoebox under the cabinets. I used to keep them in a drawer, but I got tired of pretending I'd never look again. Depositions. Transcripts. My name in bold at the top of every page. *Olivia Grayson: Witness for the Prosecution.*

I kept or printed every single article of the fallout. The most recent headline:

Another Victim of the Grayson Fraud Comes Forward

Below it, a family photograph. Two kids. A golden retriever. A caption about losing their home.

My husband had conned hundreds of millions from his clients. They lost everything. Entire families—generations—lost everything. Homes. Retirements. Reputations. Matthew Grayson ruined so many people's lives. It was absolutely devastating.

Once I was acquitted, I packed what little remained of my belongings and drove west, 3,500 miles away from my old life, to a tiny, blink-and-you'll-miss it oceanside town called Wilderport.

I look away, willing away the sickening dip in my stomach.

The sink is full of last night's dishes. I rinse a mug, trying not to think about the hundreds of lives destroyed because I didn't ask enough questions. Because I smiled for the cameras. Because I let Matthew convince me ignorance was safety.

My garden saved me, at least a little. Watching something small grow again—the fact that it *can* grow again. That's what my therapist says, anyway. (My *AI* therapist. Real ones are too expensive.)

I still have moments of shock at how different my life is now. I was rich, now I'm poor. I had staff, now I am the staff. I was complacent and stupid, now I'm... what? A survivor? My AI therapist insists I am. I'm just not fully buying it yet.

I glance down at my ankle where the roses are inked—one pale, one crimson. *For Maurice and Nora.*

Matthew would've hated it. Which is exactly why I got it.

I turn back toward the window. Outside, the fog is beginning to lift, revealing the faint shimmer of the ocean beyond the trees. The view is different every morning—gray, green, silver—but never predictable.

Neither am I anymore.

FIFTEEN

OLIVIA

Dust motes sparkle in the slanted sunlight as I refill my coffee, then settle in at the small, antique desk that sits in front of the window. I love this spot because it overlooks the garden in the back yard.

I power up my laptop and check my email, expecting bills or spam.

But there's a new message in my work inbox.

Subject: Restoration Inquiry – "The Dancer"

It's from someone named Micah Graves. He found me through a local social media page I use to support my one-woman business, Fine Lines. It's an art restoration company. When I moved here, I knew I needed a way to pay the bills that wouldn't require me to engage publicly—without navigating the web of lies I'd need if coworkers or locals ever got curious.

But since then, it's become more than that. I absolutely love it. Restoration is careful work. Slow. Precise. Quiet. You take something damaged and you bring it back, inch by inch. You don't erase the flaws. You preserve them. Respect them. You learn where the cracks are and why they formed.

Turns out, I'm pretty good at that.

The money is shit, though, let's be honest. I am barely scraping by.

Micah writes asking if I'd be willing to restore a small sculpture that's been in his family for generations. Attached is a photo.

I click it open.

It's a delicate bronze dancer, arms arched overhead, back curved like a crescent moon. One leg is broken at the ankle. A hairline crack runs through her ribcage. Someone has tried to hide the flaws—bad epoxy, painted over carelessly. But the damage is still visible if you know where to look.

I do a quick social media check—nice house, expensive car, probably drinks lattes with almond milk—decide to charge him double, and hit the respond button:

Yes, I'd be happy to take a look. I'll be at Mariner's Coffee around 10 if you'd like to meet there. – Marie

I hit send, then, without thinking, open the local community page. It's a mess of farmers' markets, lost dogs, beach cleanup announcements, and bickering over parking. I scroll past it all.

Then something catches my eye.

A new post:

Quiet tenant looking for a room. Respectful, neat. Prefer long-term. References available.

No name. Just a generic handle. But it pulls my gaze like a magnet.

My eyes lift to the window, to the far edge of the garden, where beyond the lilacs and the sloping hedge sits the guesthouse, tiny and weathered. Just one open-plan bedroom with a kitchenette, and a bathroom.

I haven't set foot inside in nearly six months.

I begin chewing on my bottom lip.

The extra income would be amazing. And maybe... maybe it's

time I remembered how to hold a conversation that doesn't involve chlorophyll.

Am I even capable of that anymore?

I close the laptop, sip my coffee, and let my gaze linger on the guesthouse.

For no reason I can name, I suddenly hear Matthew's voice in my head—*Confidence first. The rest will come.*

SIXTEEN

MATTHEW

Ten years earlier...

It starts with rain. The kind that makes people rush, heads down, shoulders hunched, desperate to escape. But she doesn't rush. She stands outside the cafe door, wrestling with her umbrella, hair damp, eyes narrowed in frustration.

I notice her before she notices me. Of course I do. She stands out in a way I can't quite explain—brown hair darkened by the rain, loose strands clinging to her cheek. Not polished, not practiced, not pretending, just... real. And somehow that makes her more arresting than anyone else on this crowded street.

The sidewalk is crowded, people brushing past, muttering on cell phones. A man clips her shoulder hard enough to make her stumble. He gives her a dirty look and keeps going.

I step forward, steadying her elbow before she can fall. "Easy there."

She glances up. Those eyes catch me—clear, cautious, searching. I let go as soon as she regains her balance, because men who hold on too long are the ones women remember for the wrong reasons.

"Thank you," she says, her voice soft, wary.

"People forget their manners when it rains." I smile.

The umbrella clicks open in her hand, finally cooperating. She laughs, quick and unguarded, and I feel the sound land somewhere inside me.

"Coming or leaving?" I ask, gesturing to the cafe.

"Coming."

I open the door. "After you, then."

She hesitates a fraction of a second, then nods and slips inside. The warmth of coffee and cinnamon rolls wraps around us, but I'm not paying attention to that. I'm watching the way this woman tucks a damp strand of hair behind her ear, scanning the tables for a place to sit. The way she lingers near the door instead of rushing, which tells me she doesn't like making the wrong choice. The way she presses her lips together as she thinks, like she's steadying herself. And then there's the way her eyes flick to me. Quick, uncertain. Like my presence has thrown her off balance. Like she's not sure why she's checking for me, only that she is. Every move is small, ordinary, forgettable to anyone else. But I see them.

I straighten my shoulders. In this moment, I'll pretend I'm already the man I plan to be—Matthew Grayson, successful investor, the name everyone in town will know. I don't need to tell her that right now my "firm" is a rented office and a stack of business cards I had printed on credit.

Confidence first. The rest will come.

Only one small table is open. I could take it. I should take it. Instead, I step back.

She notices. Her smile is small, grateful, the kind reserved for strangers who surprise you.

She sits, pulls a book from her bag. I order coffee, then claim the stool at the counter near her table. Not too close. Not far enough to be forgettable.

From here, I can hear the scrape of her pen against paper, the way she sighs when she reads a sentence twice. She's alone, but not lonely. That's rarer than people think.

I sip my coffee, careful not to stare too long.

When she looks up, our eyes meet. I hold it just long enough to let her know I see her. Then I look away, leaving space for her to wonder if she wants me to look back again.

SEVENTEEN

From: tworosesandatwine@zmail.com
To: jakecarlson@promail.com
Subject: Room Rental Inquiry

Hi Jake,
I saw your post inquiring about rooms for rent. I have a guesthouse available on my property. It's a one-room studio/rock cottage with a small bath, a kitchenette, and questionable water pressure. But it's clean, quiet, and comes with an ocean breeze and a neighbor who talks to her plants (me).

Are you local, or planning a move? What kind of length of stay are you looking for? I'll need references and first month's rent up front. No parties, no guests, no drama.

—Marie

From: jakecarlson@promail.com
To: tworosesandatwine@zmail.com
Subject: Re: Room Rental Inquiry

Hi Marie,
Good to hear from you. I'm not local. Looking to relocate. I work remotely.

No guests, no parties, no drama.

I can pay first month and provide references.

If it's still available, I'd love to see it.

—Jake

From: tworosesandatwine@zmail.com
To: jakecarlson@promail.com
Subject: Re: Room Rental Inquiry

Yes, the guesthouse is still available. I'm attaching a few photos. Let me know if it looks like something you'd be comfortable calling home for a while.

What brings you to this little corner of the world?

—Marie

From: jakecarlson@promail.com
To: tworosesandatwine@zmail.com
Subject: Re: Room Rental Inquiry

The kind of air you can't smell through a screen.

The guesthouse looks great.

I can come by tomorrow. Morning or afternoon—your call.

—Jake

From: tworosesandatwine@zmail.com
To: jakecarlson@promail.com
Subject: Re: Room Rental Inquiry

Let's shoot for Thursday afternoon, if that works. I'd appreciate your references before meeting. Can you send those over?

—Marie

From: jakecarlson@promail.com
To: tworosesandatwine@zmail.com
Subject: Re: Room Rental Inquiry

Of course. I'll send them in a separate email. On that note, if you wouldn't mind sending over your plants' names, I'd appreciate that, too. I'd hate to add undue stress to the family dynamic.

—Jake

From: tworosesandatwine@zmail.com
To: jakecarlson@promail.com
Subject: Re: Room Rental Inquiry

Well, well, well. What is it about me that says this woman names her plants?

—Marie

From: jakecarlson@promail.com
To: tworosesandatwine@zmail.com
Subject: Re: Room Rental Inquiry

You mentioned you talk to your plants, and also your email handle gives it away. I'm guessing *tworosesandatwine* names all vegetation, likely has strong opinions about petunias, and trust issues with ferns.

Am I wrong?

—Jake

From: tworosesandatwine@zmail.com
To: jakecarlson@promail.com
Subject: Re: Room Rental Inquiry

Not wrong.

Frank the Sword Fern betrayed me in '24 and I've never fully recovered.

I also think you know more about plants (and people who talk to them) than you let on.

—Marie

From: jakecarlson@promail.com
To: tworosesandatwine@zmail.com
Subject: Re: Room Rental Inquiry

I've known a few Franks. None of them trustworthy.

As for plants (and people), I observe more than I interfere.

Have you spoken with my references?

—Jake

From: tworosesandatwine@zmail.com
To: jakecarlson@promail.com

Subject: Re: Room Rental Inquiry

Yes. I'll see you Thursday. If you're ready to move in that day, and if you have the first month's rent, I'll ensure the space is ready. I'll send the address separately, along with the names of the rest of the family—minus Frank, of course. RIP.

—Marie

EIGHTEEN
OLIVIA

I'm nervous.

So I'm cleaning.

Obsessively cleaning.

It's just after ten at night. Jake arrives tomorrow—and it is *all* I can think about.

I move barefoot through the guesthouse, dirty rag in one hand, half-drunk vodka in the other. I opened the windows to usher in the cool sea air. The curtains breathe in and out with the breeze, sighing like they're glad for the company. I wonder if I'll feel the same way.

I clean in silence, letting the rhythm calm me.

The space feels tinier than I remember. But it's quaint, really. A single open room with worn wood floors and a sloped ceiling I painted sky blue. There's a bed in one corner, made up with mismatched sheets and a quilt I found at a secondhand shop. A chair near the window. A small fireplace. A kitchenette with a few outdated appliances, now scrubbed to a shine. And finally, a teeny-tiny bathroom tucked behind a sliding door.

I built the fireplace mantel myself, from a log I dragged in from the woods, then polished down until it gleamed. It's imperfect, knotty, and veined with quartz, but beautiful in a quiet way. Like the kind of thing someone might overlook unless they were really paying attention. I'm proud of it.

Nothing here is fancy. I can't afford fancy. Olivia could, not Marie.

I glance toward the door.

Just the thought of Jake's arrival sends a flutter through my chest. Another human being in my proximity. Breathing my air. Using my mugs. It will be the first person to step foot on this property other than the meter-reader guy who calls me *Chief.* I have no idea why. I could probably get him fired if I reported it.

I re-check the towels I folded, the bed corners I tucked tight. I move the chair, then move it back.

I wonder if I even remember how to have a normal conversation.

I once wore Oscar de la Renta and Tom Ford. Now my closet is a graveyard of discount finds and secondhand bargains, anchored by an alarming number of tribal kaftans, like the one I'm wearing now. (Come to think of it... maybe *that's* why the meter-reader guy calls me Chief.) And for the cherry on top, Crocs are now my footwear of choice. Yes, Crocs, the fashion equivalent of roadkill.

God, I look different. I used to worry someone would recognize me, but now... that thought is almost laughable.

I feel a flash of something that sits somewhere between shame and longing. The old me was beautiful. This new me is, well... bare minimum me.

I shake my head, hard, to toss away the thought.

That woman doesn't exist anymore—and why am I even thinking about what Jake will think?

I cross to the counter, drain what's left of my vodka, and set the glass down too hard.

The sound echoes in the small space, louder than it should.

Outside, an owl calls from the trees.

I exhale a shaky breath.

He's just a tenant.

Nothing more.

NINETEEN

RACHEL

It's a gray, bleak spring day.

I step into the lobby of Oakland Assisted Living, clutching a coffee cake I purchased from a pastry shop a few streets down. The automatic doors seal shut behind me with a loud hiss. The lobby is... sad. An artificial fern droops next to two threadbare canvas chairs, its plastic leaves covered in a layer of dust. A fake water fountain gurgles pathetically in the corner, the water barely trickling over a chipped ceramic swan.

Behind the front desk, a woman in mauve scrubs lifts her head and offers a practiced smile, one that doesn't quite reach her eyes. She picks up a clipboard.

"Hello. Name?"

"Rachel Sinclair. I'm here to visit Hilda Winslow."

She types on the computer. "Yes. She's in room 207, just down that hallway. Just fair warning... the notes say she's having a bit of a rough day. More confused than usual."

"Oh." My stomach tightens, and I adjust the red scarf around my neck. "Okay, thank you... Which...?"

"To the left."

"Thanks."

I'm both relieved and nervous. I called no less than a dozen assisted living facilities before finding Matt's mother. All he ever told me was there'd been a falling out in the family years ago and they were estranged and now she lives with full-time care. That's it. He always got quiet when I asked, so I never pressed.

I walk slowly down the corridor, my footsteps muffled on the paisley print carpet. The walls are lined with faded photographs—some black and white, others in dull, sun-bleached color—showing the facility's founders, a handful of residents clutching holiday crafts, nurses with strained smiles. Each photo is trapped behind a flimsy plastic frame, all barely hanging onto the thumb tacks.

Somewhere down the hall, a burst of canned laughter echoes from an old game show. Farther down, someone coughs, deep and wet and unrelenting.

I grip the coffee cake tighter. My heart is racing. I don't know why I'm so nervous. Maybe it's the aura of the place, or maybe it's just that I can't tell what I'm walking into. Hilda doesn't even know I exist. For all I know, she won't remember her son's name, let alone be able to talk about him.

But I have to try.

The air grows colder the farther I go, like I've entered a part of the building no one visits anymore.

When I reach room 207, I pause, peering through the small glass window.

Hilda is sitting by the window in a worn recliner, gazing at the landscape. Outside, a large bird feeder sways in the wind, dozens of tiny sparrows flitting and diving. A blanket rests across her knees. Her pale, veiny hands are folded neatly in her lap.

The resemblance knocks the breath out of me.

She looks just like him. Same nose, sharp jawline. The faint crease between her brows that makes her look like she's thinking even when she's not.

I'm here because I have no one left to ask. This woman is my last resort to figure out what happened to the love of my life. The man I was going to leave my husband for, begin a new life with.

It's been a little over a year since that last text:

> Had something come up. Leaving town for a bit,
> will message when I get back.

After that, I never heard from him again. What we had together was replaced by salacious headlines, conspiracy theories, a secret life I never knew about—and still don't think I really believe.

At first, it consumed me, trying to make sense of it, scouring headlines, obsessively studying his "wife" Olivia Grayson, playing back every word of our final conversation. But, at the end of the day, I had my own family to worry about. Children. Responsibilities. I couldn't just fall apart, and I couldn't exactly go around asking questions about *Matt the bartender* without raising eyebrows.

As the days dragged on, I *knew* he was dead. Because Matt would never have left me like that. Matt, with his crooked grin and strong hands and impossible dreams. Matt, who made me feel seen for the first time in years. Who told me I could have a life that was more than just "fine." Who looked at me like I was the future.

My future was gone. I stopped sleeping. Stopped eating. Fell into a depression so deep I wasn't sure I'd ever crawl out.

Paul moved out last month. He's renting a shoe-box apartment over the pizza place downtown. We haven't said the word *divorce*, but we both know it's coming.

The day he carried out the last of his boxes, the fire reignited. With Paul officially out of my life—and me having much more time on my hands—I could begin investigating what *really* happened to Matt. Because I know, deep in my bones, that Matt didn't jump off that bridge. Matt didn't kill himself. Someone else did, and I'm going to find out who.

I take a deep breath and press my hand to the cold glass before knocking gently. A nurse appears from a corner of the room, and opens the door.

"Hi," I whisper to the nurse. "I'm here to see Hilda."

She nods, her expression grim. "I'm sorry to say she's having a bad day today. In a bit of a fog."

I nod, swallowing the lump in my throat. "Can I sit with her a while?"

"Of course."

The nurse steps out.

Matt's mother acknowledges me as I settle into the wooden chair beside her and unwrap the cake and place it on the tray table. The smell of cinnamon and sugar fills the room.

"Hello, Hilda. I'm Rachel," I say.

A long moment passes.

Finally, she speaks.

"The birds..." Her voice is so soft and sweet I almost miss it. "They always come in pairs... They used to bring me feathers when I was a girl," she says. "Did you know that? The birds. Always little blue ones. I kept them in a shoebox."

I smile. "I like watching the birds, too." I mindlessly tug at my scarf. "I'm—I'm sorry about your son. Matt." I go to reach for her hand, but pull back. "I was, um, I was close to him."

She doesn't respond, just watches a sparrow hop across the sill. I'm assuming she knows her son is dead, but maybe her brain has chosen to block it.

"Hilda, do you mind if I ask you a few questions about him?"

She doesn't respond and the silence stretches between us. I try again.

"Do you remember the last time you spoke to Matt?"

Her brow furrows slightly. "No."

"Do you remember... did he ever mention anyone named Olivia?"

Hilda tilts her head, brow furrowed. I'm not sure if it's by the question, or the bird that has just joined the sparrow on the sill.

"Olivia Grayson," I repeat, beginning to feel bad that I'm questioning her at all. She's clearly somewhere else.

But then she looks at me. *Really* looks. And for just a second, her eyes sharpen with something close to lucidity.

"You love him, don't you? My Matt. I can tell in your voice. You love him."

I nod. "Yes, I do."

Her lips press together in a faint, sad smile.

Then, she closes her eyes and drops her head against the headrest.

A tear slips down my cheek.

I glance around the room—at the yellowed curtains, the tray of untouched food on her table, the stack of crossword puzzles never filled in.

"Thank you for raising him," I whisper as she seems to slip far, far away.

Outside the window, one of the sparrows lifts from the feeder, wings flashing as it disappears into the gray.

I pull the red scarf tighter around my neck, holding onto the last warmth it carries.

And I stay.

Not because I expect her to say anything else.

But because I know what it's like to feel left behind.

TWENTY

OLIVIA

Finally, at dusk, a red pickup truck pulls into the driveway.

I leap to my feet so fast my knees pop. I've been sitting on the couch, staring at the driveway for nearly an hour like some kind of crazed neighborhood watchdog.

He's here. My new tenant. The man who paid *double* market rent without blinking.

Angling myself just out of his line of sight, I watch as the engine shuts off and the driver's side door opens.

Jake steps out and into the slanted evening light and, for a second, I forget how to breathe.

He's tall. And handsome—*no*. Jake is tall and *hot*.

A dark Henley clings to a thick chest, its sleeves pushed to the elbows in that sexy way that only men with defined forearms can do. His jeans are worn, boots dusty. Stubble covers a sharp jaw, giving him that sexy weathered, outdoorsman vibe. When he looks up, the last shard of sunlight slices across his face, and a pair of piercing pale gray eyes catch the light.

My heart stutters and—God help me—a slight pulse begins to drum between my legs. I haven't felt that in a *long* time. Good to know it still works down there.

I bolt from the window and duck behind the door so he doesn't think I've been watching. Which, of course, I have.

He knocks once. Firm. Polite.

Make him wait, Liv.

My heart is galloping.

He knocks again.

Answer the door, Olivia. You're not a teenager trying to impress the star quarterback. You're a grown woman in a kaftan with mud under her nails and gray in her roots. Answer the damn door.

I suck in a breath and open the door.

He looks up at me. Blinks.

A moment passes between us—charged.

"Marie?" His voice is like gravel. Very *sexy* gravel.

"Yes. You must be Jake."

He nods. "It's a pleasure to meet you."

We shake hands, his strong and calloused. My gaze flickers to the deep scar above his right brow.

"This is the main house," I say quickly, "where I live. The guesthouse is out back."

He nods again, his eyes shifting over my shoulder, taking it in.

It's then that I notice he only has a single duffel slung over his shoulder. Only one bag.

I sweep past him, closing the door, thankful I'd added an extra dab of perfume before taking post on the couch.

"How was your drive over from..."

He follows me down the porch steps. "Chicago."

"Chicago?" I glance over my shoulder.

He nods.

"Wow, now I understand your desire for fresh air. That's one heck of a drive. You must be exhausted."

"Not too bad."

I lead him through the garden path. The wind picks up, rustling the foliage as if they're waving to him.

"So, yes, I *do* speak to my plants and name them. These two are Maurice and Nora," I say, pointing to the roses. "The feuding lovers who inspired my email handle. They've been in a bit of a standoff lately."

He glances at the rosebushes. "I'll keep my distance. They look territorial."

I laugh. It comes out more like a breath, but it's real.

We continue along the path, the gravel crunching beneath our feet. Just before we reach the guesthouse, Jake's attention shifts to the detached one-car garage on the opposite side of the yard. It is the most decrepit building on the property. After every strong gust of wind, I check to make sure the thing hasn't blown down.

"Is that the home of Fine Lines?" he asks.

Seeing my frown, he adds, "I've seen a few of your posts while I was searching for rooms for rent. Figured it was the same Marie. Small town."

"Ah. Yes. That's me, Fine Lines. And yes, that's where I do my work."

"You run the business alone?"

The way he says it makes it sound like more than it is—*run your business*—like I'm someone with clients, contracts, a proper income. Not someone scraping by restoring cracked heirlooms and forgotten sculptures.

I nod.

"I'd like to see it."

I pause mid-step, caught off guard. My brow arches. "Oh."

He doesn't smile. Doesn't soften the request with an *if you don't mind*. Just looks at me, level and unreadable.

My heart skips because this is the one place I didn't obsessively clean while in wait-mode today.

"Okay," I say carefully. "Sure. It's just... a little messy."

"I don't mind messy."

The garage door sticks when I attempt to open it, and I push it with both hands.

Inside, the space is narrow and intimate, scented heavily of linseed oil. The old plank walls are covered in framed botanical sketches and old auction flyers. A leather apron hangs from a rusted hook near the sink. One long workbench runs the length of the left wall, cluttered with brushes, chisels, and sculpting tools. A heavy-duty magnifying lamp angles down over a velvet-lined tray where a tiny porcelain face stares up in permanent surprise. The (slightly crooked) shelf above is packed with small glass jars full of gold leaf flakes, ceramic powders, and hand-mixed pigments. In the far corner, shelves hold half-restored sculptures, broken pottery, and a box labeled *fragments* in my handwriting.

He steps inside slowly, eyes moving over everything.

It's the first time I realize how personal this space really is.

He doesn't speak for a moment. Just looks, absorbs. His expression is hard to read. Thoughtful, maybe. Or something else? I can't tell.

"You've done all this?" he finally asks.

I nod. "Mostly. When I'm not working on something for a client, I like to pick up things at garage sales and practice on them."

He crouches to examine a Romanesque carving of a woman's face, the edge of her crown flaked and fragile. "You're... precise."

"I pay attention to detail." The moment the sentence leaves my mouth, I'm startled by a flashback of my old self, designer suits, everything precisely curated.

Like restoration work.

Control. Precision. The same ache for perfection still lives inside me, now, it's just... different tools.

This man has been here exactly ten seconds and is already making me see things I'd rather not.

I clear my throat. "Well, that's the tour."

He turns toward me. Nods. "It's good work."

I smile tightly, desperate to leave the garage and all the thoughts that have come with it—with him. "Thanks. I'll show you to your room now."

The guesthouse glows golden in the dusky light. The lamp I left on spills from the window onto the pebbled walkway. It looks like a little cottage straight out of *Lord of the Rings*.

I open the door for him. "Here it is."

He steps inside, and I follow.

"It's simple," I say, surprised by the niggle of insecurity. "But I restored most of it myself."

He runs a hand over the polished wood mantel. "This?"

I nod.

His brow arches. "Impressive."

I smile. He noticed. Just like I've noticed that he smells like cedar and soap and has a very—*very*—perky ass.

"Kitchenette's here," I continue. "Linens are in the drawer near the bed. The water pressure is... optimistic."

A ghost of a smile brushes his lips. "Good to know."

There's a brief silence. Not awkward, but electric, like the moment we first laid eyes on each other.

I wonder then... could he be attracted to me?

"Well," I say, suddenly needing to escape the gravitational pull of this moment, "I'll let you settle in."

I hand him the key. His fingers brush mine.

Sparks.

"Thank you." His gaze lingers.

I nod. "Do you need anything right now?"

He hesitates, eyes on mine.

"I think I'm all set."

"Okay. Good night, Jake."

"Good night, Marie."

I walk back to the main house quickly, pulse fluttering, feet barely touching the path. The porch creaks loudly as I hurry across it, like it's mocking me. *You have a crush, you have a crush...*

I close the door behind me and lock it out of habit. Then I walk to the kitchen window, drawn to it without thinking.

I gently push aside the curtain and peer out past the garden, to the small house now occupied by someone new.

And a thought flickers, so fast I almost miss it:

Have I seen him before?

Here in Wilderport?

Somewhere else?

I close my eyes, trying to catch the memory, but it slips away like smoke.

Probably nothing. A face that reminds me of someone. A stranger I passed at the grocery store or gas station.

When I open my eyes, a breeze moves past the curtain, carrying with it the scent of lilacs.

TWENTY-ONE
MATTHEW

Seven years earlier...

The driver opens the door and I step out into the kind of evening that feels made for this moment—warm air, bustling city full of energy, lights from the river catching the glass towers like sparks. A faint sweetness drifts from a line of potted lilacs outside the restaurant, their scent cutting through the city's metallic haze.

This is the life I promised myself. And tonight, I get to show her.

Olivia is already waiting at the entrance, her brown hair caught in a loose knot at the nape of her neck, a dress the color of champagne skimming her shoulders. For a second I just watch her—because sometimes anticipation is half the pleasure. She glances around, spots me, and a smile blooms across her face.

I slip my hand to the small of her back as I greet her, low and quiet. "You look like trouble."

Her laugh bubbles out, soft and surprised. "That's not very gentlemanly."

"Neither am I," I murmur.

She shakes her head but the smile lingers as I lead her inside.

The maître d' ushers us through the velvet-roped entrance to the rooftop, a table waiting with a view that makes the city look like ours alone. The kind of table people assume belongs to someone important. I like that assumption.

The bottle of wine I ordered ahead of time is already waiting.

Olivia sits, glancing at the skyline before leaning in. "How did you even get this reservation? I've heard there's a three-month wait."

I pour her a glass of wine, slide it across. "Let's just say I know a guy who owes me a favor." I don't mention that the favor was hard-won, a hundred late-night hours, endless meetings, endless pitching. She doesn't need the scaffolding, only the picture I build on top.

She tastes the wine, eyes widening. "This is... incredible."

"I remembered you liked the Bordeaux at that little place downtown," I say. "This one's from the same vineyard."

Her eyes sparkle. "You remembered that?"

Of course I remembered. I remember everything about her. That she taps her thumb when she's nervous, that she hates orange in desserts, that she curls her legs under her when she reads. People reveal themselves in pieces; I made it my job to collect hers.

"I pay attention," I tell her, leaning back in my chair. "Especially when it comes to you."

She blushes, looks down at her glass.

The waiter brings the first course, but I barely touch mine. Olivia talks about her day, her voice quick and animated, and I watch the way the candlelight glances off her cheekbones. The way she gestures with her hands when she's passionate.

When she finally pauses, embarrassed, I shake my head. "Don't stop. I could listen to you all night."

Her lips curve. "You're ridiculous."

"Maybe," I admit. "But I meant it."

Between courses, I steer the conversation to my company— Grayson Investments. Not too heavy, not too light. Just enough to let her glimpse the world I'm building.

"We closed a big deal this week," I say. "Real estate portfolio in Atlanta. It's the kind of thing that puts us on the map."

Her eyes widen. "Matthew, that's amazing. You've worked so hard for this."

I let myself sigh, relax a bit. "Some days I still feel like the guy eating dollar-slice pizza at midnight, wondering if I'd made a mistake. But then..." I glance at her, hold her gaze steady. "Then there are days like this. When it feels worth it."

Her hand brushes mine across the table. "I'm proud of you."

The words shouldn't matter—I know my own worth. But hearing them from her? They land deeper than I expect.

I cover her hand with mine. "I couldn't have done it without you, Olivia."

I pause, let the moment breathe, then lean closer. "Actually, there's something else I need to tell you. A surprise."

Her brows lift. "What kind of surprise?"

I smile, savoring the anticipation. "A big surprise."

"What? Just tell me!" She leans forward eagerly, like a child.

I take a slow sip, watching her over the rim of my glass. She rolls her eyes at how deliberately I'm dragging it out,

"Tell me, Matthew!"

"I paid off your student loans."

For a second, she freezes. Then she just blinks at me, as if the words don't make sense. Then her eyes widen, her lips part. "Matthew—what? No. You... you didn't."

"I did," I say softly, feeling my insight lit up with joy. "Every penny. You don't ever have to think about them again."

She stares at me, speechless. Tears start to gather, disbelief written across her face.

Her lips tremble. "What do I owe you?"

I shake my head, squeeze her hand. "You don't owe me anything, Olivia. It's my pleasure to do this. Before my mother died, I realized she was still paying off her college loans. I couldn't believe it. The stress she carried right to the end. So, no, Olivia, you don't owe me anything. Not money, not favors. Just... let me love you. That's all I'll ever want in return."

Tears slide down her cheeks.

Her reaction is more than I expected.

"You don't have to work yourself ragged anymore," I continue. "If you want to quit your job, quit. If you want to stay, stay. But you don't need to carry that weight. It's my honor to take care of you."

Her voice breaks when she whispers, "I don't know what to say."

"Say yes," I murmur, brushing my thumb over her knuckles. "Say you'll let me give you the life you deserve."

Dinner lingers into dessert, a dark chocolate soufflé that appears at our table without us ordering. "Compliments of the chef," the waiter says, winking.

Olivia blinks. "Did you...?"

I grin. "I may have mentioned you like chocolate."

She laughs, shakes her head, and I let the sound wrap around me. It feels like triumph.

Later, when the city lights stretch across the river and the last of the wine is gone, I walk her to the car. She leans into me, her perfume faintly floral, and I lower my mouth close to her ear.

"You know," I whisper, "everything I'm building—this life, this future—it's not about the money."

She tilts her head, searching my face. "What is it about, then?"

"You."

The word hangs there, electric. She doesn't answer, just stares at me, caught.

I kiss her, tasting wine and laughter and the faint sweetness of chocolate on her lips.

TWENTY-TWO

OLIVIA

It's been just over a week since Jake moved in.

Mostly, he's kept to himself. We've had a few polite encounters —a nod in passing, a shared smile over a clumsy moment at the mailbox, the occasional "Morning" or "Evening." But beyond that, nothing of real substance. He's respectful. Quiet. Predictable. And in this phase of my life, predictable feels like a luxury.

At first, I was on edge. Every door creak, every footstep on gravel had me stiffening. But slowly, something strange started happening... I've been *sleeping*. Not just closing my eyes and blinking through hours of restless nothing—I mean actual, deep, restful sleep. For the first time since everything fell apart in Potomac, my body is starting to relax. My chest doesn't ache the same way it used to when I lie down at night. My mind doesn't race quite as hard.

Maybe it's the subtle comfort of knowing someone else is nearby. Or maybe it's something about Jake. That quiet strength he carries without trying. The kind of presence that says he could take down an intruder with one hand while sipping his coffee with the other. It's that unshakable, built-for-battle protector vibe—and apparently, that's exactly what my nervous system has been waiting for.

Of course, I still watch him through the kitchen window, though I've graduated to binoculars now. I keep them tucked behind the curtain above the sink, which is something I'm not proud of but have stopped apologizing for, even in my own head. I tell myself it's precaution. That it's responsible to know who's living thirty feet from my back door.

Also, I'm just plain curious.

Here's what I know so far:

Jake spends almost all day on his laptop—hours at a time, barely moving, barely blinking. I'll glance out the window and see him there, bathed in the blue glow of the screen, completely still except for the occasional flick of his fingers across the keys. Hours, sometimes without even getting up. He keeps a notepad beside the laptop. Bullet points written in small, tight handwriting that I can't discern. But the weird thing is that he always shuts the notepad when he walks away—even if it's just to get a drink or step outside for air. Once, I watched him walk out to the porch to take a phone call. He checked over his shoulder before answering—twice. The call lasted over an hour.

No wedding ring. No phone calls that sound like a relationship. No visible signs of a love life. Just Jake, his laptop and notepad, his very serious conference calls, and whatever quiet world he's brought with him.

I've just poured my nightly vodka when I hear a knock. Three gentle taps.

I freeze, glass in hand. This is the first time he's visited.

I quickly check my reflection in the mirror by the door. Still the kaftan. Still the messy bun. Still Crocs. I suppose if he hasn't run screaming by now, this version of me isn't the worst he could encounter.

I open the door.

Jake stands there, dressed in a soft black T-shirt and faded jeans, that blend of rugged and unreadable.

"Sorry to bother you," he says. "There's a weird clanking in the pipes behind the bathroom wall. I think it's just air in the line, but I didn't want to start messing with anything unless it was okay with you."

I snort, leaning against the doorframe, cradling my glass. "Clanking pipes. Ah yes. I'm very familiar with those clanking pipes. It's the guesthouse's version of welcoming you."

He gives a small nod of amusement.

I continue, "They've been making that sound since I moved in."

"Ever had them checked?"

"Nope."

"Might if I give it a go?"

"That depends—

"Free of charge, of course."

"Then nope," I say with a smirk, "I don't mind one bit."

The corner of his lip curls into an *almost*-smile. There's something about his low-key intensity that gives me butterflies—and also reminds me how long it's been since anyone has worked on *my* pipes.

I clear my throat. "Thanks for checking before you began knocking holes in the walls."

He blinks. "Well. One, thank God you didn't give it a go because clearing air from pipes does *not* involve knocking holes into the walls."

I shrug.

Amusement flickers in his eyes, then, "I will need to turn off the water supply for a bit, though. I'll give you a heads up."

"That's fine. What's two?"

"Two, I wanted to ask because I don't take you for the type who appreciates surprises."

"Not unless they come in a bottle."

His gaze flicks to the drink in my hand, then back up. "Vodka?"

"Always."

There's a loaded pause...

"You want a beer?" I ask, overly casual, nodding toward the fridge. "I keep a stash for emergencies."

He cocks a brow. "Am I the emergency?"

"To be determined." I wink.

He smiles, just slightly, then follows me inside.

I make a conscious effort to keep my head up and shoulders back, projecting a confident, casual air—despite the sudden sheen of sweat on my skin from the rush of excitement.

I grab the bottle from the fridge, pop off the cap, and hand it to him.

"Come on," I say. "Let's take it out to the patio."

We step out into the breeze, the scent of lavender and rosemary trailing in from the garden. The sky is soft and pink, the last of daylight stretching across the horizon like brushstrokes.

He sits in the wooden chair I cleaned earlier this morning, secretly hoping for this very thing. I settle across from him, my legs curled under me, vodka glass in hand.

"You've got a good view here," he says, eyes scanning the dusky line of the garden.

"You can see a sliver of the ocean between those trees over there."

He nods, gazes.

"It's why I got the place. It's peaceful." I reply. "Though peaceful can turn into isolating if you're not careful."

He glances over. "You moved here to be alone?"

"Yes."

He takes a slow sip of his beer. Doesn't ask the obvious follow-up. That on its own makes me like him a little more.

"You any good at it?" he asks instead.

"At being alone?"

He nods.

I pause, tipping my glass slightly. "Honestly? I don't think so."

"Why?"

"I don't think we're meant to be alone. Not really. Not for long."

"I disagree." He leans back in the chair, posture easy. "There's a lot of noise out in the world. Too much of it. Being alone is the only way to clear it."

"True. Noise, constant streams of information, advertisements, people screaming their worst opinions into the void. Bad people. Bad things."

"You know bad people?"

"I do."

He's quiet. Then: "I'm sorry."

"Thanks. I'm still standing."

He cocks his head. "But alone."

"Not anymore," I say, clinking my glass gently against his.

His smile is small again, but real. "Why do I get the feeling I'm your dry run back into society?"

"Why do I get the feeling you've got more secrets than I do?"

He arches a brow. "That obvious?"

"Just a guess."

"I don't think it's a guess." He leans forward, placing his elbows on his knees, dangling the beer between his fingertips. "I think you've been watching me."

"I would never."

"The binoculars you've got hidden behind your kitchen curtain tell a different story."

"Ah. Busted." I shake my head with a laugh. "But, honestly? I'm not sorry."

"Good. You shouldn't be. Your safety should always be your first priority."

We stare at each other for a long beat.

"Do you really have secrets, Jake?"

"Everyone has secrets. I think what you're really asking is if I'm dangerous."

"Are you?"

"Only if you come between me and my morning coffee."

"That's interesting because I've been told not to trust people who can't make it through the day without caffeine."

"I've been told not to trust people who talk to their plants."

"Then we're at an impasse."

"I've been in worse standoffs."

The silence that follows crackles with sexual tension. The kind of intensity that makes you aware of your own heartbeat. Of the way your knees are angled just slightly toward his. Of how your throat goes dry for no good reason.

Jake and I have chemistry, no doubt about it.

"Seriously though," I say, looking away from him because suddenly, I no longer trust myself. "Thanks for the company. I didn't realize how long it had been since I... talked to someone."

I feel his gaze on the side of my face.

"Do you miss Chicago?" I ask, meeting his eyes.

"Absolutely not." He says it with zero hesitation. "I felt like a fish out of water there. I've always preferred nature and quiet."

"Not a city boy then."

He doesn't respond. Just leans back in his chair, watching the last light fade.

I stare into my glass. I can almost feel the electricity humming between is. Attraction? Maybe. Curiosity? Definitely.

I catch him looking at me.

I sip my drink. Maybe I shouldn't be drinking right now. This pull between us is... ridiculous. Too strong. Too fast. I can't let him see me wobble under it.

"Well," I say, rising from the chair, "I should let you get to work on those pipes."

He stands too. "Thanks for the beer."

I nod, pretending this was just a casual moment. But the truth is... I feel something shifting between us.

When I return to the kitchen window, drink still in hand, I watch him walk back toward the guesthouse. He moves with that same steady rhythm I've already come to love.

He opens the door, pauses, his hand on the knob.

He glances over his shoulder.

Our eyes meet—just for a second—then he disappears inside.

I'm about to turn away when his silhouette reappears in the window.

He reaches up slowly...

And closes the curtains.

TWENTY-THREE
RACHEL

I have become obsessed. Like Alex Forrest from *Fatal Attraction* obsessed. Except I am not obsessing over a man—I am obsessing over a woman. Olivia Grayson, the famed widow of Matthew Grayson.

My Matt.

Since leaving the assisted-living facility, I've done nothing but think, pace, and stare at walls that offer no answers. The image of Hilda's pale hands, folded neatly in her lap, keeps haunting me. That flicker of lucidity in her eyes when she said, "You loved him." I did love him. I still do.

I've taken time off work and the kids are with Paul for the night, and thank God, because I can't eat, can't sleep. I can't do anything but try to understand how the man I was going to run away with had an entirely separate life, thousands of miles away.

It makes no sense.

My home has become a war room of coffee cups, sticky notes, and laptop tabs open to every scrap of Matt's digital life—pictures in the local newspaper, social media profiles. I spend hours at the kitchen table, timeline sprawled across scraps of paper, writing in my best handwriting: the times he's at the bar, the gym, dates (that I can recall) of our secret meet-ups.

Then I cross-reference all that with the extensive research I've done on wealthy power couple Matthew and Olivia Grayson. I've written it all down—timelines, events, trying to match them to when Matt and I met up.

Nothing adds up.

And I am going crazy.

I force myself up from the table and onto chores. I clean in frantic bursts, as if wiping the counters and straightening cushions will somehow order my thoughts. My phone buzzes. Paul. *The kids are doing fine,* he answers, in response to my last check-in. When he asks what I'm doing, I click out of the text and turn the phone face-down. I don't owe him explanations. Not anymore.

By late afternoon, I've made a plan. Next week Paul has the kids. I am going to use the opportunity to hunt down Olivia Grayson.

I return to my laptop, fingers trembling slightly as I type her name again—*Olivia Grayson Potomac Maryland address.* I've searched this before, a hundred ways, always ending up at dead links and outdated articles.

I've done this search before, more times than I can count, but this time something new appears. A government-hosted database link I must have overlooked.

I click.

Owner of record: *Matthew & Olivia Grayson.*

Property status: *Seized.*

Custodian: *U.S. Marshals Service – Asset Forfeiture Division.*

My pulse quickens.

I scroll down the deed history, the black-and-white text blurring as adrenaline rushes through me. Less than a year after his death, there's another entry:

Transfer of Deed: *Estate of Matthew Grayson – Olivia Marie Grayson.*

Consideration: *Settlement Agreement.*

So the home was forfeited. Then given back to her.

Is she still there? Or did she sell it?

Either way, it's the only lead I have.

I jot down the address, my handwriting shaking.

I book the plane tickets, the rental car, the last shred of my dignity.

Then I pack methodically, almost mechanically: laptop, notebook, pens, charger, snacks, jacket—everything I might need in Potomac. I force myself to eat a granola bar while reviewing every scrap of information I have.

By evening, I'm spinning with adrenaline. I'm ready. Map marked. Bags packed. Notes organized. Every ounce of doubt shoved aside like trash in a bin.

I will find Olivia Grayson.

I will find out what really happened to Matt.

And nothing—not distance, not fear, not the seeming impossibility of it all—will stop me.

TWENTY-FOUR
OLIVIA

It's been two weeks since Jake moved in, and somehow, we've settled into a rhythm.

Every evening at sunset, we meet on the patio with drinks in hand. Nothing formal, nothing planned—just a quiet agreement between two people who aren't quite strangers anymore. The conversation always starts light: garden mishaps, small-town gossip, his polite observations about how my ferns appear to be staging a coup.

It's easy. *He* is easy. And after years of holding my breath, Jake's presence feels like something close to relief.

Something safe.

"Water's still running smoothly," he says, nursing a beer. "No more clanking."

"Thank you," I say, then add, "for not knocking a hole through the bathroom wall."

He chuckles. "Hey, you're the one who suggested that, not me."

"Where'd you learn how to fix pipes anyway? You make it look easy."

He takes another sip of beer, then says, "I grew up on a farm. Out there, if something broke, you had to figure out how to fix it or you went without. My dad was a carpenter—taught me how to work with my hands before I could even reach the workbench. Plumbing, wiring, fence posts, tractors. If it needed fixing, we fixed it." His mouth curves faintly. "Guess some of it stuck."

We sip in silence, listening to the low hum of cicadas.

I glance sideways, my eyes snagging on the pale line that cuts across Jake's eyebrow.

Before I can stop myself: "Can I ask how you got that scar?"

For a long moment, he doesn't answer. He just rolls the beer bottle between his palms, his gaze fixed somewhere beyond the tree line. Then he exhales, slow, like the question weighed more than it should.

"Army," he says finally. "I enlisted right out of high school. Thought I'd see the world, make something of myself."

I wait, sensing there's more.

"I did a couple of tours overseas," he goes on. "On one, we were on the wrong street at the wrong time. I was the lucky one. Only walked away with a cut above my eye." He lifts a finger to the scar, almost absently. "The guy next to me didn't make it home."

His jaw works, and for the first time I see a fracture in his usual calm — a shadow of guilt, grief, maybe both.

"I'm sorry," I whisper, and I mean it.

He shakes his head. "Part of the job. You sign up knowing the risks. But..." His eyes flick to mine. "Some things stay with you, whether you want them to or not."

The cicadas fill the silence that follows. I can feel the heaviness of his words, and yet, it doesn't push me away. It draws me closer.

"Thank you for telling me," I say quietly.

His mouth curves, not quite a smile, more like an acknowledgment. "Most people don't ask. They just stare."

"Well, I've never been good at minding my business."

This time he does smile, brief but real. And for the first time, I realize just how badly I want to keep unraveling him.

Then his eyes drift toward the garden, specifically the tangled trellis where Nora and Maurice continue their petty marital standoff.

"You know," he says slowly, redirecting the conversation, "if you want those two to grow together, you might need to trim the competing roots. Give them a chance to expand and reach for each other."

My brows arch. "I hadn't thought of that. You know about plants?"

"A little. Sometimes two things are compatible, but the soil's just too crowded. They need room to lean."

"You sound like a plant therapist."

He smiles, but I can tell he's serious. "Just saying—maybe they're attracted to each other. Maybe one of them just needs to be brave enough to make the first move."

My stomach explodes with butterflies.

"Are we still talking about roses?"

He doesn't answer. Just gives me that look again—the one that makes me forget my own name.

And suddenly, I'm finding it hard to control myself.

My neck flushes. My chest tightens. There's a buzzing beneath my skin, like my body is waking up after a long, frozen sleep—and it wants things I'm not sure I'm ready for. Whatever is happening between us is unraveling me.

I want to kiss him. I want to feel him. I want to stop thinking altogether and just *let go*.

I set my glass down before I drop it. My hands are trembling.

What is *wrong* with me?

Can he see hives working their way up my neck?

God, I need a moment. A moment to remind myself that this man is my tenant, that this is temporary, that I cannot get involved with him.

I stand, saying I'll refill our glasses, but when I turn, the hem of my kaftan catches on the leg of the rocking chair.

"Whoa—" I gasp, stumbling, yanking my leg, trying to jerk free from the grasp.

The fabric rips from the chair and the momentum sends me tumbling forward. Like a ninja Jake surges from his seat, catches me with one hand, the other still holding his beer. He pulls me in close, steadying me.

"You okay?" His voice is low, his breath warm near my temple.

I nod. If being so embarrassed you could cry while also suddenly being unable to breathe is okay.

"I'm so..." I steady myself, stand before him and look up.

He stares down at me, eyes dark and searching.

There is no doubt what is going to happen next.

Jake threads his fingers into my hair, wrapping his hand around the back of my head. Then he tightens, fisting gently at the nape of my neck. He tilts my chin up, his touch no longer gentle, but *commanding*.

My heart slams against my ribs.

His gaze drops to my mouth and there's no hesitation, no pause for permission. He kisses me like I'm the only thing he's wanted in days. Weeks. *Years*.

His beer hits the patio with a soft thud. Both arms wrap around my waist, pulling me hard against him.

My knees weaken as the kiss deepens, grows hungrier.

I whisper, breathless, "Would you like to go to my room?"

"Yes."

We move fast—stumbling through the door, across the floor, lips locked, hands roaming. I tug at the hem of his shirt, desperate to feel skin. He yanks it over his head and tosses it aside.

His boots hit the floor, jeans following in a rush.

His hands are everywhere—urgent, reverent—sliding beneath fabric, cupping, kneading, guiding.

My breath catches as he presses me against the hallway wall, kissing me like he doesn't care if we ever make it to the bedroom at all.

But we do—barely.

The backs of my knees hit the bed, and I sink into it—into him—finally too tired to keep holding myself together anymore.

TWENTY-FIVE
OLIVIA

I lie curled against Jake, his arm tucked beneath my neck, my fingers tracing lazy circles over his chest. His breath is slow and even, one hand resting low on my hip. The sheets are twisted around us, cool against my back where the breeze from the opened window drifts in.

The sky outside is black now, speckled with stars. I stare at the dark silhouette of the trees that encircle my property, feeling a kind of full-body peace I've never felt before.

This is bliss.

This is *everything*.

This is... what, exactly? What just happened between us?

It wasn't just good. It was earth-shattering. The best sex I've ever had. Because unlike Matthew—who made it feel like a transaction, or a way to reclaim power—Jake was present. Attentive. Giving in a way I didn't know men were capable of.

Where Matthew was selfish and impatient, Jake was deliberate. Focused. Like every touch had meaning. Like he wasn't just trying to take something from me, but offer something back.

And when it came to my pleasure, he didn't just care. He *prioritized* it. He listened to my breath, my body, my hands, and he adjusted accordingly. Jake knew exactly when to be gentle and when to be commanding. And not once did he cross a line. Not once did it hurt, not once did I feel the need to shrink, or disappear into myself, or count the seconds until it was over.

Matthew never cared if I finished. Jake made it his mission. *Twice.*

(A first time ever for me.)

I breathe in slowly, and even that feels different. I'm already addicted to Jake's scent. Soap and cedar and salt air. Matthew always reeked of imported cologne. It was overpowering, like everything else about him.

I don't feel the urge to bolt, like I used to. I don't feel hollow, or ashamed, or like I need to pull on my armor before the next blow comes. I feel... full. Content.

Honestly? It kind of scares me.

Jake shifts slightly, his lips brushing the crown of my head. I smile into the curve of his shoulder and exhale.

Just then something outside catches my eye.

A shape—a person—just beyond the tree line. They're staring at the house—at the *window*.

My stomach drops.

I push up on one elbow, squinting through the glass. The curtains shift with the breeze making shadows dance across the floorboards. For a second, I swear I see the shadow move.

I slide out from under Jake's arm, my pulse climbing. He's just fallen asleep and doesn't stir.

I tiptoe across the room barefoot, and pull the curtain aside an inch. Nothing. Just the garden, silvered under the moonlight. The lilacs sway, restless.

I move to the kitchen window for another angle. My reflection blurs in the glass—wide eyes, pale skin, shallow breath. Still no one there.

"Probably just a deer," I whisper.

I check the front door next, fingertips brushing the deadbolt. Locked. I peer through the window next to it. Nothing unusual.

A branch snaps somewhere beyond the hedge.

I freeze.

Every hair on my arms lifts.

Silence follows.

I force a shaky laugh and press a hand to my chest, feeling the wild thud of my heartbeat. "Just a deer," I mutter. "You're fine."

I step back into the bedroom, closing the curtain tight before returning to bed. Jake hasn't moved. His breathing is slow, even.

I slip under the covers beside him, but sleep feels a thousand miles away.

TWENTY-SIX
OLIVIA

I wake to birds chirping outside my window and sunlight spilling through the curtains, and for a few seconds, I forget everything. I'm just so *happy*, it's like my brain is vacant.

Then I shift, and the memory returns in a rush. Jake's hands on me, his mouth, the way he kissed me like he needed to memorize every part of me. The way I came apart—the way *we* came apart together.

Twice.

I smile to myself, curling tighter into the sheets. My body aches in that delicious way I thought I'd never feel again.

Jake.

He quietly crawled out of bed just before sunrise. I kept my eyes closed, pretending to still be asleep, though I sensed him pause for a moment, as if debating whether to say something. But then, he left, gently closing the door behind him.

I fell right back to sleep.

It's not time to talk. Not yet. And honestly, I'm grateful because my body is still humming with contentment. I don't want the feeling to leave. I haven't felt this alive since I can remember.

I shift slightly under the covers, pressing my cheek into the pillow that still smells like him. My stomach flutters with nervous excitement. Will it happen again?

God, I hope so.

...What if it doesn't?

What if that was a one-time thing, a beautiful slip of a moment that has already dissolved away?

I chew on the inside of my cheek. He's my tenant. This is complicated. It's messy.

On a deep sigh, I roll onto my back, sheets tangling around my legs, and stare at the ceiling.

Do I go to him?

Do I wait?

Do I pretend it never happened?

I shake my head, rolling my eyes. *It's seven in the freaking morning, Olivia. Much too early for spinning.*

I take a long, hot shower, then slip into a kaftan—pale gray, like Jake's eyes—and dab a touch of perfume behind my ears. By the time I step out of the bedroom, it's after eight.

Barefoot, I pad into the kitchen and head straight for the window. The guesthouse curtains are drawn, but I can see the glow of his computer screen on the table. His silhouette moves back and forth—pacing. On a call, I assume. The man takes a million calls a day, it seems.

While I grind the coffee beans and set the coffee to brew, I make a decision: I'll bring him a mug, leave it on the doorstep, knock, and walk away. A quiet peace offering. A silent message that says, *I'm okay and I hope you are too.*

Yes. Take charge, Olivia. Be a grown-up.

I pour the coffee into one of the heavier mugs, and reach for the creamer.

I freeze, a gasp escaping my lips.

There's a cufflink sitting dead-center on the kitchen counter. Silver with a tiny diamond in the middle.

I am aware of two things in the moment: One, the violent, almost visceral reaction I have to it, and two, it's *not* Jake's. Jake wears flannel and Carhartt and boots that look like they've seen war. This? This is wealth. This is champagne and million-dollar deals.

This is *Matthew,* my dead husband.

The air rushes out of my lungs at once.

It looks *exactly* like the ones he used to wear.

I pick it up with trembling fingers, flip it over, and in an instant, I am pummeled with flashbacks...

We're in Italy. A vineyard. A waiter pouring my wine, complimenting my dress. Matthew didn't like it. He didn't speak to me the rest of the night. The next morning, I found the dress stuffed in the trashcan, covered in stale wine that made it look like someone had been shot in the dress.

A gala in D.C. I laughed a little too long at Senator Blakeman's joke. Matthew's grip on my arm as he guided me out. His accusations, his threats. The next morning, a Cartier watch waited at my seat at breakfast. I wore long sleeves for a week.

The silk sheets. The chandelier flickering above the bed. Matthew's weight crushing down on me, his hands gripping too tightly around my throat. The panic that bubbled up. Despite my pleas to stop, he pinned me down and watched the tears fall down my cheeks while he finished. The next day, a box appeared on my pillow. Inside, diamond studs.

The cufflink slips from my fingers and I stumble back, clutching the edge of the counter for balance.

How did it get here?

This makes no sense.

The cufflink wasn't here last night. I cleaned the entire kitchen before Jake came over. We shared drinks. We kissed. We—

God.

A sick swirl of nausea rises in my gut.

Why does it suddenly feel like I just cheated on Matthew?

But that's crazy. He's dead. *I saw the body.* I *personally* identified my husband's dead body. Everything from the scar on his collarbone to the seahorse-shaped birthmark on his left ribcage.

It's *not* him.

Relief rushes out in a long exhale.

Then whose is it? And more importantly—how did it get into my house? And why is it sitting here like it's begging to be found?

My gaze lifts to the guesthouse.

Jake?

It has to be. It's the only thing that makes logical sense. He's the only other person who's been inside my home. Unless someone broke in while we were sleeping?

I spin around, scanning the windows, remembering seeing someone—or something—outside last night.

A chill creeps up my spine.

I bend down, sweep the cufflink off the floor, holding it tighter this time.

I need to ask Jake if it's his.

TWENTY-SEVEN

MATTHEW

Five years earlier...

The chandelier light catches on Olivia's dress as if it was stitched with fire. Gold silk, cut low in the back, skimming the shape of her shoulders. She's breathtaking, and she's officially mine.

I take her hand as we step into the ballroom. The swell of music, the hum of conversation, the clink of glasses—it all blends into a low elegant hum in the background.

People look at us when we enter. Their eyes linger.

Olivia straightens the cuff of my tux where a gold cufflink gleams beneath the light.

I bend my head toward her. "Perfect," I whisper, lips brushing her ear. "Every head in this room will turn twice tonight."

She smiles, a nervous laugh escaping as she tugs at her clutch. "They're looking at you, not me."

"Wrong, darling. They're looking at us." I tighten my hand around hers, lead her forward. She needs to feel my confidence until she finds her own.

There's a rhythm to presentation, a sequence that never fails if followed exactly. Appearance, composure, synchronicity.

The president of the bank approaches, his wife trailing behind in a sequined gown. We exchange pleasantries, the kind that sound important but mean nothing, and when the wife asks Olivia about her work, I feel her hesitate.

"She doesn't need to worry about work anymore," I say smoothly, answering before she does. "She's free to focus on the things she loves, like her charity work."

Control the conversation, contain the narrative before it can run wild—check, check.

Olivia glances up at me, surprised. I give her hand a reassuring squeeze, my smile easy, practiced. She laughs softly, nods, and the moment passes.

Later, when we're alone near the terrace, she bites her lip. "I could have answered that, you know."

"Of course you could," I say, brushing a strand of brown hair from her cheek. "But you don't need to. You don't owe anyone an explanation, Olivia. Not anymore."

Her eyes search mine, uncertainty flickering there, then fading. "I suppose."

"You're not meant to be another tired woman in an office cubicle. You deserve more. This." I gesture to the glittering skyline outside, the champagne in her hand, the music carrying through the glass doors. "This is your world now."

She exhales, soft, almost relieved. "It feels... unreal sometimes. Like I shouldn't have it."

I cup her chin, tilt her face up to me. "You deserve every bit of it. And I'll make sure you never have to give it back."

Reassure—check. Affirm—check. Anchor—always anchor.

Her shoulders soften. She leans into me, the doubt dissolving as quickly as it came.

Inside, dinner is served—white linens, silver domes lifted in unison. I guide Olivia's chair before she can reach for it herself. She thanks me, but I see the faint blush that colors her cheeks. She's getting used to this life, though she doesn't want to admit it.

Halfway through the meal, a man at the table asks about our honeymoon plans.

"We've been so focused on the company's growth," I say, "but soon, yes. Somewhere warm, maybe Italy."

Olivia smiles, nods.

When dessert arrives, a delicate custard crowned with spun sugar, I lean close, my hand resting on her thigh beneath the table.

"You're handling this beautifully," I murmur. "You belong here."

"I'm trying."

"You don't have to try," I tell her. "Just let me lead. I'll take care of you."

TWENTY-EIGHT

RACHEL

I roll to a stop at the edge of a circular driveway that has a fountain bigger than my bathroom. For a full minute, I just sit there, staring up at the last known address of Matthew Grayson's wife, Olivia Grayson.

It's massive. Stone pillars, manicured hedges, ivy crawling up one side like it's from a movie. It's the kind of place where people host silent auctions and drink wine with names I can't pronounce.

My stomach is in knots.

I don't know what I'm going to say when I meet her (if she even still lives here).

Hello, my name is Rachel, and I was having an affair with your husband, who really lived in Canada and was a local bartender—not a multi-million-dollar business mogul. Sound crazy? Yeah I know. Because it's impossible. So let's figure it out together. What do you say? Oh, also, I totally don't think he jumped. I think someone killed him.

My heart is pounding, and I feel like I'm going to throw up.

"Get out of the car, Rachel," I mutter. "You came all this way. Get out of the damn Prius."

Using the exhale-through-a-straw technique, I blow out a long breath, and step outside. The driveway is so clean it sparkles, like someone comes out here with a toothbrush. I take a few steps toward the grand double doors when—

"Well, hello there!" a syrupy sweet voice calls out behind me. "Can I help you?"

I freeze, then turn.

A woman is hurrying up the driveway. Tory Burch head-to-toe, sunglasses too big for her face. A second woman appears beside her —Lululemon everything. Blonde, skinny, glittering with jewels.

"Oh. Hi. I'm..." I hesitate, clearing my throat. "I'm looking for someone. Olivia Grayson. I think she lives here, or used to, maybe?"

A cloud of perfume hits me as they approach—sharp, floral, and so thick it makes my eyes water.

Tory Burch arches a sculpted brow, then juts out her hand. "I'm Beverly and this is Elaine. You are...?"

"Rachel Sinclair. Do you live nearby?"

"Yes," Beverly says. "We were Olivia's neighbors."

"Were?"

"Yes. She left town ages ago. After all the drama. Anyway this home was recently bought by a woman named Sherri Tolan."

"Oh, really? What kind of drama?" I ask, feigning curiosity.

They exchange a look, their eyes lighting with the thrill of their favorite pastime: Gossip.

"Oh, honey," Elaine glances at the threadbare red scarf around my neck. "You must not be from around here."

"No. I'm from Ontario."

"*Canada?*" Beverly gasps, like I flew in from Pluto. "What in the world brought you down here?"

"Business," I lie.

"What kind of business?"

Shit.

Think, Rachel. Think.

My eyes flick to Elaine's leggings.

"Yoga," I blurt.

"*Yoga?*"

Panic rushes through me. Of all the damn things I could have said. These women probably *invented* yoga. If they ask me a single follow-up question, I'm busted. So, in pure desperation, I add—

"I mean, uh, goat yoga."

A slow blink.

Another.

"I'm sorry—*goat* yoga?"

"Yep." I force myself to hold eye contact. "I'm scouting locations for a luxury goat yoga retreat center. It's really big in Canada. We like, uh, nature... and stuff."

OMG Rachel.

Elaine's mouth opens, closes. Beverly tilts her head like she's trying to picture it.

"Well." Elaine begins fidgeting with the billion-carat ring on her finger. "We *do* have quite a few yoga studios. But goats?"

"They're the new wave," I deadpan. "Very mindfulness-meets-nature. Very exclusive. Very *Gwyneth*-adjacent."

"Oh, wow," Beverly murmurs, clearly torn between calling the HOA and requesting a new class be added immediately.

"Anyway," I smile politely, "do you know where I might find Olivia?"

"I'm sorry, I'm confused..." Elaine says. "You're here to discuss goat yoga with Olivia Grayson?"

"Among other things. Personal things. Yes."

There's a long pause before either of them answers, both women squinting at me like they're trying to decide whether I'm just a normal idiot... or someone with information they could spread like wildfire.

"Washington," Beverly says finally. "Olivia moved to Washington state. Some little coastal town—Wilderport, maybe? It was all very hush-hush. She left in the middle of the night."

"Why so hush-hush?"

"Because the whole neighborhood had been swarming with police and news vans for months. Her husband—poor thing—jumped off a bridge. Can you imagine?"

I can.

I'm *trying* not to.

"It was crazy, but you know, she was always a little... *off*... if you ask me," Elaine adds with a conspiratorial tone. "One of those women who were just too perfect, you know?"

I nod, though I can say with full confidence that I have never met one of *those* women.

"You wouldn't happen to know her new address, would you?" I ask, keeping my tone as casual as possible.

Beverly gives me a slow once-over, her curiosity sharpening. "Actually, I do. She left so quickly she didn't even clean out her locker at the clubhouse. When I brought it up to the staff, they got a mail forwarding address." She cocks a brow and looks away. "I might've gotten a peek at that email."

God, this woman.

"Can I have it?" I ask.

The silence that follows is so loaded I'm certain she's going to say no. Then, after a glance between them, Beverly shrugs. "I'm sure I jotted it down somewhere. You're welcome to swing by the house—if you don't mind a little mess."

She wants more gossip. Specifically, why a goat yoga enthusiast from Ontario is sniffing around a woman who vanished in scandal.

"That would be lovely," I say, forcing a bright smile as my brain scrambles for every yoga term and goat-related fact it's ever absorbed.

TWENTY-NINE
OLIVIA

The mystery cufflink is now buried deep in the kitchen trash, beneath coffee grounds and vegetable peels. Jake said it wasn't his, and I believe him.

I've convinced myself of three possibilities: it belonged to the previous owners, it slipped from a secondhand jacket I bought, or it survived the move from Potomac, tucked in a box I never fully unpacked. That last one feels the most plausible—so I tossed it. I won't let it haunt me.

Now, Jake is asleep beside me, one arm slung over my waist. The sheets are tangled around our legs, still warm from the kind of sex that leaves your limbs heavy and your mind blissfully empty. I haven't felt this relaxed in years. Maybe ever.

I don't know what's happening between us. I'm not even sure I want to define it. All I know is that I feel alive and beautiful again. Like a woman instead of a ghost, and I plan to hold onto that feeling for as long as he'll let me.

I stare out the bedroom window, my cheek resting against the crook of his shoulder. Beyond the glass, the trees sway in the breeze. The moon is low, casting a silver glow over the property. I've found myself looking for that silhouette again, scanning the same patch of woods where I thought I saw someone watching.

Suddenly a floorboard creaks from somewhere in the house.

I freeze, my heart leaping in my throat.

I hear it again. It's subtle—barely audible over Jake's quiet breathing—but I definitely heard it.

I lift my head, squinting at the doorway. Wait.

Another creak. This one closer.

I look at Jake—at his peaceful expression. I don't want to wake him. It feels too early in... whatever this is... to expose him to my midnight paranoia. Besides, I feel safe with him here. He's huge, intimidating, and would definitely wake if I screamed. So, I carefully slip out from beneath his arm and slink out of bed. Adrenaline is already kicking in, giving me a burst of energy. I grab my robe and slide it on, not bothering to tie it.

At the bedroom doorway, I peek around the corner. The hallway is dark. Now that Jake sleeps with me, I don't keep the lights on.

I wait a beat, letting my eyes adjust to the darkness.

Nothing.

I take a cautious step. It's that time of night when the silence presses around you, now broken only by the faint groan of the house settling. A cold draft of air carries the briny scent of salt and pine from a window I must have forgotten to close.

I move through the house like I'm underwater. Every step slow, soundless. The living room is empty. So is the kitchen. I flick on the porch light and peek out—garden, gate, path. All empty.

Maybe it was the house settling. Maybe the old pipes shifting.

Or maybe I'm losing it.

I kill the light and creep deeper into the house, past the old bookshelf, the creaky linen cabinet, the empty guest bath.

Nothing.

When I finally return to the bedroom, Jake hasn't moved. The sight of him, bare chest rising and falling, sends a wash of warmth through me.

I slip back into bed and tuck myself against his side.

But I don't go back to sleep.

THIRTY
RACHEL

It's just past 11 a.m., and I'm sitting at Gate C19, my red scarf wound tightly in my lap.

The airport is buzzing—businessmen with rolling carry-ons, families juggling strollers and snack bags, a *very*-important person yelling into a phone two rows over. I've got a six-hour flight to Seattle, then after a lengthy layover, a connection to Wilderport, a blink-and-you'll-miss-it town on the Washington coast. The kind of place people go to disappear. This only makes me more intrigued by Olivia Grayson, and more suspicious that she knows *something*.

It will be late by the time I arrive.

After leaving Beverly and Elaine's house yesterday, I spent the rest of the afternoon snooping around Potomac Crossing, hoping to glean anything I could about the Olivia and Matthew Grayson scandal. But it turns out a year is all it takes for a neighborhood to move on. The whispers have dulled. The headlines have faded. The mansion is just another house now. And Matthew is just another man who fell from grace—and off a bridge.

I haven't told Paul where I'm at or what I'm doing. Just a "thumbs up" response to his texts here and there.

I stare out the giant glass window at the runway, sunlight

bouncing off the tarmac in hazy waves. Somewhere out there is a plane that will carry me to the truth.

For you, Matt.

I'm going to find out what really happened to the love of my life. Even if the answers aren't what I want.

Even if I'm not ready.

I tighten my grip on the scarf and wait for them to call my name.

THIRTY-ONE

OLIVIA

It's just after eight in the evening, and I'm still in the garden. The last bit of daylight lingers in a muted blue light. It's chilly enough that I've thrown on a sweatshirt. I clip a few wild sprigs of rosemary and trim back the mint bush that has threatened to take over the entire back yard.

My gaze shifts to the driveway, as it has a hundred times. Unfortunately there is nothing but deepening shadows and a curl of mist hanging low over the gravel.

Jake's been gone since late morning. Where? I have no idea. All he said was, quote, "Going to run into town for a bit. I'll be back later."

My fingers twitch against the gardening shears. I tell myself I'm being ridiculous. Not because I think something has happened to him, or that he's currently giving some other woman the most incredible sex of her life—but because of how uneasy and vulnerable I feel without him here.

It's a jarring realization: I've become dependent on Jake. On his presence, his steadiness. It snuck up on me like a wave I didn't see coming until I'm already breathless in the undertow.

I didn't have this with Matthew. In fact, it was the opposite. The only time I ever felt *unsafe* in my home was *with* him. Every conversation felt like a test, a minefield. Every glance, a calculation. I never knew which version of my husband I was going to get— charming and generous, or cold and cunning.

Jake is nothing like that.

Jake has become the calm to my chaos.

I shake my head and look back toward the driveway.

Where *is* he?

The light fades quickly, and I'm suddenly aware of how dark it's getting. What remains of the sun is nothing but a thin band of orange on the horizon. The trees beyond the garden are pitch-black.

My skin prickles.

I gather the herbs in my arms and retreat to the house, locking the door behind me with more force than necessary—but not before checking the driveway one more time.

Inside, the air feels too still. Everything is just too quiet. God, I miss him.

I light a few candles, move through the rooms slowly, flipping on lamps and pretending I'm not checking corners or glancing toward the windows.

I need to relax. A bath, maybe. Yes. With hot water and lavender oil. And bonus, when Jake walks in and sees me soaking, he will be none the wiser that I've spent the entire day pacing like a lunatic, waiting for the sound of his truck in the driveway.

I pour a glass of vodka, step into the bedroom—and jolt to a stop like someone's slapped me in the face.

There, propped on my nightstand like it's always belonged there, is a framed photo of me and my dead husband.

On our *wedding* day.

I gasp, my vision tilting like I've been shoved out of time.

The frame is antique silver with tiny etched roses along the edges. I remember it—just like I also remember throwing it in the trash after smashing the glass with my boot.

This *exact* one.

The vodka slips from my fingertips, shattering on the wood floor beneath my feet.

In the picture, I'm beaming, the veil swept back from my face. My hair is shiny and curled just right. My lips are painted the softest rose. I look like a woman in love.

Matthew stands beside me, one hand on my hip, the other cradling the back of my neck. His smile is polished. His gaze, proud. He always knew how to pose for the camera. How to play the part.

What no one knew was that I cried in the bridal suite before the ceremony. Or that he yelled at me on the car ride to the venue for being five minutes late. Or that the necklace I wore in that photo was a frantic last-minute purchase—because mine "wasn't good enough."

I stumble backward, slipping on the spilled vodka before catching myself on the doorframe.

Someone has been in my house.

In my *bedroom*.

I spin on my heel and dart to the front door to ensure it's locked. I check the windows, one by one. Living room. Bathroom. Kitchen. All locked.

I hurry down the hall, checking each room. Guest bath. Laundry closet. Even the pantry.

My gaze swings toward the guesthouse. It's so dark now I can barely see it without any lights on inside.

I scan the tree line, every muscle pulled tight, searching for the silhouette I now *know* I saw days earlier.

Nothing.

My eyes shift to the trash can with the cufflink buried in the bottom. There's no convincing myself that the creepy things that have suddenly been happening is just a crazy coincidence. Not anymore.

Because now, deep down in the depth of my soul, I am certain of two things: That cufflink once belonged to my husband. And I destroyed that photo.

Which means someone has been in my house. *Twice.*

Someone knows who I really am. Not the simple, quiet new-girl-in-town "Marie," but Olivia Grayson, idiot wife of the biggest con artist of the decade.

I stare at the photo, staring back at me like it's a living breathing thing.

Someone is messing with me. Sending a message?

Why?

Is it one of Matthew's old clients? Another collector—just like the ones who broke into the Potomac house? Did they track me all the way out here?

My heart hammers as my gaze drifts back to the guesthouse—and then a thought hits me so hard it knocks the air from my lungs:

All of this weird stuff started happening the moment Jake moved in.

What if the man I've been sleeping with isn't here to find fresh air—

He's here to find *me.*

The *real* me.

THIRTY-TWO

RACHEL

It's dark outside by the time I settle into the cheapest rental car the airport had available. It's an old white sedan that smells like cigarettes.

I'm running on five hours of broken sleep and no less than five bad airport coffees. One of my flights was delayed, the other had me wedged in the middle seat between a man who snored like a chainsaw and a woman with a toddler who screamed every time the seatbelt sign came on.

The drive to Olivia's new home takes me along a winding two-lane road carved through a thick forest, the kind of road that vanishes on GPS and feels older than the trees themselves. The moon is bright and full overhead, casting long shadows along the cracked pavement. The roads are wet from a recent rain, and it's so humid that my pin-straight hair is suddenly curly.

I roll down the windows to fight the fogging glass. The briny scent of ocean washes through the car. I can hear the distant crash of waves, and for a moment, it soothes me.

It's been a long time since I've been to the ocean. Years, maybe. Life has a way of getting away from you when you're making sandwiches and paying bills and pretending your marriage isn't disintegrating.

I get this crazy fantasy in my head—me and Olivia walking along the beach, barefoot in the surf, wind in our hair, maybe even laughing. Like we're friends. Two women who somehow got caught in the same hurricane, finally comparing storm damage.

I've spent hours contemplating the woman behind the headlines.

I've read all the articles, all the online forums and the comments. They painted her as a cold and manipulative house-wife, and maybe even complicit in whatever scam her husband was running.

I picture her now: thinner, tired, maybe a little hardened, but still holding on. Maybe she hates him. Maybe I'm supposed to hate him, too. Maybe we'll compare notes. Maybe we'll put the last pieces of this puzzle together and finally get some answers.

I'm not planning to knock on her door tonight. Just drive past for now. Get a sense of the place. I'll get a motel after that. Then tomorrow, I'll visit first thing in the morning, coffee and muffins in hand, and introduce myself, reciting the speech I practiced on the flight over.

My fingers tap anxiously on the steering wheel.

I reach down and turn on the radio, settling on a Van Morrison song.

It feels like I've been driving forever. I wonder if Olivia intentionally relocated to a place this remote. Probably so.

That's when it hits me: This *is* the middle of nowhere. If I were to get a flat tire out here, I would be screwed—and also, very, very scared.

I ease off the gas just slightly, my hands tightening around the wheel as I glance around. Dense forest presses in on both sides of the road, black and impenetrable beyond the arc of my headlights.

A flicker of unease curls in my stomach.

I am utterly, completely alone out here.

Then my imagination, the little tyrant, takes control of my thoughts. I begin recalling all the old ghost stories I've ever heard—

cars breaking down on forgotten roads, a man appearing with an ax, smiling like he's been waiting.

I remember a story my brother told me once about a woman named Carina who vanished while searching for her dog who'd darted into the woods late one night. She found the dog, dead, on the doorstep of an old decrepit cabin that seemed to appear out of nowhere. Inside lived an old woman, missing one eye, who practiced witchcraft. The Widow of Weeping Pines, she was called. They found Carina's body ten days later at the base of an old fire tower, her eyes sewn shut, her hands missing.

I was eight when he told me that. I didn't sleep for a week.

Now, the only thing separating me from that kind of fate is a rental car with questionable tires and a tank just under half-full.

My grip on the wheel tightens. My eyes flick to the gas gauge. Then the treeline. Then the road.

It's fine. I'm fine.

And then—out of nowhere—a deer darts into the road.

I scream and slam the brakes, tires screeching as the animal flashes past, a blur of pale legs and panic.

The car skids to a stop.

I sit frozen for a second, eyes wide, lungs heaving.

"That's it. I'm turning around." I say out loud.

Heart still lodged in my throat, I press the gas, looking for a shoulder wide enough to turn around.

Suddenly, headlights appear in my rearview mirror.

Oh you've got to be kidding me.

Nerves explode in my stomach.

There are no houses out here. I haven't passed a single gas station in miles. And suddenly, now when my fear is peaking, someone's behind me?

I grip the wheel tighter and pick up speed.

The headlights come closer.

I ease down on the gas a little more. Thirty-five miles per hour. Forty. Forty-five. Way too fast for the curves in this road.

The other car matches me.

My pulse skyrockets.

I begin to sweat.

What are they doing?

I scan the roadside for any exit at all. An old hunting road. Driveway. Anything.

I keep glancing back at the headlights.

When I was a little girl (and when my brother wasn't telling me ghost stories), my mother told me to never ignore my gut instinct. "It's always right," she'd said. And right now, that instinct is screaming at me that I am not safe.

The police. Yes. *Call the police, Rachel.* At the very least, they'll know my location and what happened leading up to my death (God forbid).

I look again at the rearview.

It's a truck—and it's edging even closer.

I feel like my chest is constricting. Everything is going too fast. My pulse, the car's speed, my trembling fingers as I try to unlock my damn phone.

"Come on, come on." I curse the screen when it doesn't accept my passcode, unquestionably due to my shaking hand.

When I refocus on the windshield, the road ends at an abrupt T in the road.

"Shit!"

I drop the phone, yank the wheel to the right. Tires scream against wet pavement. I slam the brakes. The car fishtails, skids sideways, and launches off the road, crashing through brush until the nose drops hard into a ditch.

I jolt forward, the seatbelt snapping tight across my chest. My ears ring.

A bird bursts from the brush in a frantic blur of wings, slamming against the windshield before vanishing into the night. I scream, hands white-knuckled on the wheel.

I sit stunned for a beat, heart thundering, staring into two beams of light illuminating the skeletal trees right in front me.

And then I remember the truck.

I twist around.

It's right *there*. Parked on the road *right behind me*—with the lights off and the driver's door standing open.

Oh my God.

Weapon.

I need a weapon.

My breath comes in ragged gasps as I fumble for anything—an umbrella, a tire iron, a lip liner that I can stab into someone's eye.

Then—

Footsteps. Slow and deliberate on the wet asphalt, like some terrifying horror movie.

That's when I remember my window is down.

I freeze, my stomach dropping to my feet.

A large dark silhouette appears at my door, dressed in all black.

My blood turns to ice.

"Hello, Rachel," he says in a low, gravely voice. "Surprise."

THIRTY-THREE

OLIVIA

I'm sitting on the porch when Jake's headlights slice through the trees. As the Chevy rounds the bend in the driveway, the light hits me square in the eyes. I squint but don't move from my spot on the porch swing. One hand is clenching the photo so tightly my fingertips have gone numb. My other hand rests near the cushion—just above the knife I tucked beneath it.

The truck groans to a stop. The engine cuts out.

The driver's door opens.

I hear his boots on the gravel. Hear the plastic crinkle of grocery bags.

Then stillness as he must notice the look on my face.

"Marie?" His silhouette freezes.

I don't answer.

"What's wrong?" He takes a step forward, instinctively setting the bags down. His voice is cautious now. "Are you okay?"

I lift the photo. It glints off the headlights that haven't timed out yet.

He stops moving.

"I found this," I say, my voice barely recognizable. "On my nightstand."

His brows draw together. He doesn't speak.

"This is me and my ex-husband—my *dead* ex-husband," I continue, rising slowly from the chair, the photo held out like evidence. "On our wedding day."

He crosses the driveway, slowly this time. "Okay..."

"Okay?" My voice cracks, volume rising. "You don't find that strange?"

Jake's eyes flick to the picture, then to me. "I'm sorry—I don't understand..."

"You did this, didn't you? *You* printed this." I take another step toward him. "You found it online, you printed it, and you put it on my goddamn nightstand. Right after you somehow found his old cufflink and left it in the kitchen for me to find. What kind of twisted game are you playing with me? What do you want from me?"

His expression shifts—confusion melting into disbelief. "What?" He stops just before the porch steps. "Marie, no. Why would I—?"

"You tell me!" I snap, the words ripping from my throat. "First the cufflinks, and now this. Tell me why it only started after you moved in!"

"You think *I'm* doing this to you?"

"I don't know what to think!" My voice breaks on the last word. My hands are shaking. "Everything was fine before you got here. And now this. I thought I was losing my mind but I'm not. Someone is doing this—and it has to be you."

Jake sets down the grocery bags. Eyes locked on mine, he ascends the steps, hands raised, voice gentle. "Marie. Look at me. I don't know anything about that photo. I swear to you."

The calm in his voice only makes my panic feel louder. I back up a step.

His eyes flick briefly toward the cushion that's hiding a knife. Smart man.

"I'm not going to hurt you," he says.

"I don't know that," I whisper, my control wavering.

It's a lie, though. I do trust him. God help me, I trust him and I don't know why.

"I didn't realize how badly the cufflinks scared you—or that you were scared at all," he says. "I never should have left today. I'm sorry. If you think someone's coming into the house, I believe you. You should have called me."

"And said what? That someone is leaving me haunting reminders of my *dead* husband?" I shake the photo at him. "That someone might know who I really am?"

It's a test. I need to see his expression when I say it.

He blinks. Frowns. "What do you mean, who you really are?" His face drops. "Your name isn't really Marie, is it?"

"No," I whisper.

Neither of us moves.

For a long moment, we just stare at each other.

I swallow deeply. "One of two things have happened here, Jake. One: You're lying. You printed this photo and you are messing with me. If this is the case, then you know who I really am because you would have had to Google this photo under my *real* name. Or two..." Tears pool in my eyes. "Someone else here knows who I really am, and I have no idea who they are, why they are doing this, what they want, or how they found me."

"Marie, or whatever your name is," he says, closing the distance between us. "Can we sit?"

When I don't respond, he reaches out and takes the photo from my trembling fingers. His touch is careful, deliberate, like he's trying not to startle a wild animal. He turns the frame over and sets it facedown on the railing.

"I have to trust you," I blurt, emotions finally cracking. "I *need* to trust you. I can't be betrayed again. I can't be betrayed by another man. Not again. I won't... I won't recover this time. I can't, I can't, I can't—"

My brain starts replaying the old scripts: the lies Matthew told, the way he used my silence to build his empire, the way he always made me feel crazy for asking questions he didn't want to answer.

And now Jake—calm, steady Jake—is looking at me the same way Matthew did in the beginning. With patience. With softness. With a look that suggests *I'm* the one unraveling—not him.

My chest tightens. What if I've done it again? What if I've let another monster slip past my defenses just because he smiled like he meant it?

The fear is so loud, it drowns out everything else.

My knees buckle before I even realize I'm falling.

His arms are around me in an instant, catching me against his chest, just like he did before our first kiss.

I begin sobbing—gut-wrenching, choking sobs—letting my weight sag into him like a wet washcloth, hating myself for needing him, and hating the part of me that still wants to believe he's safe.

Jake guides me onto the porch swing, steadying it with one hand while holding me with the other. The wood creaks under us as we sit.

"I don't care what your real name is..." His voice softens as he brushes the hair from my face, his thumb grazing the edge of my jaw. "I truly don't care."

Tears spill down my cheek. He wipes them away.

"I don't care who you used to be. All I care about is the woman in front of me now." He leans in closer, gaze steady. "Listen. I'm falling for you, whatever-your-name-is. Fast. And I'm trying not to screw it up by pushing too hard, too soon. That's why I haven't asked too many questions. I knew you were hiding something, and so I told myself we'd take this at your pace. But now... with this... I can't protect you if I don't know the truth. And I want to protect you. I want to be the one you can count on, not the one who breaks you."

He takes my hand into his.

"I will walk away if that's what you want—if you look me in the eye and tell me you don't trust me, that you don't feel what I feel. But if there's even a part of you that believes I'm not the enemy here, then let me stay. Please."

I look down at our hands.

His voice is so steady, so certain. It terrifies me more than it comforts me. Because if he is lying, he's good at it. *Just. Like. Matthew.* And the scariest part is... I don't know if I care. I am falling in love with this man.

"My real name is Olivia Grayson. Marie is my middle name." I force the words out. "My husband was Matthew Grayson."

His expression remains neutral.

"You might've seen the headlines about the man who conned billions from his investors. He ruined so many innocent people's lives." My voice cracks. "Before I go on, you need to know—I didn't know. I swear to you, I didn't know."

Still no reaction. Not judgment. Not disbelief. Just patience.

I continue.

"We lived in Potomac Crossing in a massive, obnoxious mega-mansion. Designer everything. Couture this, one-of-a-kind that. Very different to this," I snort, gesturing to the property. "And then one day, the very expensive walls started crumbling. Quietly at first —little cracks I didn't want to look too closely at."

I swallow, the bitterness still fresh on my tongue.

"Matthew's business was drowning in debt. He tried to keep the illusion going until it finally swallowed him whole. I know now that the SEC had been secretly investigating his company for a year. I think he knew that too, and instead of facing consequences for his actions, my husband jumped off a bridge."

Jake exhales slowly.

"I drove up on the scene. I identified him at the morgue." I whisper. "It was awful."

His thumb begins stroking the back of my hand.

I close my eyes. "Then came the media firestorm. I was questioned. Accused. The FBI, SEC—everyone came for me. The media tore me apart. One night, a debt collector for one of his clients broke into my house and threatened me. I've never been more scared in my life. Before he left he advised me to, quote, 'run.' He told me there would be a lot more people coming for my money." I laugh a humorless laugh. "But then I lost everything.

Most of my things, the cars, the money. My name. My friends. My sense of safety."

Jake shifts beside me, his hand still threaded through mine.

"I didn't get convicted," I continue. "There wasn't enough to charge me. But that didn't stop the media from turning me into his accomplice. I was guilty by association. And those who didn't think I was involved in his business dealings, blamed me for his death. Said I'd driven him to it. Because it's always the wife, isn't it?"

I look at him fully now, stomach churning.

Tell him, a voice whispers in my head.

Tell him the real *truth.*

I open my mouth, but the words get caught somewhere between the comfort of his stare and fear that he'll leave once he knows what really happened.

"And then you left?" he asks.

I swallow deeply.

"Yes. I packed what I had in the back of my car and left in the middle of the night. Drove here, and started a new life as Marie. I never give anyone my last name. And until that cufflink showed up... until the photo... I thought I'd buried it all."

He doesn't say anything else, but holds me while I cry... not just for what happened, but for the part of me that still isn't sure I deserve comfort.

THIRTY-FOUR
OLIVIA

The days that follow are both the quietest and the loudest of my new life.

Jake doesn't leave my side—not even once. Not when I water the garden, not when I walk down to the mailbox, not when I curl up on the porch swing with a book I won't remember reading. He moves through the cottage like the shadow I never knew I needed. Not invasive or suffocating, just steady and constant. Like a wall braced behind me, ready to hold me up when I can't do it myself.

Jake wanted to call the police.

"No." The word came out sharper than I meant.

He studied me. "Why not?"

Because one 911 call and everything unravels. Because I'm not ready to become that woman again—the one who jumped at shadows and hid in closets.

"Not yet," I said quietly. "Please."

His jaw worked, but finally he nodded. "If anything else happens—we call the police. That's the deal."

"Okay. I promise."

"Good. Now. Do you have any idea who might be behind this?"

"It has to be someone from Matthew's world," I'd said. "A former client who still thinks I have something left to steal, to make up for what my husband took from him."

Jake's response?

"If they come back, they're going to wish they hadn't."

I feel lighter since confessing (almost) everything to Jake. Like I'm not carrying it all alone anymore.

Tonight, we're making dinner together. It feels comfortable. Domestic. I'd nearly forgotten how to laugh like this. He chops herbs while I stir the sauce, hip to hip at the stove. The wine is open, the music soft.

He reaches past me for a spoon and murmurs, "You always cook without a bra?"

I wiggle my eyebrows. "Only when I'm trying to seduce someone."

He smirks, places a kiss on the top of my head.

We eat at the small table by the window, gazing out at the setting sun.

The wine warms me, loosening words I wouldn't usually say out loud. My eyes catch on the faint scar along Jake's eyebrow.

I set my glass down. "Can I ask you something?"

He quirks a brow. "You just did."

I roll my eyes, but my smile fades. "Can I ask about your scar? About... what happened that day? The guy next to you who didn't make it home." I watch his face.

For a moment, he just studies me, unreadable. Then he sets his fork aside, leaning back in his chair. The sunlight catches on the curve of his jaw as he exhales.

"His name was Keller," he says finally. His voice has gone low, gritty. "We were on patrol, outskirts of a village that barely showed up on maps. Quiet day, nothing unusual. I actually remember thinking—relieved—that it had been a calm day. He was on a motorbike behind me. My job was point. Focus half a click ahead, eyes on the road, looking for anything off. I told myself the path was clear."

He pauses, jaw tightening. "I didn't see the wires. They were buried under loose dirt. One minute we're driving, the next, the windshield is exploding. When I looked back... Keller... there wasn't much left of him." His throat works. "The main explosion happened after I'd crossed. I tripped the wire, my buddy paid for it. I was supposed to keep him safe. That was the job. And I failed."

His voice roughens, quieter now. "You know the part I can't shake? I keep replaying the moment I chose the left path instead of the right. One decision, one street. Wrong place, wrong time. And it cost him everything."

My chest aches for him.

I reach across the table, covering his hand with mine. "Jake... you can't carry that forever. You couldn't have known."

His eyes meet mine, stormy and unguarded. "Maybe not. But I swore to protect him, and I failed. That stays with you."

He squeezes my hand, firm but gentle. "That's why I don't make promises lightly, Olivia. When I tell you I'll keep you safe... I mean it. I don't get second chances. Not with you."

The air between us shifts, charged, intimate. I can feel the truth of his words in the press of his fingers, in the quiet vow lingering in his gaze.

And God help me, I believe him.

And it loosens something inside me, makes me want to tell him everything I've kept locked away.

"My lawyers painted me as the clueless housewife," I say, shaking my head. "It was like even the people who were trying to save me were stripping me of my last shred of dignity."

Jake's expression doesn't change. "You weren't clueless," he says quietly. "You were surviving."

"It honestly felt like that sometimes. I lost everything," I whisper. "My mind, almost. I—I used to wake up and not remember what day it was. I had panic attacks. I couldn't leave my house for a long time. I just hid, in the closet mostly."

"Your safe space."

I smile. Jake has caught me crying in my "safe space," more than a few times lately.

"Why a closet?" he asks softly. "And why always pretzels?"

I shrug, a half-laugh breaking through. "My parents always argued in the living room, and my room and closet were at the far end of the house. The small space made me feel safe. And pretzels... Growing up, they were all we ever had. Bread, peanut butter, pretzels—the kind that came in the big plastic jug. I guess I developed a taste for them. We were really poor. Which is probably why I clung so hard to the security Matthew gave me. Anyway," I inhale deeply, "I spent a lot of time there."

"You were grieving," he continues. "Grief does that. And you weren't only grieving your husband, but yourself, your life, your reputation, your lifestyle, everything."

He looks at me thoughtfully. "Did you love him?"

It is the most intimate question Jake has ever asked me.

"In the beginning I thought I did. But that's a conman for you, isn't it? They are skilled at making people like them. Very charismatic, good-looking. Promise you the world. But it wasn't long until those initial feelings faded."

"What do you mean, you *thought* you did?"

"I didn't know what real love was."

His gaze intensifies.

"Do you now?" he asks.

Yes, I think. But something stops me from saying it, and I don't know what—or why.

So instead, I say, "I'm not ready to answer that question yet."

He stares at me for a moment, then nods, and refocuses on dinner.

When I fall asleep that night, it's with my head on his chest.

And then the dream comes.

I'm in Potomac again. My old kitchen. I'm hosting a party. But no one has a face. They drift like mannequins, their mouths moving soundlessly. I try to speak, to call out, but no one can hear me. I'm mute. And then I see Matthew, near the fireplace, glass of scotch in hand.

Standing beside him is Jake.

They're talking like old friends. They turn to look at me in perfect unison.

I jolt awake with a gasp, drenched in sweat, heart galloping. Jake is there instantly, arms around me.

"It's okay. You're okay, Olivia," he murmurs against my hair. "It's just a bad dream. I've got you."

I want to believe him. But something cold settles over my skin.

I snuggle closer, careful to stay still until he falls back to sleep. It doesn't take long.

Tracing a circle over his bare chest with my fingertip, I stare out the window, below the clod-hung moon, into the trees at the edge of the property, where I saw the silhouette before. Shadows shift and stretch between the trunks, catching my attention. Every rustle makes my muscles tighten.

And then—I see it again. A figure standing between two pines.

"Jake," I whisper-hiss, scrambling upright.

He startles awake. "What—what?"

"I think I see someone," I whisper, voice dry as ash. "Between the pines."

He bolts out of bed, grabs the flashlight from the nightstand. His attention shifts to the window. "Where exactly?"

I point. "Just past the garden fence. By the left-most tree. I'm not sure..." Jake is already tugging on his jeans, slipping into his house shoes. "I think someone was standing there."

"Stay here," he commands. "I'll check it out."

I wrap the blanket around my naked body. My eyes stay glued to the window as I listen to Jake's heavy footsteps tracking through the house. The sound of him flicking on lights. The subtle creak of the back door opening, then clicking shut again.

My heart pounds against my ribcage.

Outside, the flashlight beam sweeps the darkness as Jake hurries through the garden. But instead of heading straight for the trees, he rounds the edge of the guesthouse, disappearing behind it. I lean forward, squinting, and wait.

Seconds pass.

He emerges again, stepping back into the moonlight. Only now, he's carrying something in his other hand.

A gun.

THIRTY-FIVE

OLIVIA

There was no one lurking between the trees. That was good news, but the gun Jake had hidden was, well, surprising news.

He told me he's always carried a gun. He's trained to shoot, has a concealed carry license—he even showed me the card.

"I didn't tell you when I moved in because I didn't want to scare you," he said this morning. "But I promise, it's only for protection."

I nodded, but honestly, it puts me on edge—and I was already on edge to begin with.

I can feel myself slipping back into the version of me who triple-checked every lock. Who woke at every creak. Who hid in her closet for hours on end. The panic-stricken woman who lived in Potomac is resurfacing, and I don't know how to stop her.

I've started watching Jake more closely—every move, every phone call, every time his expression flickers with something I can't quite read. Why? Because I can't ignore that everything started happening the moment he moved in. I feel caught between my emotions and my common sense. And it's wearing me thin.

Everything is.

Now, it's just after five in the evening. I've settled on the couch with a glass of wine. The windows are open, the curtains fluttering in a cool ocean breeze. The smell of garlic and rosemary fills the room. Jake's in the kitchen behind me, sleeves rolled to his elbows, chopping herbs. It's his night to cook.

I turn on the TV and scroll without purpose. Reality shows. Nature documentaries. Then something catches my eye—a bright red banner blinking across the bottom of the screen.

Breaking News: Woman Missing

It's the local news.

I sit up straighter and increase the volume.

"...Authorities are continuing the search for thirty-nine-year-old Rachel Sinclair, a tourist from Ontario who was last seen two days ago around 10:30 p.m. at the Beach Trail Road gas station. Surveillance footage shows her purchasing a water bottle and protein bar before returning to her rental vehicle. That vehicle has since been found abandoned. Her purse and phone were still inside."

A photo flashes onscreen. The woman is beautiful. Blonde hair. Freckles. Her smile is natural, caught mid-laugh like she wasn't expecting the photo to be taken.

The story continues, *"...a mother of two. Described by family and friends as loving, grounded, and devoted. Her husband, Paul Sinclair, is working closely with authorities..."*

Jake enters, wiping his hands on a towel, a frown on his face as he focuses on the screen. "What's going on?"

My eyes remain glued to the story. "A woman went missing while here in town."

He steps deeper into the room, his expression sharpening.

The camera cuts to a female reporter standing on a cracked two-lane road deep in the woods. Behind her, a strip of yellow tape is strung between the trees.

"This is where Rachel Sinclair's vehicle was discovered late last night," the reporter says, her voice somber. *"It appears she was*

possibly driving too fast, took the sharp corner, then fishtailed and ran off the road. According to the sheriff's department, Sinclair's phone and wallet were still inside the vehicle, and there were no immediate signs of struggle."

The camera pans to the skid marks on the road, then to the backend of a white sedan. The front is in a ditch, mere inches from the trunk of a massive oak tree.

"Oh my God." I launch my torso off the pillow I was leaning against, sloshing a splash of wine onto my lap. "That's right down the road! I recognize it." I twist to look at Jake. "You know that T in the road a few miles from here? Left comes to my driveway. It looks like she went right."

The crease between his brow deepens.

The reporter continues and I twist back around. *"Search and rescue teams have begun combing the surrounding forest, but the terrain is dense, and with temperatures threatening the first frost of the season tonight, time is critical."*

I gasp. "The person I saw in the middle of the night, between the pines? Oh my God—what if that was her? What if she was stranded and looking for help?"

"If you have any information regarding this woman please call the number listed..." A second image of Rachel fills the screen—this one more posed. She's sitting in a back yard with two small children in her lap, a swing set in the background.

Jake doesn't respond right away. His eyes stay fixed on the screen.

"They said she was last seen two nights ago?" he asks.

I look at him, nod. A flicker of tension pulses in my chest, though I don't know what to make of it.

"I'll be right back," he murmurs, setting the dish towel on the counter.

I watch him walk into the guest room where he keeps his duffel bag. The door doesn't close, but I can't see inside. Just hear the rustle of fabric. The zip of a bag.

My mind begins to race.

Last seen two nights ago...
And then it hits me—
That was the night Jake was gone for hours.

The night I found the picture of me and Matthew on the bedside table.

THIRTY-SIX

OLIVIA

There is an undeniable unease pulsing through the house since Jake and I saw the missing woman on the news. We hardly spoke at dinner. And we didn't have sex after. First night since we began sleeping together.

Jake excused himself to the guesthouse, saying he had a conference call.

It's the first time he's left me alone in the house.

Now I'm curled on the couch, legs tucked beneath me, a throw blanket draped over my legs, laptop balanced on my knees. A refilled glass of red wine sits on the end table, nearly full. I haven't touched it.

I open Google and type: *Rachel Sinclair, Ontario.*

Her social media pops up immediately. Facebook. Instagram. Pinterest.

She's stunning, in that effortless suburban-mom way. Long, straight, blonde hair, bright eyes, fit but not obsessive. Her posts are filled with smiling family photos, snapshots of hiking trips and birthday parties. Her last Instagram post is from just weeks ago, showing her laughing at a local farmer's market, holding up a giant head of lettuce like it's a trophy.

She loves to cook. Recipes fill her Pinterest board: crockpot meals, sourdough tips, kids' lunch hacks. She's also into fitness—running selfies, a few gym boomerangs with encouraging hashtags like momswholift and strongnotskinny.

I click into her husband's page.

Paul Sinclair.

He's average. Red hair, pale skin, not nearly as fit as Rachel. He might have been handsome once, but he looks like someone who has given up on life and let themselves go.

The latest post on his feed is a news interview.

He stands outside their home, gripping the hand of his son, who is mid-sob and clutching his thigh. The other child, a little girl with big blonde curls, stands stiffly beside him, holding her own hands and blinking at the camera like she understands too much.

The caption of the video reads: *Help Us Find Rachel.*

Paul's voice shakes. "She wanted to take a few days to herself. Sightseeing in D.C., she said. She said she just needed to reset."

He wipes his mouth, his hand trembling slightly. His eyes flit toward the kids—one now sniffling, the other chewing nervously on a sleeve.

"When she stopped responding to my texts," he continues, "I began checking her location using the tracking option we both have on our phones." His throat bobs with a hard swallow. "I... I just wanted to make sure she was safe."

The reporter—a sharp-eyed woman in a beige coat, hair pulled into a sleek knot—nods solemnly. "And what did you find?"

"The day after she arrived in the U.S.," he says, voice hollow, "she booked a one-way flight to a small oceanside town in Washington state. Over three thousand miles away from where she visited."

"Where exactly around D.C. did she visit?"

"A place called Potomac Crossing."

My jaw drops.

My blood turns ice cold.

"And she was only there for a day?"

"Right, and then she left, and her cell phone location has been in the same place since hours after she landed—well, was, before the cops took the phone."

"In the middle of the forest, correct?"

"Yes."

"And," the reporter presses gently, "that didn't strike you as odd?"

"No, I mean, yeah, I guess."

"But not enough to report it at that time."

Paul shifts his weight.

"Does she know anyone in Wilderport?"

"Not that I'm aware of."

A long pause. The reporter shifts slightly, her tone soft but deliberate. "Paul, some critics online are questioning the timeline. They're asking why you waited days to report her missing, especially with the odd location of her cell phone."

A flicker of defensiveness crosses his face.

"We—we aren't exactly in a good place right now. We informally separated and so technically wherever she was wasn't any of my business. And I didn't want to panic," he says. "And I was hoping she'd just... answer. Or call me back."

The reporter lowers her voice. "Is there any indication Rachel left voluntarily? Another relationship, perhaps?"

"No," Paul says firmly, jaw tightening.

The reporter nods slowly but doesn't look convinced. "So, while she was in Potomac Crossing for the day, did she do anything unusual?"

Paul reaches into his pocket, pulls out a note card. "The phone's tracker showed she drove straight from the airport to a gated community. She stopped at one house. I gave the address to police."

"Whose house?"

He squints down at the card. "A woman named Sherri Tolan. The home recently changed owners. Looks like she bought it a few months ago."

The camera pans slightly, lingering on the notecard shaking in his hand.

But I don't hear the rest—because I know that house.

It's *my* house. The one Matthew and I shared. The one with marble countertops, glass chandeliers, and secrets rotting beneath the floorboards.

The one I ran from after the trial.

Rachel Sinclair visited my old home in Potomac Crossing. And then she flew here, to the location I chose to begin a new, secret life.

And now—she's missing.

<h1 style="text-align:center">THIRTY-SEVEN</h1>

OLIVIA

Jake returns from the guesthouse.

He pauses in the doorway, immediately sensing the shift. "Olivia?"

I don't answer.

He steps closer. "What is it? What happened?"

I turn the laptop screen toward him, freeze-framed on Paul Sinclair's tearful plea. "This is Rachel Sinclair's husband."

He frowns.

"This interview says she visited Potomac Crossing before she disappeared." My voice is shaking. "Not just Potomac. *My* house. My *old* house."

He stares at me.

"Rachel Sinclair visited the home Matthew and I shared before he died. And then she flew here. To *this town*. And now she's missing."

When he still doesn't respond, I surge off the couch and spin around, face flushed.

"This is crazy, Jake! Jake—you're the *only* one who knows who I really am and where I live now." I drop the laptop on the couch and jab a finger in the air. "*You*."

"Incorrect," he says in the cool, calm tone that usually grounds me. Now it's absolutely maddening. "Me, and the US Postal Service, *and* whoever keeps watching the house, *and* if I had to guess, someone from the gated community where you used to live, probably to forward mail."

I open my mouth to argue, but I can't, because he's right. I left Potomac in such a hurry, I didn't think about covering my tracks. I gave the country club a forwarding address without thinking. Yes, I use my middle name here, but I never changed my last name legally. Yes, I bought the cottage under an LLC, but I'm sure anyone could link that back to me. God, I was so stupid.

"Olivia." His expression darkens. "Do you still seriously think I had something to do with this?"

"Why wouldn't I?" I snap. "I can't ignore the fact that everything started the moment you moved in. The cufflink. The photo. The silhouette outside the window. And now a missing woman who somehow traced my exact path from Potomac to here? And who just so happened to go missing the night you went into town? What am I supposed to think, Jake?" I fling out my arms. "Huh? What?!"

His jaw ticks and for the first time I see a hint of anger in his eyes. "I'm getting kind of sick of this, Olivia. When we sat outside on the porch swing, I asked if you trusted me. You said yes."

"That was before a woman went missing!"

His eyes narrow. "You think I *kidnapped* a woman?"

I turn away, begin pacing. I don't know what the hell to think.

Jake closes his eyes and takes a long, measured breath. "I believe someone who knows who you really are, is targeting you, or at the very least trying to rattle you."

I spin around. "But *why*?"

"I don't know. But I do know that I have had *nothing* to do with any of it." He takes a step forward. "Olivia, it's time. It's time you talk to the authorities. You promised. If anything else happens, you promised you'd call them. This definitely qualifies as something else happening."

He's right.

But God, I don't want to.

I don't want to ruin what I have here.

I pace away from him, arms wrapped around myself. "So what? I just drive to the local station and what—start from the beginning? Start with my husband's business fraud? The press? The trial?"

"I'm not talking about calling the local sheriff. I think you should call the federal agents who knew you back then. Who interviewed you. Who know the truth."

I swallow back a sob and look away.

I can't believe I'm back here. Back in the one place I swore I'd never return to.

THIRTY-EIGHT

OLIVIA

A black SUV pulls into the driveway just after nine the next morning. Government plates. Black tinted windows. Black rims. Lights where there shouldn't be.

Jake watches from the kitchen, arms crossed over his chest, jaw locked tight.

I wipe my palms on my jeans as I open the door (didn't feel like a Kaftan-appropriate occasion).

The man who steps out is tall, mid-fifties, broad-shouldered in a dark blue suit. Silver hair. No sunglasses, just piercing blue eyes and a jaw so square it looks like box.

He looks exactly the same.

Agent Ryland was the only one who didn't treat me like a naïve, gold-digging trophy wife during the interviews. His card was the only one I held onto.

"Agent Ryland," I say, smiling despite the anxiety pulsing through me.

"Good to see you, *Marie*." He winks, then holds out a familiar red-and-white Starlight mint.

I smile wider, unwrapping it without hesitation.

Never once have I seen Ryland without a peppermint in his mouth.

The first time we met, he'd been sucking on one of those mints. Seeing how nervous I was, he offered me one. Ever since then he always had one ready for me. It's a weird little ritual between us now. A small thing. But it feels like a trust commitment of sorts— you help me, I'll help you.

"Come in, come in." I step back and open the door wider.

Jake appears in the doorway between the kitchen and living room, posture relaxed but eyes sharp.

"This is Jake," I say, watching them both closely. I wasn't sure how to navigate the introduction, so I figured keep it simple and address it immediately. "He rents the guesthouse. He's been here since everything started, and is familiar with everything I have to say."

As they shake hands, Ryland says, "I'll need to speak with you separately at some point."

Jake nods. "Of course."

We sit in the living room. I make iced tea, mainly to keep me busy, and set out a few muffins Jake picked up at the farmer's market earlier.

I press my knees together and suck on the mint like it's a lifeline.

Ryland flips open a slim leather notebook.

That's another thing I liked about him. While every other agent typed notes on tablets or dictated into handheld devices, Ryland wrote everything by hand. I once asked him why, and he just shrugged and said, "Tech can fail. Ink smears."

He glances up, eyes sharp but kind. "You alright if we start from the beginning?"

I nod, the mint tucked between my cheek and tongue. "Yeah. Let's start."

"Begin with the cufflink and go in order—the cufflink, the photograph, the figure in the woods. Tell me it all, in your own words."

I explain how each thing felt small and explainable in isolation —but together, the pattern formed, along with the gut-punch certainty that someone knows who I am, and is playing a game I don't understand.

"And when I saw a woman went missing just down the road—days after she visited my old home—I felt like I had no choice but to call." My gaze flickers to Jake. "Something is happening, and I don't know what or why, but I believe it's connected."

"Do you still have the cufflink and the photo?"

"Yes."

Jake, already holding the Ziploc bag we sealed them in earlier, hands it over. He dug the cufflink out of the trash immediately after the photo was found.

"I'm assuming you both have your fingerprints all over it?" Ryland asks, lifting it carefully.

"Only hers," Jake answers. "I never touched either one before bagging them."

Ryland nods. He pulls on a pair of latex gloves.

"We'll do what we can to pull fingerprints," he says, examining the bag's contents more closely.

"How long will that take?" I ask.

Ryland exhales. "Depends. If the prints are clean, we can have a partial or full lift in under forty-eight hours."

"But if the person wore gloves," Jake adds, "we get nothing."

"Right." Ryland nods grimly.

He seals the bag in a padded evidence pouch and scribbles something on a chain-of-custody tag.

"We'll be in touch the moment we get anything. Even a partial could tell us something." Ryland sets the bag aside and leans forward. "Now to the missing woman. You said you've never seen Rachel Sinclair before?"

"Correct. I don't recognize her."

Jake interrupts. "Are you planning to speak with the local authorities about it?"

"Yes," Ryland confirms. "Right after this."

"Will you be taking over the case?"

Ryland pulls a fresh mint from his pocket, glances at me, and lifts a brow.

I open my palm just in time to catch it mid-air. He takes one for himself. We untwist the plastic at the same time.

"I've got to speak to them first," he says finally, popping the mint into his mouth. "If the investigation crosses state lines, which it does, or involves potential foul play—like evidence of abduction—then yes, we'd be the ones to step in. Right now, the fact that she traveled from Canada, to D.C., to your old residence in Potomac, and then here? That already has our attention."

"So technically, it could fall under federal jurisdiction?" I ask.

"Yes. Especially if the local departments don't have the resources or reach."

Jake adds, "And especially if the case involves stalking, breaking and entering, right?"

"*If* her disappearance links to you, yes." Ryland leans back in his chair, sucks hard on the mint. "It's not just about where she went missing—it's about why. And if someone's targeting you, using this woman as part of it... then it's not just a missing person's case anymore. It's part of a much bigger thing."

With that, Ryland flips to a fresh page in his notebook. "Now—let's go back to the day you identified Matthew's body. Walk me through it."

THIRTY-NINE

OLIVIA

The question catches me off guard. "What does that have to do with anything?"

"Well, that's when it all started, right? And it seems like it's all coming back, right? A cufflink that looks like it belonged to your husband, a photo of your wedding day, a woman visiting the old house you two shared together then going missing..."

I nod, then recount it slowly... and carefully. The argument we'd had, me leaving, then not hearing from him for days, then returning home to breaking news of a body found washed up on shore—and how somehow, deep in my gut, I knew that it was him. I tell Ryland about driving to the bridge, then to the morgue. About the look on the coroner's face before he pulled back the sheet. The blood and swelling and bruising, the dirt, the smell of river water soaked into the fabric of his shirt that I'd only just ironed. The scar on his collarbone. The seahorse-shaped birthmark on his ribcage.

When I finish, Ryland's pen stops moving. His expression doesn't change, but there's a flicker—barely there—like he's running my words through a filter.

"And in between now and then, to confirm, nothing like this has happened before? No weird items left in your house? No... feeling like someone was watching you?"

"That's correct. I left Potomac, came here, began using my middle name, and have lived in relative peace since then. "

"Until now..." He watches me a beat too long, eyes narrowing slightly before he scratches his chin. "So what's happened between then and now that might've triggered whoever's doing this? What's changed?"

It's the question that's haunted me for days—the one my mind keeps chasing, even as my heart begs me to let it go.

My eyes flick toward Jake.

Ryland follows my gaze.

The room stills.

The message doesn't need to be spoken aloud: Jake began living on my property (and between my sheets).

Jake is the one thing that's changed.

Ryland nods slowly, reading between every line. Then he says, "Okay. Is there anyone who would take issue with you allowing a new man into your life?"

"No. No one even knows I'm here. It makes no sense."

But even as I say it, something unsettles in my chest. Because it *shouldn't* make sense. But the answer is yes, I do know someone who would take an issue with my new relationship, my new state of happiness. My husband. My very-possessive, dead husband would take a *huge* issue with it.

His gaze lingers again—just long enough for it to feel like a question he hasn't asked.

I hold it. I don't blink.

Then, finally, he looks down at his notepad, thinking. "So you believe no one locally knows you're actually Olivia Grayson. If that's true, then it's someone from your past who has tracked you down. We need to know if this person also knows Rachel Sinclair. If there's a connection." He looks up. "Olivia, *think*. Is there anyone—*anyone*—from your past that knows both you and a woman from Ontario?"

He stares at me expectantly almost like he's trying to coax the answer from me.

"No," I say finally, feeling like I just failed some sort of test.

"Okay." Ryland closes his notebook. "I'll be in touch very soon."

When Ryland leaves, I don't exhale. I just stare out the window, heart pounding, wondering who from my past is coming after me.

And, more importantly, what do they want?

FORTY

OLIVIA

I am going crazy.

I haven't slept in two days. Not really, anyway. A few minutes here and there, maybe, but nothing deep enough to dull the anxiety that feels like it's eating me from the inside out.

Every sound is nefarious now—the creak of the floorboards, the wind against the windows, the rustle through the trees. Even the silence feels suspicious. My home is no longer my sanctuary.

I've begun hiding knives.

One in the bathroom drawer. Another under the console table by the front door. Another underneath the couch cushion. Yet another inside the pocket of my robe.

Jake doesn't know.

He's been trying to distract me—meals, movies, long walks along the bluff—but nothing works. I smile and nod and play along like I'm fine, and then I go back to digging trenches in my mind, preparing for war.

Because somehow I know it's coming.

I'm in the laundry room when he finally catches me.

I don't hear him approach. I'm too focused on securing a blade behind the dryer vent.

"Olivia."

His voice is quiet, but it might as well be a gunshot. I whirl around, eyes wide, heart in my throat—hand behind the dryer.

His frown shifts from confusion to something closer to heartbreak. He blows out a breath, steps into the room.

"Sweetheart. What are you doing?"

The knife clatters to the floor behind the dryer.

"Olivia..."

I step aside. Jake kneels, picks up the knife, stands up again and then studies me. Not with judgment, but concern.

I *hate* it.

"Hey," he says, "come here."

I shake my head, tears springing to my eyes. "Please don't look at me like that."

"How should I look at you?" he whispers. "Like someone I care about? Someone who's clearly terrified and trying to survive?"

He sets the knife on the washer and pulls me in.

I begin sobbing.

"I can't do this again," I murmur between tears. "I can't live like I did back then, Jake. I was scared all the time. Scared of the lawyers, scared of the press, scared of the people who I knew would stop at nothing to get their clients' money. And now it's happening again, only I don't even know who the threat is, or what they want." Then, like an unhinged, hormonal teenager, I wail, "I don't have any money, Jake!"

"Oh baby," he squeezes me tighter. "There's one big difference between then and now. You're not alone this time."

"That's something else... I still don't know if I fully trust you."

He tenses for a moment, but then lowers his chin to the top of my head and just holds me.

We stand like that for a long time.

"I'm scared I'm losing my mind," I whisper.

"You're not. You're doing what people do when they feel like they're being hunted. You're preparing. You're fighting."

"I don't want to fight. I just want to feel safe."

"Then that's what I'll give you. Somehow. We'll figure this out. But I need you to promise me something."

I lift my head, eyes glassy.

"Promise me you'll tell me before you hide another knife."

A broken laugh stumbles out of me, tears still streaking down my cheeks.

"Deal."

He brushes a strand of hair from my face, gaze locked on mine.

"Good," he says quietly. "Because next time, I want to be the one who hands it to you."

I stand barefoot at the kitchen window, a mug of tea cradled in both hands. I haven't touched it. It's just something warm to hold. To distract me.

Outside, Jake kneels in the dirt beside the roses, swaying gently in the breeze.

Maurice and Nora.

He's shirtless, sweat on his neck, jeans streaked with soil. There's a small spade in one hand, a watering can in the other, and a coil of twine tucked in his back pocket. He's tying them together, just above their base, so they'll support each other as they grow.

Something about it guts me.

I press my forehead to the glass and watch as he works. He knows how much this means to me. Like tending to these roses will dry my tears, banish my fear.

He adjusts the soil at their base, patting it gently, and then sits back on his heels. For a moment, he just studies them.

"Please don't hurt me," I whisper.

Then, as if sensing me, he turns toward the window.

I don't move.

Neither does he.

We just look at each other.

He dips his chin—*you okay?*

I nod back.

No words. Just deep understanding. And yet, my gut twists, because somewhere deep inside, I still can't shake the feeling that something is coming.

Something neither of us is ready for.

FORTY-ONE
OLIVIA

It's the middle of the night.

The trees, motionless, loom like sentinels outside the window. There's no moon—just a low stretch of clouds that blocks everything out.

It's the coldest night of the season.

A candle flickers on the nightstand, casting soft golden waves across Jake's bare chest. He's on his back, breathing slow and steady, a hand resting on my hip. We're naked. My thigh is hooked over his, skin pressed to skin, our bodies still humming from sex.

I should be sleeping.

But I can't.

I'm wired and restless.

I shift, and press a kiss to his collarbone, then another. His eyes open, slow and warm. A low smile curves his lips.

He rolls toward me, grabbing my hands and pinning them above my head as he settles on top of me. Our fingers thread together. My breath catches as his mouth finds mine—hungry, commanding.

This is what I need.

Him. Again.

And again—and *again.*

His lips trail down my neck. I tilt my head back, eyes half-closed, lost in the rhythm of his breath against my skin—and then something feels wrong.

Off.

A prickle crawls up my spine, sharp and instinctive, like my body senses it before my mind can name it.

My gaze slides toward the window.

Someone is standing there, in the dark shadows just beyond the window. Wearing all black—eyes fixed straight on me.

My breath catches, every muscle locking tight. The candle flickers, and for a heartbeat the light stretches across a face—half in shadow, half lit. *No.*

No, it can't—

My pulse rockets. I blink hard; once, twice, desperate for the image to dissolve.

It doesn't.

The flame gutters again, and this time I see him clearly.

Matthew.

Standing there.

Staring at us.

My dead husband.

I scream. The sound rips so violently from my lungs I barely recognize it as my own. I scramble backward, hurling Jake off me, knocking the candle off the nightstand, sending it crashing to the floor. I fall off the bed, hitting the ground hard, arms scrambling for something—anything—to protect myself.

Jake is already halfway to the door, boxer shorts hanging low on his hips, gun clutched in his hand.

He must have seen the person, too.

He sprints out of the room, disappearing down the hall, front door slamming open a second later.

Candle.

Still burning.

Still on my knees, I grab the water from the nightstand, splash it over the still-lit candle now shattered on the floor. Then I scramble back to the side of the bed, gripping the nightstand as I drag myself up on shaking legs, eyes fixed to the window, heart pounding like it's trying to escape my chest.

The figure is gone.

Jakes words echo through my mind: *If anything else happens— we call the police. That's the deal.*

I spin around and grab my phone. Drop it once, twice. My fingers fumble as I dial 911.

"Nine-one-one, what's your emergency?"

"My husband," I gasp. "I saw my husband outside. He's supposed to be dead—he *is* dead—but somehow he's here—he's—"

"Ma'am, please stay calm. Are you in a safe location?"

I spin back around and stumble to the window, scanning the tree line for any sign of movement.

Jake's flashlight swings wildly as he sprints across the back yard, past the garden, and into the trees.

I don't see Matthew—or a second flashlight—anywhere in the distance.

The 911 dispatcher's voice buzzes in my ear. "Ma'am, can you hear me?"

"Yes, yes, sorry..."

"To confirm—did you say your husband? Is he currently threatening you?"

"No," I whisper, breathless. "He didn't say anything. He was just... standing outside the window. Watching us. But... he's dead. I —I identified his body at the morgue over a year ago. I don't understand what's happening."

There's a pause. "Alright. We have officers en route to your location. Stay on the line with me. Are all your doors and windows locked?"

"Yes."

I scan the woods frantically, searching for any trace of Jake's flashlight. My knees nearly give out beneath me, so I grip the window frame for support.

"Do you have a weapon?" the dispatcher asks.

"I—no. My boyfriend does. He took his gun—he went after him—"

"Do *not* attempt to engage, ma'am. Do you understand? Stay in a secure area of the house..."

Finally, just past the tree line, a bobbing sliver of white light flickers in the dark. A figure emerges through the trees. His flashlight dangles in one hand, his gun in the other.

Jake.

"I—he's coming back..."

"Your husband?"

"No, my boyfriend."

I squint as he comes into view. He's panting, his bare chest scratched and smeared with dirt. His boxer shorts are soaked from sweat. He's barefoot, and I see the dark glisten of blood across the top of one foot.

"Oh my God." I drop the phone, sprint through the house, out the back door, and run toward him. "Are you okay?"

"I'm fine," he says between breaths, grabbing me by the shoulders. "Are *you* okay? Are you hurt?"

I shake my head violently. "Did you see him?"

Jake's jaw tightens. "He had too much of a lead. I chased him all the way to the creek bed, where I lost sight of him. I didn't want to go farther and leave you here alone."

"Oh my God." Tears of panic well in my eyes. "He's alive, Jake. I saw him. It was him. I *saw* him. I know it sounds crazy, but it was Matthew."

"Did you call the police?"

"Yes."

"Good." He grabs my face, kisses me hard on the forehead. "Good girl, Olivia."

He takes my hand and hurries me inside.

"Do not leave my side, okay?" he says, keeping one hand on my lower back and he guides me into the living room.

I nod but I'm already scanning the windows again.

Because my husband is alive.

My *dead* husband has somehow come back from the grave—and I know exactly what he wants me from me.

And it has nothing to do with Jake.

FORTY-TWO

OLIVIA

A patrol car hums quietly in the driveway, engine still running, its exhaust curling into the night air. The temperature has dropped significantly. A uniformed officer stands near the porch, speaking low into a radio. His voice is calm, like this is just another routine call. But inside, it's anything but routine.

I'm curled tight in the corner of the couch, wrapped in a blanket that Jake draped over my shoulders. My fingers twitch against the soft fleece. The moment feels surreal, just like when I saw my husband's body in the morgue just over a year ago. The difference now is he's not a memory anymore.

Matthew is alive.

The small-town responding officer doesn't believe me. Because of course he doesn't. So I had to go through the whole song and dance of telling him who I really am—my real name, my past, my connection to the man who supposedly died. His jaw dropped. His eyes widened.

He knew the name.

Now it's all out there. My identity. My trauma. The tangled, humiliating truth of the life I escaped. The only thing missing is the local news showing up.

I have a feeling they'll arrive by morning.

There's no taking it back now. No hiding anymore. I feel exposed all over again. Like someone peeled off my skin and left me shivering in the open.

I flinch when a hand grazes my shoulder.

Jake kneels in front of me, places his hand on my knee. He looks like he's been through a war zone. Streaks of dirt mingle with the angry scratches on his neck and arm from chasing Matthew through the woods. I had to force him to clean and bandage the gash on his foot before the cops arrived.

"Babe," he says softly. "They need to ask you a few more questions."

I nod, barely.

The officer steps inside, phone in hand, his flashlight clipped to his belt. He's young. His tone is patient, but I can see in his eyes that he still doesn't believe me. Hell, I don't blame him. How often does someone come back from the dead? He probably thinks I'm delusional from the lingering trauma. Or on medication, maybe.

"Did the man you saw outside your window make any attempt to enter the house?" he asks gently.

"The *man* was my husband," I snap. "Matthew Grayson from Potomac Crossing."

He glances at Jake, then back to me.

"And no," I continue, growing more and more frustrated, "he was just standing there. Watching. And I know he has Rachel Sinclair, the missing woman—I know it."

"How?"

"I just do. She came looking for me, then she disappeared, and now Matthew has appeared. He has her."

The officer opens his mouth, closes, then asks. "When he was at the window, did he say anything? Threaten you in any way?"

"No. I screamed, and he ran."

He's asking the right questions. But there's a weight of awkwardness in the air. Like no one can truly grasp what's happening—because I barely can myself.

We turn our attention to a car pulling up the drive.

The officer excuses himself.

Jake goes to the window, watches, then turns back to me.

"It's Ryland. He's speaking with the officer outside."

"*Ryland?*" My eyes pop. Because if the FBI is here already—if the local cops knew to call *him*—then someone understands the threat.

I bolt upright. The blanket falls off my shoulders. "Ryland will believe me. He was there. He worked the case. He'll listen to me. I know what I saw."

I turn to Jake, scowling, even though he's been nothing but supportive. I speak to him like he's the one questioning me—because maybe I need to say it out loud just one more time. "It was him, Jake. I am one hundred percent sure of it. Just like I'm one hundred percent sure that I *identified* him in the damn morgue. I saw his face, his body. I looked straight at it. The seahorse birthmark on his ribcage, I saw it all. I signed the papers. How can he be alive?"

"Olivia—"

The placating tone breaks me.

"No, Jake! How can he be alive?" I yell, shattering the calm.

The voices on the porch outside go quiet.

I don't care. I'm shaking so hard my teeth knock together. How *the hell* can this be happening?

Ryland walks in, face tight with concern.

"Ryland," I hurry across the room. "How could this happen?"

He grabs my arm to steady me. "We're on it, Olivia. Don't worry. I've got a team on their way to scan the woods immediately, specifically where Jake saw him last. Olivia..." He squints, leaning to demand my total focus. "You're *sure* it was Matthew Grayson?"

"Yes!"

"Okay. Okay. I believe you." He reaches into his pocket, tosses me a mint.

We both go through the rhythm, unwrap, toss paper, pop into mouth.

He asks, "Can you walk me through exactly what you saw—start to finish?"

I retell the story for what feels like the hundredth time in thirty minutes.

"What was he wearing?"

"A black shirt and a black baseball cap."

"Did you notice any distinguishing marks, features, or gestures?"

"No, but it was him. He was just standing there, watching me, like he wanted to scare me. That's what he's doing. He's scaring me. He's making me suffer."

"Making you suffer for what?"

It's the first time I break eye contact.

"I don't know," I lie.

Ryland turns to the officer. "Will you give us a moment, please?"

The officer nods and murmurs something about checking the perimeter again. The door clicks behind him.

"He has her." I say, voice trembling. "I don't know why or how I know—and it makes exactly *zero* sense—but Matthew has Rachel, the missing woman. I know it. I know it in my soul. She came looking for me, and he took her. Have you found her? You *have* to find her."

"Not yet," Ryland says. "We've got a team combing through everything we have. Her hotel, bank activity, rental car. We're looking for any connection between her and Matthew and your past life."

"What about her phone?"

"We've got it. It was found on the front seat, battery pulled, wiped completely. We've got our forensics team trying to recover deleted data, but someone knew exactly what they were doing. They scrubbed it clean."

Jake mutters something under his breath, fists clenched.

"We've also subpoenaed her cloud account and are working

with cell providers to get a timeline of her pings—texts, calls, GPS. So far, the last confirmed ping was near your road."

My stomach sinks.

Jake advances slowly, arms crossed. "What about video surveillance?"

"We've already pulled footage from surrounding traffic cams and convenience stores in town. But it's a remote area. Gaps in coverage everywhere. We're also checking for burner phone purchases in the last month across the tri-state area. That said, with this latest development, we'll pull the footage again looking for Mr. Grayson, too. Did he look the same?"

I nod. "Like death never touched him at all."

"Have you spoken with the medical examiner who dealt with his body?" Jake asks.

"That's number one on my to-do list." Ryland nods.

"What about Rachel's husband? Does he have any connection to Matthew?" Jake continues.

"Paul Sinclair is cooperating, and no, we haven't found a link yet. I've spoken to him twice a day since she disappeared. He's devastated. He said she didn't know anyone in this town. No friends. No family. He said she didn't know you, Olivia Grayson, and has no idea why she would come looking for you."

"I don't know why either!" I yell, snapping under the weight of fear and confusion.

A beat of silence passes.

"Well, I think one thing everyone agrees on is that it appears Rachel was digging into your life, or Matthew's, or both," Ryland says, more gently now.

"How did she get my address here, do you know?"

"A busybody neighbor named Beverly, who got it from someone who works at the front office."

I curse under my breath.

Ryland continues, "We're working under the assumption she didn't just come here on a whim. She came here to find you, or someone sent her. If Matthew is alive, maybe that someone is him."

"Meanwhile," Jake adds, voice tight, "Olivia's home is broken into and someone leaves a cufflink and a photo of her and Matthew. There is no way it's not him, or he paid someone to do it. He is messing with her."

"Agreed, but we have to prove it."

"It doesn't make sense—can I have another mint?" I say.

Ryland tosses me another.

I begin unwrapping, grateful for something to do with my hands. "Why would Rachel Sinclair investigate me? Maybe... could she have worked at Matthew's company? Or maybe she was a client?"

"She didn't and she wasn't. We checked."

Silence falls between us, thick and awful.

I feel Jake's presence step behind me.

"Do you think she's dead?" The question just slips out and I regret it instantly.

Ryland hesitates. "We're treating it as a disappearance under suspicious circumstances. That means we're not assuming anything yet. But we're escalating resources. If we can't get traction soon, we'll be bringing in the behavioral analysis team." He takes a breath. "Listen. We're not giving up. But if what you saw tonight is real—if Matthew is alive—then this isn't just about Rachel anymore."

"What do you mean?"

"If your husband is alive, and he somehow faked his death... it changes everything. It's fraud. It's federal. It means every legal proceeding that followed—his will, his estate, your acquittal, the end of the investigation—was built on a lie. His death certificate is falsified. His insurance claims, if there were any, are now fraudulent. The morgue records? Tampered with. The autopsy? Either forged or someone else's body entirely. And if that's the case..."

He pauses, as if trying to find a softer way to say it.

"Then someone helped him do it. No one just disappears from a federal investigation without assistance. Someone else knows the truth, now. Whether they are still alive or not, I don't know."

Jake places his hand on my shoulder, squeezes.

"Could Rachel have helped him, maybe?" Jake asks, quietly.

Ryland shrugs. "Maybe."

I feel like I have officially entered an alternate universe.

Ryland presses on, voice low. "Faking one's death is a felony. Combine that with conspiracy, fraud, theft, evading federal charges, and possibly obstruction of justice? If he's caught, he'll face decades in prison. Multiple agencies would get involved—FBI, SEC, even the U.S. Marshals. This isn't just about a disappearance anymore, Olivia. It's a federal fugitive case."

A federal fugitive case.

I look up at Jake, needing to see him there. Something to anchor me.

Ryland's tone softens. "But what matters more right now is that we do believe you're in danger, Olivia. If Matthew went to these lengths to escape justice, and he's back now, it's not random. It's intentional. He came back for a reason and he's targeting you."

Jake slides his other hand onto my other shoulder.

"And if Rachel Sinclair is part of that reason that he resurfaced," Ryland says, "we may be dealing with something much worse than fraud."

Ryland turns his focus to Jake. "May I speak to you outside?"

As the door clicks shut, I stare down at my hands. But in my mind's eye, all I see is Rachel's smiling face from her social media posts. Her children—those beautiful, innocent children. Her husband's panic.

Matthew's done this before—played with lives like they were disposable. And now Rachel Sinclair has been dragged into his sick orbit. Every part of me knows it wasn't willingly.

And every part of me believes that if she's still alive, she's in grave danger.

Tears sting my eyes, guilt wrenching through my stomach.

One decision.

Just one.

A single choice I made just over a year ago. At the time, I told myself it was the right one.

Now a woman may die because of it.

And if I don't stop him this time, then I'm no better than he is.

FORTY-THREE
RACHEL

I come to slowly, my mouth dry, my head pounding like a drum.

The air smells faintly of mildew and sewer pipes.

Where am I?

For a second, I can't open my eyes. My lashes are stuck together—crusted with sleep, I think? I'm not sure. But I feel... strange.

Have I been drugged?

When I finally manage to pry open my eyes, only one opens. The other is swollen shut.

Blinking, I take in my surroundings, trying to put it all together. I don't know how I know this, but I get the sense I've been right here for a while. Days maybe.

The ceiling above me is low and yellowed, a water ring blooming like a bruise around the light fixture. A dim bulb flickers overhead, casting a sickly orange glow over the room.

When I wince as my eyes adjust to the light, the pain in my face registers—and it all comes back to me in one dizzying rush. The sharp corner in the road, the silhouette at my window, the hand that grabbed a fist-full of my hair and slammed my face into the car door.

Terror snaps through me like static.

I try to sit up but I can't. My wrists are cuffed to the bed.

A strip of duct tape covers my mouth.

I begin thrashing, kicking, screaming as much as I can through the tape. When I finally stop my chest is heaving and I look around —*really* look around.

I'm alone and inside what appears to be a tiny cabin. The kind of one-room cabin you'd rent for fifty bucks at an off-season campground. No insulation, no locks worth a damn. Filthy. I'm chained to a single bed with a matted floral comforter. The walls are rough-hewn planks, dotted with mold. A space heater rattles in the corner. The single window is covered with blackout curtains, duct-taped at the corners. Across from me there's a counter with a rusted sink, a mini fridge buzzing like it might explode, and a small television set on the national news channel. The volume is too low to make out the words.

I think of my kids. Their beautiful, little faces.

The guilt slams into me.

If I hadn't had an affair with Matthew, if I hadn't become obsessed with finding Olivia, I wouldn't be in this mess.

I have to get out of here—wherever the hell I am.

FORTY-FOUR
OLIVIA

After the last brake lights disappear into the woods, the door clicks closed and it's just us.

I sit on the edge of the couch, knees drawn up. The blanket Jake obsessively keeps draping around my shoulder is puddled around my waist. I've stopped pulling it up.

Jake sinks into the couch next to me and releases a long exhale. For a full minute we say nothing.

He rests a hand on my leg. "What can I get you?"

"I need to look for Rachel," I whisper, my throat raw from screaming. "We have to find her."

"I need you to leave that to the authorities, Olivia. Right now, we need to focus on you."

"I can't." I fidget with the hem of the blanket. "Jake, he's going to come back. I can feel it—I know it in my gut."

Jake's jaw twitches and his eyes narrow. "That's what I'm counting on."

"No," I shake my head. "You can't get involved in this. If something happens... I'd die if you went to jail for assault—or worse."

"Look at me." He squeezes my thigh. "I *will* protect you. No matter what the cost, Olivia."

Tears blur my vision. It's everything I've ever wanted to hear, and yet, my heart aches under the weight of it.

I am in love with Jake. There is no trying to convince myself otherwise. And that terrifies me because I know how a love story can end.

What if Jake hurts me, like Matthew did?

What if something happens to Jake? What if he gets hurt because he's been pulled into my crazy, fucked-up orbit. Like Rachel.

What if Jake betrays me?

What if the very thing I'm clinging to is the thing that will shatter me all over again?

I choke on a sob. "Jake, I've lived through this before. I've had everything torn away. My name, my life, my future. You weren't there when the press crucified me and painted me like an accomplice. When they whispered behind my back in the courtroom. When people crossed the street just to avoid looking me in the eye. When masked men *broke into my house* and *threatened* me." I look down, biting back tears. "You have no idea how bad this can get. He's going to take everything from me again. I know it. And if you get in the way, he'll make sure you pay."

Jake lifts my chin with one finger until I'm looking straight into his eyes. "I'm not afraid of him, Olivia. You are *not* facing this alone. Not anymore. No one's getting to you. Not while I'm here. And no one's getting to me, either."

A single tear spills down my cheek. Then another. I can't stop them.

Jake wraps his arms around me, pulling me tight against him. I let myself melt into him, the only place I've felt truly safe since my world unraveled. Even when I've doubted him, I still felt *safe* with him. It's a weird place for my heart to sit.

His lips brush against my temple. "Let me protect you," he whispers. "I will protect you, Olivia. I just need you trust me."

Trust me.

As I bury my face against his chest, my stomach twists.
The tables have turned, haven't they?
I didn't trust Jake in the beginning...
Now he's the one who shouldn't trust me.

FORTY-FIVE

RACHEL

My thoughts scramble for a plan, but stop the moment a key rattles in the lock.

The door creaks open. A man steps inside and gently closes it behind him. He's not dressed like a villain—no mask, no gloves, no visible weapon. Just a crisp navy-blue golf shirt and tapered joggers, the kind that scream casual wealth. A sleek, expensive watch gleams on his wrist. In one hand, he carries a small grocery sack.

It's Matt.

But also *not* Matt.

I squint, blinking wildly, wondering if it's possible I'm seeing some sort of apparition. According to the news, Matt is dead... so is this his ghost? Or is it the drugs? The blow to my head, maybe? This man looks exactly like my Matt—but it's not him. The build and weight are different. The way he holds himself, even the way he moves, different. It's not Matt.

Still... he's devastatingly handsome, like Matt. A better-looking version, even. A wealthier version, who looks like he came straight off the golf course.

Matt-lookalike studies me quietly as he crosses the room.

"I'm really sorry for the restraints," he says in a calm, measured tone, "but I couldn't risk it." He smiles, soft and apologetic, and even winces, like he genuinely feels bad. "I'm sure that's so uncomfortable."

He even sounds like Matt.

He sinks onto the edge of the bed like this is just some awkward conversation between friends. My muscles tighten beneath the cuffs, but my heart doesn't race like it should. I don't know why. Maybe it's the drugs, or maybe because he's so calm. Also, he doesn't *look* like a killer.

My captor sets the bag beside me and starts pulling things out. Painkillers. Eye drops. A blue gel ice pack that's already sweating. A bottle of water. Peanut M&Ms.

"I saw the ones in your purse—or what was left of them," he winks. "So I got a few packs. I figured it was a safe bet. M&Ms help everything, right? Mom always said that."

He takes a breath and his shoulders fall, as if he's been carrying something heavy. "I know you're confused, Rachel. I don't blame you. But I need you to understand—I'm helping you. I know it doesn't feel that way, and I'm sorry I hurt you. I hated doing it. But you would've run, and that would've been much more dangerous."

He reaches up, brushes a strand of hair away from my face.

I notice that I don't flinch.

"You weren't supposed to come here," he says softly. "You couldn't just let go, and the worst part is that you didn't even realize what you were getting yourself into you. You, Rachel, were digging yourself into a hole that very likely could've buried you."

The way he says my name... it's like he's known it his whole life.

"I know you're here to track down Olivia Grayson, but you need to know that Olivia is not who she says she is. She's not the grieving widow. She's not the sweet girl-next-door. She's a master manipulator. Charming, clever, polished to perfection. But underneath it all? Olivia is a cold, self-serving, calculated liar. She can lie with the kind of ease that makes you question your own memory. For years, I watched her twist people around her finger, then walk away without a second thought. And she did it all with a smile. She is not who she pretends to be."

He pauses, hurt shining behind his eyes. Or is it betrayal? "You're not the only one who came looking for the truth. So did I. But the truth about Olivia is, she'll always protect herself first. Even if it means letting someone else burn for her sins."

I recall the dozens of articles I'd read. The questions and insinuations that Olivia had something to do with Matthew's death. *Everyone* doubted her. Then I think of the way her neighbors described her as off and "too perfect." And for a split second—for the first time ever—a flicker of doubt sparks through me. After all, why would she run away? Innocent people don't run away, do they? Especially not clear across the country and buy a house out in the middle of nowhere.

Maybe he's right. Maybe *he's* the one who's telling the truth. Or he's lying. That's how manipulation starts, isn't it? A seed of doubt. A whisper of warning.

I close my eyes and remind myself that this man bashed my head into my car door, drugged me for days (I think), and tied me to the bed.

As if reading my thoughts, he adds, "Again, I know you're confused, Rachel. I know you don't know if you can trust me right now. I'd really like to explain everything, and I'd really like to remove that awful tape from your mouth, but I need you to promise me you won't scream, okay?"

I don't answer.

He lifts a brow.

Finally, I nod.

"Good. Thank you. Okay. I'm going to take it off—nice and slow."

The tape is carefully pulled away. My lips crack as they part.

We stare at each other for a minute, my captor waiting to see if I'm going to scream, and me waiting to see if he's going to kill me.

There's something about the way he doesn't move away from me, doesn't even seem remotely concerned that I am going to hurt him, that makes me think *he's* not going to hurt *me*. I could technically knee him in the kidney right now. It wouldn't kill him but it would hurt. But why would I do that while he's being so... calm?

"Thank you." He smiles after I don't scream and I feel like I passed some sort of test—and that pleases me. Then he lifts a bottle of water, tips it gently to my mouth, and dribbles it between my lips. I swallow greedily, savoring the cool fluid.

He lifts the corner of the comforter and dabs my chin. "Better?"

I nod again.

Without another word, my captor stands and walks to the sink, keeping his back to me. Again, why is this overly comfortable demeanor so disarming?

I hear the faucet run, and when he turns back, he's holding a damp washcloth.

"Let me help." The Matt lookalike crouches in front of me and presses the cool cloth to the swollen side of my face. The sudden cold makes me flinch, but his touch is light. Almost tender.

"There we go," he says softly. "I know it hurts. You should've seen it earlier. It's gone down a lot."

He sets the cloth aside and lifts the ice pack. "Here. Just for a bit. You'll want to keep that swelling under control. It will keep it from bruising too badly."

I'm stunned into stillness as my captor eases the ice pack into my hand, curling my fingers around it like he's teaching me how to hold it.

Then he pulls out a familiar orange pill bottle, rattles it once, and begins unwrapping the packaging. "Ibuprofen. You've got to stay ahead of the pain."

I shake my head.

"What? Oh." He closes his eyes and sighs. "You think they're drugs disguised as ibuprofen. No, they're not." He shakes out two pills and places them in his palm. "Take a look for yourself."

I do, and they look exactly like the kind I take. Also, I watched him literally remove the foil from the top.

I nod.

"Good." He smiles, pleased, then lifts the water bottle after easing the pills into my mouth. "Small sips. Don't choke."

The Matt lookalike studies me for a second longer, then sets the water aside, and leans forward, resting his forearms on his knees. "I was going to grab something to eat on the way back," he says conversationally. "But I didn't know if you had any allergies or preferences. I figured I'd check with you first—didn't want to assume."

My stomach growls at the mention of food, and he grins like he's just scored a point. "I knew it! Pizza? Thai? Or something lighter? I can go right now. Won't take long."

I blink, disoriented. Dizzy from the interaction. This man is treating me like a guest. Like *his* guest and he's here to serve me. To *help* me so that I didn't make a dangerous mistake.

"I know this is all overwhelming," he says. "But I need you to trust that I'm not your enemy, Rachel. I've done a lot of wrong things, I'll admit that. But everything I'm doing now—everything— is to protect us."

Us.

FORTY-SIX

OLIVIA

I haven't slept—*again*.

Every time I close my eyes, Matthew's there. Staring at me through the open window. An expression not filled with rage, or hatred, but something scarier. A predator's smile just behind his eyes, as if he is savoring every second of my unraveling. Like he's saying: *I know exactly what I'm doing. And I'm going to enjoy destroying you.*

Jake stayed beside me all night, holding me when I trembled, feeding me bites of toast when I didn't want to eat, listening when I rambled, then sitting beside me in silence for hours.

Sometime around five in the morning, we gave up trying to sleep and moved to the living room. Jake built a fire to fend off the last cold snap of the season.

Now, as the late morning light filters through the curtains, I slip off the couch, careful not to attract Jake's attention. He's on a call, outside on the patio. Something for work, he said.

I grab my phone and tiptoe into the bedroom closet, the place I go to unravel, to gather myself, or just hide from the world. Right now, I'm hiding from Jake. Because I know he'd try to stop me from making this call.

I find the number for the Potomac County Morgue and press call.

My pulse picks up as I listen to the ring.

"Potomac County Coroner's Office. This is Dr. Pittman."

"Hi. This is... Olivia Grayson. You might remember me..."

A pause. "Yes. I remember, and your timing is impeccable. I've already spoken with a federal agent. Ryland, I believe."

"I figured." I exhale, relieved I don't have to rehash the story. "I know this sounds weird, but I just need to hear it from you. The night I identified my husband... it *was* my husband, right? I saw the scar on his collarbone. The seahorse birthmark on his ribcage. We both did."

"Yes, I remember," he says in a way that suggests he's been thinking about it as much as I have. "You identified him personally. There was no doubt."

"Right?" I begin chewing on my nail. "But did you do DNA testing? Anything more conclusive?"

"No, and I told the feds that, too. You—his *wife*—gave a confirmed ID. And I recognized him, too. Hell, he and I chatted at the grocery store just days before. We even played golf together a few times. I personally recognized him along with you. Doing additional DNA testing didn't seem necessary."

"Yeah..." I nod, though he can't see me. "Did a woman named Rachel Sinclair ever reach out to you?"

"The missing woman? No. The feds asked the same. I've never heard of her or from her." He exhales. "Listen, Ryland didn't give me much information but I gathered enough to know that there's talk your husband might be alive, but I just don't see how, Olivia. You and I *both* ID'd him. I'm as confused as you are—trust me on this."

Trust me. Those words again. Seems like everyone is telling me to trust them.

"I know," I whisper. "It's crazy, isn't it? Looking back, I just wish something else would've been done to check."

"There was no reason to do more," he says. "Protocol was followed. I did nothing wrong by not doing DNA testing."

"Did you test for anything in his system? Like, I don't know, drugs or poison, or something?"

"No. There was absolutely nothing on his body to suggest he had jumped against his will. Again, protocol was followed."

"I know, I'm sorry—I'm not saying you did anything wrong." I blow out a breath. "I just... I don't understand. If he is alive, how? And why? Why do this?"

"I can't imagine," he replies. "His mother must be beside herself."

I blink.

My grip tightens around the phone.

"I'm sorry—what?"

"I said his mother must be beside herself."

"No... wait... his *mother*?"

"Yeah. Hilda... Hilda Winslow; yes, that's it. She goes by her maiden name, she told me. Anyway, she called not long after everything happened. Said she saw it on the news. They weren't close, I guess."

"What?" I rasp, suddenly cold all over.

"What do you mean, what?" Pittman asks.

"That's not possible." I snort a humorless laugh. "She's dead. Matthew told me himself. He said she died years ago—decades ago."

Another pause. Then: "Wow. Really? Well, that's a conman for you. What a piece of shit he was."

My thoughts begin to spin. A long-ago memory of Matthew echoes between my ears: "*You don't owe me anything, Olivia. It's my pleasure to do this. Before my mother died, I realized she was still paying off her college loans. I couldn't believe it. The stress she carried right to the end. So, no, Olivia, you don't owe me anything. Not money, not favors. Just... let me love you. That's all I'll ever want in return.*"

I never even questioned it. Why would I?

Also... there is no way the FBI doesn't know that she's still alive and hasn't interviewed her. Which can only mean one thing... Ryland isn't telling me everything.

"Do you still have the number she called you from?" I ask. "Maybe on a call log or something?"

"Um..." He hesitates, then, "I'm sure Agent Ryland could—"

"No. Please—um, no. I want to speak to her myself—you know he wouldn't let me call. Please, I'm just asking for a favor."

"Olivia, I—"

"Please. *Please.*"

"Listen, this could get me fired... but I also get the feeling you're potentially in harm's way..." A long pause, then: "As long as you promise not to say you got it from me..."

"I *promise.*"

"Okay... let me see what I can find," he says. "I'll text you soon."

"Thank you so much."

I hang up and sit in the dark, my jaw hanging open.

Matthew's mother is *alive.*

And just like that, another piece of my husband's carefully constructed lie crumbles.

FORTY-SEVEN
OLIVIA

I don't get the text from the coroner until late the next morning. The moment it pings through, I lie to Jake—something about an upset stomach—and slip into the bathroom, phone clutched in my hand.

My reflection startles me.

My skin is pale with hollowed-out cheeks and purplish smudges beneath my eyes. My hair is tangled at the roots, still knotted from sleep, and I haven't showered since... when? I can't remember. The oversized sweatshirt I'm wearing is one of Jake's. It swallows me whole. The sleeves are pushed up past my elbows, the collar slipping off one shoulder. There's a faint stain on the hem from last night's wine.

I tug the curtain aside to look out the window. A line of condensation streaks the glass, and for a moment, it looks like a creepy melting handprint. I wipe it away.

Jake is on the patio, hunched over his laptop. A band of thick fog hovers just above the grass. Despite the cool air, he's barefoot, a mug balanced on the railing beside him, a thin line of concentration running between his brows.

Still here.

Still guarding me.

I close the curtain again, sealing myself into the dim cocoon of the bathroom.

The text message from the coroner is short:

> Matthew's mother's name is Hilda Winslow. She lives in the Memory Care Unit of the Oakland Assisted Living facility, just outside Hudson Bay, north of Toronto.

I thank him, then Google the facility.

The homepage loads slowly, the banner stretched across the top reading: *Oakland Assisted Living – Compassionate Care for Your Golden Years.* A carousel of soft-focus photos scrolls across the screen. Sunlit courtyards, pale green walls, paisley carpet, a woman in scrubs helping a gray-haired man into a wheelchair.

There's a tab marked *Memory Care Unit,* and I click it.

The description reads: *For patients with Alzheimer's, dementia, and advanced cognitive decline. 24/7 care, on-site medical professionals, and secure monitored access.*

I dial the number. The phone rings once... twice...

"Oakland, how may I help you?"

"Yes, hi, this is Marie Dahmer." I cringe at the fake name that came out of nowhere. Dahmer? Jesus. Maybe I should be checking into the facility, not calling it.

"How may I help you, Marie?" the receptionist repeats.

"I'm trying to reach Hilda Winslow."

"Are you a relative?"

"No. Well... yes. Long-lost, you could say."

"So then you know about her dementia?"

"Yes." I swallow deeply, suddenly aware of my pounding heart.

She pauses. "You're her second surprise guest recently."

Second?

"Oh really," I say, trying to act casually. "Who else?"

"A woman, I can't remember her name. But she was very sweet. Brought Ms. Winslow a coffee cake."

Rachel? Could she have visited the facility?

"Anyway," the nurse continues, "let me see where Ms. Winslow currently is..."

My heart pounds as I listen to the key strokes on the other end of the phone.

"Ah, okay, she just finished her mid-morning snack, so she should be awake. I can't promise you'll get much out of her today, but you can try. I'll put you through now."

A series of clicks, and the line rings again.

A soft voice answers.

"Hello?"

"Hi," I manage, clearing my throat. "Is this Hilda Winslow's room?"

"It is. May I ask who's calling?"

"Marie. I was hoping to speak with her."

"Yes of course, she would love that. She's a little foggy, but sweet as ever. Just a moment."

I hear the murmur of encouragement, the rustle of fabric, a creaky bed. Then—finally—a voice.

"Well, hello there," the woman says, warbling and bright. "Are you calling about the birds outside my window?"

I blink. "Um... no, I'm not."

"That's a shame. They're goldfinches. Loud little buggers, but I don't mind. They remind me of wind chimes."

I smile, despite everything. "That's beautiful. I love watching birds."

"Are you calling for money?" she asks abruptly, a sudden burst of anger.

"No—no. Not at all."

"Good." A long pause, a deep inhale. "Because I don't have any."

That makes two of us.

"I was actually calling about your son."

"Oh." Her voice dips, quiet and sad. "Yes. I heard he jumped off a bridge."

The words gut me. Not just the sadness in her voice but how candidly she says it. Like it's a fact that she can do nothing about.

"I was just wondering... have you... have you seen or heard from him in the last year?"

"No," she says without hesitation. "No, I haven't seen him. Not in a long time. Our family fell apart a long time ago."

"Why?"

"So many things."

I wait a beat. When she doesn't say anything else, I press, despite myself. "Can you share a few with me?"

She hums, as if pulling old memories from deep in her psyche. "Well, it all started when my husband left me with nothing."

That sounds familiar.

"And, you see, I was a selfish woman," she continues, almost sing-songy. "Always was. I made bad decisions."

"What kind of bad decisions?"

"Oh honey, many," she says slowly. "For one, I told everyone Matthew was sick. I made up a heartbreaking story, and set up a donation account to get money. People believed me, gave what they could. And on and on the lies went." She pauses so long I check to make sure the call is still connected. "Then Matthew found out, and then came the fights. On and on. A snowball. Too much to ever come back from. Sad, really."

And then, as if we hadn't been talking about fraud and betrayal and broken families, she drifts into a story about the birds outside her window. The little brown ones that flock to her feeder each morning. How one of them has a crooked wing but still manages to land just fine.

"It's the scrappy ones you have to admire," she says, her voice an eerie edge to it. "The ones who keep going, even when the wind is against them."

I listen politely, even though my heart and mind are racing.

I made up a heartbreaking story...

If what she's saying is true—if she lied for sympathy, for money, and used Matthew to do it—then it makes perfect sense why he was the way he was.

When she calls me Amanda and thanks me for chocolates, I know she's slipping. I murmur something vague and kind, and just as I'm about to thank her and hang up, she says:

"Have you ever met my other son?"

I'm stunned. "I'm sorry... your *other* son?"

"Yes. Kyle."

Kyle?

Matthew has a brother? No. Matthew never told me he had a brother. Just like he never told me his mother was still alive.

"Yes. Kyle. Matthew's twin brother," she continues, then chuckles. "I heard they called Matthew a conman on the news. I had a good laugh over that because they really got that one wrong. Kyle was the conman. Ironic, isn't it?"

My heart is pounding so hard it feels like something trying to beat its way out of my chest.

She continues, uplifted now, almost whimsical. "I always told Kyle he had too much charm for his own good. That boy could lie so smooth, he'd make you thank him for it." She lets out a chuckle. "Guess he got it from me. Now, Matthew on the other hand? He was such a sweet boy; had a lot of friends. They called him Matt. It's a shame he never did anything with his life except work at a bar. Kyle and Matthew couldn't have been more different. Emotionally, I mean. Physically they were absolutely identical."

Identical.

She laughs again, and this time a chill rolls up my spine. "You know, the only way I could tell them apart was the birthmark on Kyle's ribcage. Shaped just like a little seahorse. How funny is that? A seahorse!"

I.

Can't.

Speak.

"Hon? You there?"

"I'm sorry—the... the birthmark? What did you just say?"

"That birthmark," she says. "Right there on his ribs. Shaped like a little seahorse. Matthew didn't have any birthmarks, you see. Only Kyle."

The phone slips from my hand and hits the hardwood floor with a dull thud. I stagger back against the bathroom wall, the world tilting beneath me as a single impossible thought takes shape:

I was never married to Matthew—or "Matt." I was married to Kyle this entire time. Matthew's *twin* brother.

My Matthew *is* Kyle.

FORTY-EIGHT
MATTHEW (KYLE)

Rachel's voice is hoarse from days with tape across her mouth, and I nod as if I'm just another sympathetic ear. But while she speaks, I'm running inventory. Always inventory.

There's an order to these things. People think manipulation is improvisation, instinct. They're wrong. It's structure. It's discipline. It's knowing the rules of the game before the other person even realizes they're playing.

1. Environment:

The room has to be controlled before the person can be. Warm enough to keep her body relaxed, not too hot. A body that shivers or sweats becomes unpredictable. The heater rattles, so I let it. White noise steadies people. It disguises silences, blurs time. Curtains taped tight, no light leaks. Disorientation is a gift—when she can't tell day from night, she needs me to mark time for her. The smell is off—mildew, damp wood—but imperfection is useful too. Too much comfort breeds boldness. A little discomfort keeps her looking to me for relief.

2. Restraints:

Never rope. Rope burns escalate panic too quickly, and panic erodes trust. Handcuffs are cleaner. Professional. They leave the possibility of freedom intact. She can flex her wrists, feel her blood moving, convince herself she still owns her body. Enough freedom to keep hope alive. Hope is a leash. The tighter you pull, the harder they resist. Give slack, they follow.

3. Comfort items:

Kindness isn't a gift, it's a tool. Ice packs on a schedule, every two hours. Not sooner. Routine creates dependence. Painkillers, but only if unsealed in front of her, so that she doesn't think it's drugs. That show of honesty is worth more than the pills themselves. Water tilted slow, careful. Always clean up her chin with a cloth. People remember that kind of detail; it translates as tenderness.

4. Food:

Withholding is more effective than giving. Hunger softens edges, blurs anger, makes people pliable. When she's ready to break, then I'll offer food. She'll think of it as generosity, but it's a transaction. Timing is control and control disguised as nurture is the strongest kind.

5. Trust tests:

The tape removal was the first. No screaming, no thrashing. Good. That told me she *wants* to believe me. The next will be food. Then information. Then freedom of movement, carefully rationed. Each compliance test escalates. Each one earns me another piece of her. She won't even notice when she's given herself away entirely.

6. Body language:

Keep mine soft. Posture low. Never tower. I sit at the edge of the bed, forearms loose on my knees, casual, safe. She lies flat on her back. She could twist away, make herself small, kick. She doesn't. She tracks me with her eyes, breath uneven but steady. That means she's made a decision: she's trusting me not to hurt her —at least not right now. That's all I need.

7. Emotional cataloguing:

Her voice cracks when she says my brother's name. Emotional trigger noted. Use it later if I want tears. Avoid it if I want cooperation. People like to think their emotions make them unique. They don't. Emotions are buttons. Learn the control panel and you can run the whole machine.

8. Narrative framing:

Never give them the full truth, never give them the full lie. Too much honesty creates suspicion. Too much deceit creates rebellion. But braid them together and she'll never untangle them. She'll thank me for the lies one day, because they made the truths easier to swallow.

9. Reward and withdrawal:

Every interaction is a transaction. A smile offered, then withdrawn. A cloth dabbed at her cheek, then taken away. A kindness delayed has more value than a kindness given freely. People crave the return of what was withheld more than they appreciate what was constant. That's how attachment is forged.

Checklist complete.

I lean closer, brushing her hair back gently, the way I used to with Olivia when she had a headache. Soft hands sell the story better than words ever could.

FORTY-NINE
OLIVIA

The phone is still on the floor where it landed.

For a long second, I just stare at it, my back pressed to the bathroom wall.

Matthew's twin brother...

The seahorse birthmark... only Kyle...

Ryland.

My fingers feel like they belong to someone else as I pick up the phone. The screen is still lit, the call timer long gone. My heart is pounding so hard it makes my vision pulse.

I scroll through my contacts until I find Ryland's number. For a second, my thumb hovers. Jake would tell me to wait. To let the authorities handle it. To breathe, to think.

But I can't breathe. And I definitely can't just sit here.

I hit call.

The line rings once, twice.

"Ryland." His voice is clipped.

"It's Olivia." My voice comes out pitched and shaky, my words as confused as I feel. "I—I don't understand... I need you to tell me the truth."

A beat of silence, like he's rearranging his mental files. "Grayson. Are you somewhere safe?"

I squeeze my eyes shut. "Jake's here. He's outside. I'm in the bathroom. I just got off the phone with Hilda Winslow."

"What?" he says sharply. "How?"

"The coroner gave me her number. She's in a memory care unit near Hudson Bay." I press my fingers to my temple, trying to keep the world from spinning. "She told me Matthew has a twin. A twin named Kyle. She said the only way she could tell them apart was a seahorse-shaped birthmark on Kyle's ribs."

Silence. Then a soft curse under his breath.

"Ryland." My voice cracks. "Tell me I'm misunderstanding this. Tell me she's confused. She has dementia—she called me another name, she thanked me for chocolates I didn't send, she rambled about birds. Tell me this is just... broken memories."

He exhales, the sound heavy enough I can almost feel it through the phone. "I'm sorry, Olivia."

"For *what*?"

"For not telling you sooner."

My stomach drops. I sink to the closed toilet lid, one hand gripping the edge. "So it's true?"

"Yes," he says quietly. "Matthew has a twin brother. Kyle."

The bathroom air feels like it's slowly suffocating me. "So you knew. You've known this, and you didn't tell me?"

"I couldn't. Parts of this case are sealed," he says. "We're working multiple angles—financial crimes, false identities, missing persons. You're a witness, Olivia, and a potential victim. There were things I wasn't authorized to share."

"Well now I know, so start talking," I snap.

A long exhale, then, "They're identical twins. Same face, same build, same age. On paper, they were almost interchangeable. But personality-wise? Not even close. Matt was the stable one—the one who stayed put, worked a regular job, kept his nose clean. Kyle..." He trails off. "Kyle was talented, charming, and smart, but he used all of that in the worst possible ways. He was very cunning and very good at making people believe exactly what he wanted them to."

Charming. Talented.

My stomach turns.

"Years back," Ryland continues, "Kyle got tangled up in some serious financial fraud with some very dangerous people in Canada. When things started to close in, he panicked. He needed to disappear. So he used Matt's identity to do it."

I press my knuckles to my mouth. "How?"

"Birth certificate, social security, passport. The works. Matt didn't have a footprint in the States, which made it easier to get away with. Kyle took that blank slate and turned himself into Matthew Grayson."

"So the man I married..."

"Was Kyle," he finishes gently. "Using Matt's identity."

I feel like I'm going to throw up. "And you knew this when? When did you figure out there were two of them?"

"We suspected something was off around the time of the so-called suicide," he says. "The timeline never quite added up, the money trail was messy, and there were conflicting reports about where 'Matthew' had been and with whom. But because parts of the trail ran through Canada, we had to coordinate with their federal authorities. That always slows things down—different jurisdictions, different systems. And you had already identified the body at the morgue as your husband."

"But it wasn't," I whisper. "It was Matt's."

"Yes," he says. "That's our working theory. We are currently working to confirm this in a way that will hold up in court but we believe that under the guise of reconciliation, Kyle invited his brother to meet him. We believe he killed Matt, dumped his body, and then used his twin's corpse to fake his own suicide. It gave him an exit. Everyone thought Kyle—posing as Matthew—was dead. Clean break. We didn't make the solid connection until recently— and we've been tracking him ever since."

"So where is he now?"

"If we knew that," he says, voice bleak, "I wouldn't be on the phone with you. I'd be putting cuffs on him."

"And Rachel..." I whisper.

"Yes. She's connected to all of this. We believe she learned something about his real identity. And, as you can imagine, that created a problem for Kyle."

I close my eyes, willing my stomach to stop churning.

"Olivia... I am sorry," he says again. "If it were up to me, you'd have had every piece of this puzzle the second we had it. But it isn't up to me. What you need to know now is this: the man you married —that was Kyle. *Not* Matt. And he is not dead—and we *will* find him."

FIFTY
OLIVIA

I burst from the bathroom, Jake's name tearing from my throat.

He bolts inside, panic already on his face. "Marie? What is it?"

"Matthew isn't Matthew!" I stagger forward. "Matthew has a twin brother named Kyle—I've been married to *Kyle*. He's been using his brother's identity, and he's alive, and stalking me."

Something sparks in Jake's eyes. "How do you know this?"

"I just talked to his mother, Hilda Winslow. She said something about a twin, so then I immediately called Ryland and he told me everything."

Jake crosses the room. "Sit down, Olivia, let's—"

"No!" I shove him back, hysterical. "Don't you see what's happening? I married Kyle Grayson—*not* Matthew."

"What did Ryland tell you, exactly?"

I tell him everything, then—

"But I don't know how, Jake. *How?* I *identified* the body. I saw the birthmark, the scar—I saw them both. And according to his mom, the seahorse birthmark is only on Kyle, not Matt... so how could I have mistaken the identity that day at the morgue?"

Jake's jaw clenches as he shakes his head. "Kyle used a dermatological pigment on Matt's dead body that could last through water and decay without fading away for a few days, at least. He knew the body would be found almost immediately. We believe he'd been planning this for months."

"Wait." My stomach turns to water. "We? Who's *we*?"

Jake frowns. "Didn't Ryland tell you?"

"Tell me what?"

Jake curses again and looks away.

"Tell me *what*?" Anger ignites so fast and hot it's as if my body knows what's coming before I do. "Who is *we*, Jake? How do *you* know all of this?"

When he doesn't respond, I yell his name.

The pain on his face when he finally looks at me tells me everything I need to know.

"Oh my God." My knees buckle, and I grab the back of the couch. "*We* is you and Ryland, isn't it? You work for them, don't you? The FBI. You work with Ryland. You're one of them." My jaw drops. "*That's* where I recognized you from. That's why I felt like I'd seen you before when you first moved in. You were there, weren't you? At the interviews in Potomac?"

He nods slowly. "You and I never officially met—you only saw me once, from a distance. And yes, I do work for the FBI... I'm undercover here, Olivia. I was assigned to Kyle's case when he was being investigated for fraud years ago. We never believed he jumped off that bridge, he was far too narcissistic for that. I've been tracking him ever since."

"You mean tracking *me*, too, then."

It feels like a bomb detonates inside my chest.

"You lied to me," I hiss, my voice shaking so violently I can hardly form words. "You said I could trust you! You let me fall in love with you. You slept with me—oh my God—you *slept* me with me, Jake!"

"Olivia—"

"You son of a bitch!" I scream the words so loud they echo through the house. I grab the nearest pillow and hurl it at him. He doesn't move. Just takes the hit. "You played me! Just like *he* played me—you piece of shit. You *used* me!"

My chest rises and falls in violent bursts as I stand there, staring at him.

"Olivia." Jake steps toward me, his voice ragged, his face etched with pain and panic. "Please—just listen. I didn't come here to fall in love. I didn't expect *you*. But the moment I met you—the second you opened that damn door—everything changed. The moment our eyes met, I felt like someone grabbed my heart and squeezed it. And then when I got to know you I fell. Fast. Hard. I knew I'd do anything to keep you safe. And I have. I *have* protected you—but not because I had to. Because I *wanted* to. Because somewhere along the way, this stopped being an assignment and started being everything I've been looking for. I love you, Olivia. I *love* you. Olivia, please just—"

"Get *the fuck* out of my house."

FIFTY-ONE
OLIVIA

The storm rolls in just after sundown, as if summoned by my mood. Rain lashes the windows and wind howls through the trees. I lie curled on my side, the blankets twisted around me, a pillow clutched to my chest.

Jake is gone.

I threatened to call the police and have him arrested for trespassing and whatever laws he broke by sleeping with a woman he was supposed to be investigating.

And still, he didn't leave. He just stood there, drenched in something that looked far too much like heartbreak. He did everything short of begging—said he'd sleep on the porch, in the truck, in the damn rose garden if that's what I needed. He swore he hadn't lied to hurt me. That none of it—*none of it*—had been fake.

But I couldn't hear through all the rage and embarrassment. I told him that if he truly loved me, he'd go. That if he stayed, he'd only be proving he was just like the last manipulating man I trusted. Because even if everything he was saying to me was true, he'd still lied to his colleagues about our relationship. He couldn't deny he was a liar—and I wanted nothing to do with a liar.

That one landed, and finally, Jake left.

I watched from the doorway as he climbed into his truck and disappeared down the driveway.

And now I'm here, alone in the house that once felt like safety, now like impending doom. My throat is sore from screaming, my soul is sore from crying.

I can't believe the man I loved—the only person who's made me feel anything real since Matthew (Kyle)—has been lying to me all along. Baiting me so I wouldn't kick him out. Gathering intelligence for some case I never asked to be part of.

I *trusted* Jake. I let him in. I gave him my body, my secrets. My heart.

Just like I did with Matthew.

And what did it get me? A husband who faked his death. And now, a boyfriend who never even really existed.

I bury my face into the pillow and begin heaving sobs. A full-blown gasping-for-air ugly-cry.

I hate myself. For falling again. For believing again. For letting my guard down even an inch.

And worse—despite all that—I still love Jake.

I do.

And it's absolutely maddening.

I roll off the pillow just as a streak of lightning splits the sky outside my window, illuminating the empty corner of the room where Jake used to keep his boots.

God, he's gone.

The man I fell in love with is gone while the one who shattered my life is hunting me.

I want one back. I can't get rid of the other.

As a low rumble of thunder rolls through the air, I think: I don't even care if Kyle comes back now.

Let him come.

Let him end it.

Because I don't think I have the strength to keep running.

FIFTY-TWO
RACHEL

"I'm sure you have a lot of questions..." Matt-lookalike prompts, sitting on the edge of my bed, inches from where my hands have been cuffed for days.

I begin with the most important question: "Who are you?"

"My name is Kyle Grayson," he says. "I'm Matthew's—well, you knew him as Matt—twin brother."

My mouth drops open. *Twin* brother?

"Ah," he says hurtfully. "I see by your expression he didn't tell you about me." He shakes his head. "I guess it doesn't surprise me. Matt was really good at keeping secrets."

"What secrets?"

"I've been living here in the U.S. under my brother's identity. That's probably why he didn't tell you about me. We never knew who we could trust."

"What?"

"I know," he says softly, like he's explaining something delicate to a frightened animal. "It's a lot. I'll try to keep it simple. Years ago, I got into some serious trouble back home. My brother—Matthew—he wasn't doing great either. You probably know he dropped out of high school, didn't have many job opportunities.

Debt piling up. We were both drowning... just in different ways. So we made a plan."

He picks up the ice pack he's kept by my side, replacing it every few hours, and leans in slowly, dabbing at my swollen eye with featherlight precision.

"I'm sorry," he murmurs. "It's better but still swollen. You've got to keep pressure on it. Here—" He gently presses the cold pack against my cheek, holding it there with his palm. "There you go. Brave girl."

His words make my stomach twist, but I don't pull away. I don't have the strength.

"See?" he says, brushing hair back from my forehead. "We're already working together."

"You're doing great," he adds. "You're thinking clearly, asking questions. That's what I need. That's what *we* need."

He smiles as if we're partners on a mission.

"So," he continues, "I came to the States under Matt's name. It was the only way. He stayed in Canada, out of sight. I built a new life here. A business I'm proud of. And Matt was part of it. He had partial ownership."

"You're lying," I whisper.

"Well," he gives me a sad, warm smile, "I'm not going to pretend I haven't lied. I've lied a lot. But not about this."

A moment stretches between us and I'm surprised by the rush of emotions that flood me, just speaking about him again.

"What happened to him?" My voice cracks. "Really? The bridge... what happened?"

Kyle's eyes fall. When they rise again, they're glistening.

Now we both have tears in our eyes.

"We didn't make the best business decisions and the SEC was closing in on us," he says. "The investigation was digging up things we thought were buried. And then Olivia—" his voice hardens slightly "—she found out the truth about everything. About the switch, about the company issues. She felt betrayed. Financially, emotionally... and I don't blame her."

He exhales, then shifts closer, like he's letting me in on a secret.

But something about the movement feels off—too deliberate, too staged.

"But Olivia wasn't the type to cry and walk away. She threatened to expose everything. And when she found out about you…" He leans in farther, his eyes flicking briefly toward the window before finding mine again. "She realized she had an angle. She lied and told Matthew she'd contacted you and told you everything. Said she wouldn't allow another woman to be lied to. She told him you were furious and wanted nothing to do with him anymore."

My breath catches.

"He believed her, Rachel. He was already overwhelmed and scared and the thought of losing you pushed him over the edge. That's why he jumped."

I begin crying. I can't help it. My body trembles, and he removes the ice pack and places a blanket over my legs, then rests a hand on my knee.

"And I'm not proud of this," Kyle says, expression full of pain, "but I used the chaos to disappear. Everyone thought his body was mine. So I took my chance. I vanished. I didn't want to rot in a cell for the rest of my life. I just wanted to survive."

He squeezes my thigh. "You can't blame me for what I did. *Please* don't. And I need you to know—I lost him too. I lost my *brother*. I'm grieving too, Rachel. I'm grieving *with* you."

I can't tell if I believe him or if I'm just too broken to fight.

My head tells me it's all an act, but my heart is bleeding,

Could that be his point?

"Wait…" I sniff. "How did you even know I was looking for him?"

"The nursing facility called when you visited our mother," he says. "It's protocol. I'm alerted to non-family visitors."

"So you followed me after that?"

He nods. "For a while. Until I realized you weren't going to let it go. And now… here we are."

He stands abruptly and moves toward the counter. "You need to eat. I need to eat. I can get you whatever you want. Seriously. We'll figure this out together, Rachel."

"I'll stay away from Olivia, I promise," I say, hating the desperation in my voice. "I'll quit digging. Please let me go."

He walks back toward me, crouches beside the bed so that we're eye level. "I *want* to let you go, trust me. But you've put me in a terrible predicament."

"I have?"

He nods solemnly. "One, if I let you go, I don't know what Olivia will do when she finds out about you. I'm sure she's already put together that you were in town to visit her. Do you see? She lied to you, and she won't want that to get out. And, Rachel, she'll do whatever she needs to do to silence you forever." He bites his lip, fighting tears. "I can't risk that. I can't have that blood on my hands. Not after just losing my brother. You have so much going for you, Rachel. I have to protect you.

"And two," he continues, "I'm in a predicament because now you know *my* truth, too. You know the body in the river was my brother, not me. And if you walk out of here, I'm done. They arrest me and I'll be locked up forever. My entire life, gone."

"Where have you been hiding the last year?"

"Mexico... until you came knocking, so to speak."

I close my eyes. Why couldn't I have just left well alone?

"You know what I think?" He leans in closer, voice just above a whisper. "I think fate brought us here. Two people caught in the same storm. You're already part of this, Rachel. You're in it now. But if we work together... we'll survive it. You help me, I help you. We protect each other."

He places a hand over mine again. "You're not a prisoner. You're not my enemy. You're the only person left who knows who I really am. That means something."

He smiles faintly.

"You didn't scream. You didn't fight. You didn't fall apart. That tells me everything I need to know. You are such a strong woman, and I am honored to help you. It's you and me, Rachel. It's *us* now."

His chin begins to quiver. "I just lost the only person in the world who ever really knew me. Don't make me lose you too."

FIFTY-THREE

OLIVIA

I'm still in bed when a knock sounds at the front door.

It's late. Or early. I don't even know anymore. I must've dozed in and out.

Outside, it's pitch black and rain hammers the roof. Still. It's been storming for hours it seems.

I don't move when I hear the knock. Hell, I don't even startle. I'm all cried out of every emotion a human can feel at this point.

Let it be Kyle. I don't care. Let him come end this nightmare. And if it's Jake? He can go straight to hell.

I *don't care* anymore.

"Olivia! It's Ryland!" I can barely make out the voice through the raging storm.

Another knock, louder this time. "It's Agent Ryland. Please open the door!"

I force myself to sit up. Jake must have told him I kicked him out.

Good.

I slink out of bed, and shuffle out of the room. I haven't changed out of the oversized T-shirt and leggings I wore all day, and I'm certain my eyes are swollen from crying so much. Agent

Ryland continues to see me at my absolute worst. It's almost comical at this point.

As I walk to the door, I realize I feel more connected to Ryland than anyone else in my life right now. I trust him. He's been in every version of my hell—the morgue, the trial, the aftermath. He's seen me cracked wide open, stripped down to the rawest parts of myself. He knows my history. My secrets. My scars. Everything I've been through.

I'm grateful for him. Deeply. Weirdly.

I glance at the clock as I pass through the living room.

11:17 p.m.

When I open the door, Ryland is standing on the porch. He's wearing his usual long khaki coat, his hair damp with drizzle, and shoulders splattered with raindrops. His unmarked SUV sits parked in the driveway. Its lights are still on.

He takes one look at me and frowns. "You look like hell."

"I feel like it." I step back, opening the door wider.

"You okay?" he asks, stepping inside.

"No. Not even close."

He pauses at the threshold, careful not to track in water.

"Don't worry about it. Come in. Mud is the least of my cares right now."

I sink onto the edge of the couch as he lowers himself into the chair opposite me, rolling his Starlight mint from one side of his cheek to the other. I take the mint he offers, unwrap it silently, then pop it into my mouth.

"I spoke to Jake," he says cautiously, gauging my reaction.

I look down, begin picking at a loose threat on the cushion.

"I'm sorry I didn't tell you when you called. I was protecting him. I was protecting the operation. But I am really sorry you had to find out the way you did," he says after a long silence.

My jaw tightens, but I say nothing. What am I supposed to say to that?

Me too?

I'm sorry for pretty much my entire existence? I'm sorry for my continued ignorance? I'm sorry I married a man who built his life on lies? Sorry that I ignored every red flag, every gut feeling screaming at me to leave him?

Sorry I didn't speak up when I sensed something illegal was going on?

Sorry there's now an entire federal task force burning resources trying to fix something I didn't have the courage to face sooner?

Sorry I fell in love again, and so stupidly didn't even see the signs the man worked for the feds?

Sorry I'm the walking embodiment of bad decisions?

Ryland releases a long sigh as if reading my thoughts. "Jake is a good man," he says gently. "One of the best. You should know that."

"He's a liar."

"He was doing his job, Olivia."

"Is having sex with me part of his job, too?"

Ryland winces. "I took him off the case. He was too emotionally invested. He... didn't like that very much. Told me he wouldn't back off, wouldn't stop protecting you."

Our attention flickers to a flash of lightning outside the window. The storm is getting worse.

"So... I sent him back to Chicago. Told him I'd pull his badge if he didn't leave the state."

My stomach twists, and for some absurd reason, I feel guilty for getting Jake in trouble. For making him *actually* leave.

"I want to make sure you're clear here," Ryland continues, "Jake lied because he was ordered to. But everything else..." He rubs the back of his neck. "Listen, I've known the guy for over ten years. I can promise you that whatever you guys had... that was real. You can't fake a connection like that. I saw it. I saw it in his eyes, when he spoke about you, the desperation that snuck through when we realized you were in real danger."

I close my eyes, cursing the tears threatening to build.

Thunder booms, shaking the windows.

"Okay," Ryland clears his throat. "That's all I'll say about that. Now. We've made some progress."

My eyes snap open.

"The man who helped Kyle steal Matthew's identity confessed this morning. He works for the Social Security Administration and has been helping Kyle—gave him a clean number, a legitimate financial footprint, even a tax history. He forged business documents and used shell companies to build Grayson Investments from the ground up. Kyle's been living in Mexico under a third identity."

"And what about Rachel?"

"She wasn't just someone who knew the Grayson family," he says carefully. "She was Kyle's brother's lover. She and Matt were in love, in a relationship."

"What?"

"They lived in the same town outside of Toronto. From what we've gathered, they've been having an affair for years. We believe she became worried when he left suddenly and never returned. We believe she came to the States, looking for him. She started digging—that's possibly why she went to your house looking for you—and somehow, Kyle found out."

I close my eyes, feeling the weight of a thousand pounds settle on my shoulders. "And she was a liability. He was worried that she or I would put the pieces together, if we met."

Ryland nods grimly.

Tears spill down my cheeks. "This is all my fault, Ryland. Every bit of it."

He shifts forward in his chair, his voice low and steady. "Hey. Look at me." I do, reluctantly. His expression softens, the hard edges giving way to something quieter. "This is *not* your fault. Kyle conned many, many people. In a sense, you loved a man who didn't exist—not the way you thought he did. You believed what you were shown. That doesn't make you weak, Olivia. That makes you *human*. We don't get to choose the lies we're told—but we do get to choose what we do once we learn the truth. And you've done everything right. You came forward. You're helping us. You're trying to make it right. That's what matters now. Not what you didn't know back then."

He clears his throat and reaches into the pocket of his coat. "On that note..."

He pulls out a smooth, oval-shaped stone—faded pink with a tiny crack running through its center. He holds it out, palm open.

"My wife carried this with her everywhere once she got sick," he says softly. "She used to keep it in her pocket and rub her thumb over it whenever things got bad. She reminded herself she was the rock. Even when everything else was crumbling." He swallows deeply. "Before she passed, she told me to give it to someone who might need it someday."

He presses it into my hand, folding my fingers around it.

"I've never met a woman, aside from my wife, God rest her soul, with your kind of strength. You're the rock now. And you're not crumbling."

"I don't know what to say," I whisper, tears rolling down my cheeks.

"You don't have to say anything," he murmurs. "Just keep going. Like she did. Like I will do until the blessed day I get to see her again."

"I'm so sorry, Ryland." I wrap my hand over his. "And thank you. Thank you for everything."

He dips his chin, clears the emotions away. "Enough of that. Now for the real reason I came over. We have official confirmation now that Kyle killed his brother, and that steps things up a notch. He's no longer just a fraud or a conman. He's a murderer. And that makes him a much bigger threat. Especially to Rachel." He leans in, eyes locking on mine with such intensity that my pulse picks up. "Especially to *you*."

FIFTY-FOUR

OLIVIA

"Protective custody?" I repeat the words he just tossed out, like they're the most normal thing in the world. "What does that mean exactly?"

"It means we take you somewhere safe and secure. Usually out of state. We handle transportation, security, all of it. You're kept off the grid. No phones, no social media, no contact with the outside world unless we supervise it. It's temporary, but it's complete."

"How temporary?"

"As long as it takes to find Kyle. Days. Weeks, maybe."

I look around the seaside cottage that I love so much. My stomach begins to swirl.

"I don't want to leave my home. My life."

"I know. No one does. But that's where we're at. Remember—this isn't punishment. It's safety protocol. When there's a credible, active threat, our job is to isolate the danger and keep potential targets safe."

"And Jake?" I ask before I can stop myself. "Would he know where I was?"

"No. Not unless you authorized it. That's how seriously we take security."

The idea of being completely alone in some unknown place with no one I know—not even Jake—makes my skin crawl.

I swallow hard. "What about my house? My things?"

"It will all be here when you got back. We'd post surveillance and keep a presence around the property. All you'd need is your clothes and whatever toiletries you prefer. We'll handle everything else."

My gaze shifts to the windows, to the roses just beyond the glass—spindly and stubborn, clinging to the trellis despite the heavy rain still falling. My chest tightens. Who's going to water them? Prune them? Speak to them? Who will keep Nora and Maurice from growing too far apart? I can't explain it but those fragile, defiant blooms are the only thing I've nurtured since my world went to hell and I love them so damn much.

I choke back a bitter laugh. My entire life is crumbling, and here I am worried about whether or not my garden will die without me.

I refocus on Ryland, who is watching me intently.

"How close are you to finding both Kyle and Rachel?"

"Getting closer every day."

"You have to find her, Ryland. You *have* to."

Ryland's expression softens. "Olivia, we're doing everything we can. Her car's being combed for prints. We've subpoenaed her credit card records, travel itinerary, pulled airport footage. We're in daily contact with her husband. We're expanding the search radius every day. I promise you, I will keep you updated."

I wrap my arms around myself and stare out the window at the rain falling in sheets.

"I'm so sick of running, Ryland."

"I know."

"And the worst part is that it's all my fault. *All* of this."

"No, it's not."

"Yes, it is," I say sharply, looking at him. "I knew Matthew—Kyle, whatever—was hiding something. I saw the signs and I didn't say anything. I stayed because I enjoyed the lifestyle. How disgusting is that? I didn't voice my concerns, didn't ask questions. And now a woman is missing because of it."

"This isn't your fault, and we're going to find her," Ryland says. "I promise you, Olivia. We won't stop until we do. And until then I need you in protective custody. What do you say?"

"What if I refuse?"

"I hope you don't. But if you do, we'd put you on lockdown. We'd place someone on-site—not Jake, obviously. You'd have round-the-clock surveillance. But Olivia..." His eyes narrow. "I've been doing this a long time. I've seen how men like Kyle escalate. I need you to trust me."

"People keep telling me to trust them, but every time I trust someone I end up being played."

Outside, a gust of wind rattles the windows. Somewhere in the distance, a branch cracks like a shotgun.

"Olivia. Please. I need you to do this."

I glance again toward the garden. My stubborn blooms. My creaky porch swing.

My life.

"I'll go," I say quietly, swallow the ache crawling up my throat. "I'll do it."

"Good. That's a good decision, Olivia." Ryland stands, pulls out his cell phone. "I need to make some calls. Pack a bag. We'll leave within the hour."

I watch Ryland walk toward the front door.

I wonder if we're already too late.

Because Kyle wants revenge, and he won't stop until he gets it.

FIFTY-FIVE
OLIVIA

A little over a year earlier…

I hover at the top of the marble staircase, one hand resting on the banister, trying to make some sort of sense about the visitor we just had. A tall, tattooed, terrifying-looking man who didn't smile. Just like he didn't bother to hide the gun on his hip. It was clear immediately that the man was not law enforcement.

He was a different kind of enforcer.

I answered the door. He asked for Matthew by his first name only. And when my husband appeared at the door, he turned ghost-pale, mouth parting, eyes going wide. Then, just as quickly, he recovered. Smiled. Shook the man's hand and invited him inside.

"Would you mind giving us a moment, sweetheart?" he'd said, placing his hand on my lower back and guiding me toward the back of the house. "Go have a drink under the pergola. We'll only be a few minutes. I'll meet you out there when I'm done."

I knew better than to argue in front of a man like that. So I smiled, nodded, and walked away like a good wife.

Now the man is gone, but the feeling he left behind lingers.

Something is very, very wrong.

My flats click softly across the polished floors as I crest the stairs and veer toward the east wing. Past the media room. Past the observation deck with the white orchids Matthew bought me last week. Each step feels heavier, pulled forward by the dread coiling tighter in my stomach.

The door to Matthew's office is cracked open.

I push it.

My husband sits behind his desk—head dropped into his hands, elbows resting on the dark mahogany. I know he hears me, but he doesn't look up. Under the lamplight, his skin looks even more pale than when he first saw his visitor. His tie is loosened, his blazer tossed carelessly over the armchair.

"Matthew?" I whisper.

When he looks up, his eyes are red. He's been *crying*.

"What's going on?" I rush to his side.

When he doesn't answer, I kneel down next to his chair so that we are eye level.

"Matthew, talk to me. Who was that?"

Still, no answer.

"*Matthew*. Was that... something to do with work?"

He nods once, then drags his fingers through his hair. "One of my clients wants their money." He looks at me, his usually perfectly coiffed hair now sticking up in wild tufts. "I don't have it, Olivia. I haven't had it for a long time. That man was sent by my client to get it—by any means necessary."

My stomach drops.

"Wait." It takes me a second to find my words, if barely at all. "You don't... you don't have it? How much?"

"Too much."

Silence presses like a weight between us. The only noise in the entire house it seems is the faint ticking of a grandfather clock in the next room.

I ball my hands into fists to stop them from trembling. "How long has it been going on?"

"Years," he murmurs. "It started with one deal. One investor. I spent his money, then borrowed to cover it. Same with the next client. And the next, and the next. Then I borrowed more. Then more to cover that. I thought I could fix it. I always fix it."

I knew. I mean, I didn't *know*, but I had a very strong suspicion that my husband's business wasn't clean.

"This time you can't fix it?"

He doesn't even bother answering.

"And now men are coming to our house to get their clients' money by any means necessary."

No response.

"Matthew," I say softly. "Did he threaten you?"

"Yes."

I swallow hard. "Okay... so I'm guessing we can't call the cops because then your business becomes exposed."

"Right."

"So what are you going to do?"

"Not me." His gaze sharpens. "We."

I blink. "We?"

He drops out of his chair and lowers onto the floor with me. He grabs my hands.

"I need your help, wife."

Wife.

My heart begins to pound.

"We need to leave," he continues.

"Leave?"

He nods, solemnly.

"Why do I feel like you don't mean, like, go to a luxury hotel?"

"I mean we need to leave the country."

"*What?*"

"Olivia." He squeezes my hands, the sudden desperation on his face jarring. "One of two things is going to happen: The FBI is going to arrest me—"

"*The FBI?*" I screech.

"Yes. They've been investigating my company for months. Probably longer than that."

My jaw unhinges. I can't even speak.

"Either they're going to arrest me, or my client's debt collector is going to kill me. It's either prison for life, or death. Those are my two options now—*unless I leave.*"

I blink, stunned, trying to comprehend what I'm hearing. The man kneeling in front of me—the man I married, the one who built our empire and swept me into a life of opulence—is unraveling. And somehow, I'm being dragged down with him.

"Olivia," he says, though his voice is trembling so much it sounds like he's begging. "I've made mistakes. I know that—and I'm so, so sorry. I know I haven't been the husband you deserved. I got caught up. The money, the pressure, the image..."

His eyes brim with tears.

"But I swear to you, I've never dishonored you. I've never cheated on you. Not once. You have always been the only woman I've ever loved. I know I should have said it more. But it's true." He holds tighter. "I don't care about the houses, or the cars, or any of it. I care about *you*. I need *you*. If I lose you—I lose everything."

"Matthew..." My voice is nothing more than a whisper.

"No. Please. I'm *begging* you, Liv. We still have a chance. A real one. A fresh start. Just you and me. Somewhere warm, somewhere no one knows us. We'll disappear. Find somewhere we can live like kings and queens. We'll be happy, I swear it. I'll make it right."

He lowers his forehead to our clasped hands, his voice breaking. "I'll be better. I promise. I'll be the man you thought I was when you married me. Just... help me do this. Help me get out. Please."

The dim lamplight above us casts a golden glow across his dark, sweaty hair. His pale, clammy skin. He is a man on the verge of total collapse.

But I know my husband. Better than anyone, really. And I know how good he is at putting on a show. And yet something deep down still wants to believe him. He is my husband after all, and he *has* given me so much. And also I loved him once, long ago.

And I took a vow.

He lifts his head again, looks at me with red-rimmed eyes. His expression reminds me of a scared little child. I've never seen him like this.

"I can't do this without you, Olivia. I don't want to."

My pulse roars in my ears.

I already know what I'm going to say—and he does too because he nods, exhaling loudly, and says, "Thank you. I promise you, you won't regret it, okay?"

I nod, tears filling my eyes.

"Okay." He inhales, renewed with a rush of energy. "We're going to disappear—that's the plan. South America, maybe."

"How? We're just going to pack a bag and jump on a plane and never come back?"

He squeezes my hands again—firmer this time—and it doesn't feel like desperation anymore. It feels like restraint.

"We're going to go for a long drive, park near a trailhead, hike in a few miles, and leave staged signs of a struggle or confusion, like a dropped backpack, torn clothing, maybe. It will look like we got attacked, or into a fight or something. Then we'll exit the forest at a pre-planned spot—miles away—where a getaway vehicle is stashed, already packed with essentials. We'll drive straight to the border, using backroads and cash. It will be days before anyone even realizes we're gone, then they'll find the car, conduct a search party. By then we will be deep in South America."

My eyes must give away my shock and fear because he says, "I know. I know, sweetheart. I don't want to do this, either." His thumb strokes the back of my hand. "But we have to. Olivia, they're going to kill me or arrest me. Do you understand?"

"No." The word spits out before my brain catches up. "No. I can't. This is too much—no. I'm not doing it."

He stills, his eyes scanning mine.

"Olivia... I don't think you're fully understanding... I'm sorry to say this, but you'll go down with me. For fraud. Conspiracy. They'll consider you an accomplice. You *are* my wife, my partner.

You've been by my side since the beginning, and you've been photographed all over the globe spending all my money. Really, you're in this just as much as I am."

My body starts to shake.

He kisses my knuckles. "But I've got a plan, don't you see that? Please don't be scared. This will work. I just... I just need *you*. *Us*. We are in this together. I've told you everything now—no more secrets. There is nothing else left of me. You're the only person left who knows who I really am. That means something."

He sniffs, eye glistening. "If anyone can make it through this it's us. You are such a strong woman, Olivia, and I am honored to be your husband. It's you and me, sweetheart. Forever." He squeezes my hand so tightly that my rings cut into my skin.

My heart pounds painfully in my chest. I stare down at my wedding ring, the diamonds glinting like teeth in the lamplight.

I should say no again.

I should scream.

I should run.

But instead—I nod.

Because what else can I do in this moment?

I'm trapped.

"Okay," I whisper, lifting my chin. "What do I need to do?"

We sit there for hours. Mapping it out. A sudden disappearance. Offshore accounts. New names. A new life.

By the time I crawl into bed that night, I don't even know who I am anymore.

FIFTY-SIX
OLIVIA

Ryland is outside, phone pressed to his ear, pacing beneath the porch light that flickers against the gusting wind. Beyond him is violent rain and pitch blackness. The storm has intensified to scary levels, the rain outside coming down so thick I can't see past my window. There's no way we'll drive in this. Not until it passes.

I'm in my bedroom wondering what one packs for protective custody?

I stare at my suitcase, half-open on the bed, and feel an odd combination of dread and relief. I'm being taken away for my safety—and that's good. A smart decision, which we all know by now does not come easily to me. But leaving my house, my garden, my evening drink on the patio... the pillowcase that smells like Jake...

I release an exaggerated sigh. How can love be so maddeningly fickle? One moment I want to rip Jake's face off, feeling so hurt and betrayed that I want to scream until my throat goes raw. The next, I'm clutching his pillow, burying my face in it just to inhale the fading scent of him. The whiplash of anger and longing is absolutely infuriating. How can I hate him and miss him in the same breath? How can I ache for a man I'm still not sure I trust?

Love isn't supposed to be like this. But maybe, for me, it always is.

What a sickening thought.

I unzip the bag the rest of the way and begin packing.

One pair of jeans, leggings, and baggy sweats.

Two sweaters—one soft, one warm.

Three T-shirts, three sets of pajamas.

My favorite kaftan—because of course.

Toiletries.

Eleven pairs of underwear and one bra.

A travel-size perfume I received as a sample years ago.

My journal and two books I probably won't read.

Again, I find myself staring at the now half-filled suitcase.

For the first time since starting over, I don't have to decide what to do next. Someone else is taking over. Someone else will decide where I go, what I eat, where I sleep. There's a strange, guilty freedom in this, and yet, the relief tastes sour. Because while I'm here, zipping up a suitcase, Rachel—God knows where she is—likely isn't getting to choose where she eats or sleeps or breathes.

If she's even still alive.

And then there's Jake. He's gone because of me, too. Sent back to Chicago, yanked from the case, maybe on the verge of losing his job—all because I allowed him to get too close to me.

Yes, he never should've slept with me. But I didn't exactly stop him, did I?

A loud pop of thunder startles me out of my self-pity, and I remind myself right now, I only have one focus: to pack.

Chewing my bottom lip, I spin around my room.

What else, what else, what else?

More underwear. A woman always needs more underwear.

After officially emptying out that drawer, I return to Jake's pillow on the bed.

You know you're going to do it, a little voice whispers in my head.

Do not do it, the other voice scolds.

"Oh my God," I mutter, quickly removing the pillowcase and stuffing it deep into the corner of my suitcase.

I did it.

I'm just about to close the lid when I freeze.

A chill creeps up my spine, sharp and sudden.

I turn the moment a muffled yell comes from somewhere outside.

FIFTY-SEVEN
OLIVIA

"Ryland!"

I sprint through the living room, pulse racing. Rain lashes against the side of the house, and thunder cracks overhead like the sky is splitting in two.

I yank open the front door and lunge outside, my foot catching on something solid. I fall forward. My knees slam into the wood. My palms slip against something warm and wet. I fall onto my side, just as lightning flashes overhead, illuminating the shape I tripped over that's sprawled across the porch.

Ryland.

Encircled in the yellow glow of the porch light, Ryland lies on his back. His eyes are open and glassy. His lips are parted, slack. Sideways rain splashes into the hollow of his throat, mixing with the blood that's pooling beneath his skull. It's thick and dark and inching toward my knees.

I scream, a gust of wind whirling my hair around my face.

"No! No, no, no, no—" I scramble toward him on hands and knees, slipping on the blood-slick porch.

Gently, I lay my hand on his chest, then his neck.

No pulse.

My head spins.

Muttering pleas I rise to my knees, sobbing uncontrollably. Chest heaving, I hold out my bloodied hands in front of me. I don't know what to do with them.

There's so much blood.

It hits me then that Ryland was shot, likely multiple times—and I need to get *inside*.

I stumble to my feet, slipping in the blood, and clutch the railing to stay upright. I look toward the woods—a blurred black against the sheets of rain—and every hair on my body rises.

I trip over the threshold as I lunge back through the door. I slam it shut and lock it.

My phone. I need to call for help.

Where is it?

It's in the bedroom.

My legs barely hold me up as I stumble down the hallway, feeling like I'm about to vomit.

I round the corner, nearly falling again.

I freeze.

Kyle stands in the doorway, my phone dangling from one of his hands.

The other holds a gun.

He's dressed all in black, boots muddy from the storm. His wet hair is neatly combed back, not a strand out of place. His skin glows pale in the dim hallway light, his eyes bright and alive and so heart-breakingly familiar.

Exactly how I remember him.

Exactly.

Like death never touched him. Like the river never took him. Like he didn't just murder a federal agent outside my front door.

There's not a scratch on him. He looks calm. Collected. *Smug.*

And still, painfully—*terrifyingly*—handsome.

My blood turns to ice.

He smiles, warm and casual, like we're about to sit down for dinner.

"Hello, Olivia."

A scream builds in my chest but never makes it out.

He takes a slow step forward.

"Surprise."

I've lost count of how many days I've been cuffed to the bed in this stinky one-room log cabin.

I'm not sure what's worse—the fever or the fear. My body aches in places I didn't know could ache. My skin feels sunburned from the inside out. I'm drenched in sweat, teeth chattering, throat raw and parched. The nausea is worst though. It comes in waves now, thick and relentless, and feels like the worst stomach virus you can imagine.

Kyle keeps me sedated. With what, I don't know. But it's a serious drug. At first, he was dosing the water and the food, but when I caught on and stopped eating and drinking, he started forcing the pills down my throat with his fingers pressed to my jaw, holding my nose until I swallowed. I stopped fighting it yesterday. I don't have the strength anymore.

The duct tape over my mouth is also back.

I keep thinking about the first night he took me, and how I believed him. I was terrified, but I listened. I wanted to understand. Now, I'm certain every word he told me was a lie.

Sometime during that first night, I heard my mother's voice.

Always listen to your gut, Rachel. It's never wrong.

Every word that he has said about Matt being complicit in his scam is an absolute lie. Matt would never. And I realized then—deep down, with every trembling cell in my body—that this man isn't giving me a choice. He's manipulating me into submission. Making me feel seen, heard, understood. Making me feel like a partner.

And that's when I became absolutely certain that Kyle was going to kill me.

He killed Matt. I know it in my bones. I wonder if he drugged him the way he's drugging me. Slipped something into his drink, then whispered lies into his ear until he saw no other way out but over the edge of that bridge? Or maybe he gave him hallucinogens. I don't know, but three days of this, and honestly, I feel like jumping off a bridge right now, just to end this nightmare.

God, I miss him.

I miss my life. My children. Their loud voices and sticky fingers and cereal crumbs in the couch cushions. I miss my tiny kitchen with the squeaky cabinet door, the fridge magnets shaped like fruit. I miss the clank of the dishwasher and the way my twins would race each other to the bathroom in the mornings.

I even miss Paul—his heavy footsteps, the way he'd groan when his knees cracked, the quiet way he used to hum while scrolling his phone. I miss knowing someone was sleeping beside me, even if things between us had faded to gray.

I miss my car, my run-down little Civic with the broken air vent and the cupholder full of loose change. I miss my desk at work, even the cheap stapler that always jammed. I miss Tanya—loud, inappropriate Tanya with her leopard-print reading glasses and endless stream of gossip. I miss her laugh. I miss Excel spreadsheets.

I miss boring.

I would give anything—*anything*—to be back there. Just one more ordinary day.

Instead, I'm here.

Alone.

He's gone again—he leaves every night. Always after dark. I don't know where he goes, but I assume it's to Olivia.

He's *obsessed* with her.

Suddenly, a sound cuts through the dark.

A vehicle, but this time on the opposite side to where Kyle parks.

My heart stutters. For a second I think I'm imagining it—but then it comes again. The distant hum of an engine.

My pulse spikes so fast it hurts. I twist toward the window, straining against the cuffs until the metal slices into my wrists. Through the sliver of filthy glass, I see headlights weaving between the trees. A car. Someone's out there.

Someone's driving by.

I scream, the sound strangled behind the duct tape. The noise is muffled, pitiful. I thrash harder, the bedframe creaking under my weight. The headlights grow brighter—closer—flooding the cabin walls in white light.

I scream again, until my throat burns, until my lungs feel like they might tear. The light flares—then starts to turn away.

"Please," I try to yell. "Please, I'm here—help—"

The engine slows. For one breathless moment, I swear it's stopping.

But then it accelerates, around a corner, I assume.

Tears fill my eyes as the sound fades into the distance, swallowed by the trees. The glow of headlights vanishes from the window, leaving only darkness.

I sag back against the mattress, sobbing into the tape, wrists bleeding.

No one heard me.

No one's coming.

I am going to die out here.

FIFTY-NINE

OLIVIA

"You son of a bitch." The words barely leave my lips before I lunge forward.

Kyle raises the gun, pointing it directly between my eyes.

I stop in my tracks, adrenaline surging through my veins. The air between us tightens like a wire pulled taut.

"What do you want?" I scream, my voice cracking like the thunder in the distance. "What do you want from me?"

Lightning pops, briefly illuminating the room. The calm, terrifying look on his face.

"What do I want from you?" he mocks, tilting his head to the side and tapping the barrel of the gun to his temple. "Ah yes. That's right. To make you pay for what you did to me."

My stomach drops. Because I've known, deep down, from the very beginning this was never about a new love affair. Never about jealousy.

It's about punishment.

About revenge.

"Where is she?" I ask because that's all that matters right now. "Where's Rachel?"

"Dead."

The word slices through me, but I don't let it show. Instead, I lift my chin and clench my jaw. I refuse to cry. Because that's what he wants. My pain. My guilt. My collapse.

I don't bother to ask why. I already know. Rachel got too close and she became a liability.

I'm trembling inside. Not with fear, but with rage.

"You've been lying to me since the day we met," I seethe. "And you killed your brother, you sick son of a bitch. The brother you never told me about. You took everything from him, his identity, his life, his girlfriend. Why did you let it go this far, *Kyle*?" I spit his name—his real name—like poison. "I'll take responsibility for being a stupid, naive wife who should have left you long ago—no. I should have never even married you in the first place—"

"You fucking cunt," he snarls. Just like that, the calm demeanor is gone, replaced by something far more terrifying.

His eye twitches as he steps closer, gun pointed at my forehead. "You are such an ungrateful *bitch*. You are lucky I married you. I gave you so much—and you took it *all*. The purses, the cars, the dresses, the parties, the private jets. And what did you do in return? You betrayed me. You Spat. In. My. *Face*."

I flinch as he inches forward, his face twisted with fury. The tip of the gun trembles slightly—just enough to tell me he's not in control anymore.

I think of Jake for a flicker of a second—his voice, his steadiness, the way his hand trembled when he told me he wouldn't let anything happen to me. If he knew what was happening right now... if he saw this...

My heart hammers against my ribcage.

If I die here, Jake will come for him. He'll burn the earth to find him. That thought steadies me enough to breathe.

"This is all your fault," he continues, his voice cracking. "I didn't want to kill my brother. But once you bailed on the plan, I needed a new one. So I called Matthew, told him I wanted to make amends. Said I regretted the past and I wanted to reconnect. He drove down immediately."

"And you *killed* him."

"I didn't have a choice!" he screams. "Because of you! I didn't have a fucking choice! I had to run and I needed a body—and what better body than one that looks just like mine? So I drugged him, used a pigment to recreate my scar and birthmark, then we drove to the bridge..."

He watches me recoil—and he likes it. His eyes glisten, and a predatory smile curves his lips. "And yes, you helped," he adds, stepping closer. "You ID'd the body, remember? Your signature's on the paperwork. So really, this whole thing—Rachel, Matthew, even the feds chasing me—it's all your fault. *Everything* is your fault, Olivia."

My eyes dart to the corners of the room. I scan for anything I can use as a weapon. A lamp. A vase. An escape.

If I can just survive long enough for Jake to find me. He will. I know he will.

He leans in, and his voice turns to a whisper. "If you would have just kept up your end of the deal, but you didn't. You didn't keep your promise. That's where it all unraveled. These bodies? They're *your* fault. "

"You're wrong," I say, my voice trembling now. "And you're sick in the head. Rachel didn't die because of me. Neither did Matthew. *You* did that. You made those choices. *You* faked your own death."

In a burst of sudden movement, Kyle slams his fist into the wall. The drywall caves, a crack spidering across the plaster.

"I *died* the moment you turned your back on me!" he roars. "Everything could have worked, Olivia. But *you* made the choice. You betrayed *us*."

"Stop, Kyle." My voice cracks. "Just *stop*."

"And it's all so ironic, isn't it?" He chuckles maniacally, eye swirling with madness. "Everyone thinks I'm the conman here. But they have no idea who they're dealing with, do they? Have you told them, Olivia? Have you told them the truth?"

SIXTY

OLIVIA

A little over one year earlier…

It's still dark when I wake.

I lie there for a long moment, staring at the shadowed ceiling. My body is rigid and soaked in sweat. My heart pounds so hard it feels like it's knocking against my ribcage.

This is it. The day we've spent weeks planning. The day Matthew and I disappear—forever.

I didn't sleep. Not even for a minute. All night, I swung between fury and terror, landing on one final thought: I *hate* him. I hate my husband for putting me in this position. For dragging me into his mess. For looking me in the eye and saying *we* when he meant *me or else*.

He has left me with no choice. My back is up against the wall, and he knows it. I'm the wife, the face beside him in all the press photos. Of course they'll come for me too. Just like he said.

It's that thought of being handcuffed that's kept me up all night. Orange jumpsuits. Steel bars. No windows. No choices. My entire life, gone. And even if I did escape persecution, Matthew made sure I understood that he'll either be thrown in jail or killed— and it will be *my* fault for not going through with this plan. There isn't a save-myself option here. I am screwed either way.

I don't want to do this.

I'm *terrified*.

I swing my legs over the side of the bed and pad barefoot to the bathroom. There, I splash ice-cold water on my face.

It doesn't work. My stomach is swirling so violently that I throw up.

In the kitchen, Matthew is already dressed. The outfit he's chosen for the occasion? A pressed blue dress shirt, and slacks. Because he always dresses like he's going to some big important meeting. His hair is slightly damp from a shower, his face freshly shaved. He's ready.

I'm not.

I'm *so* not.

He looks up and smiles like it's any other morning. "Coffee?"

I nod, but don't answer. My voice is still buried somewhere under the weight of what we're about to do.

He pours two cups, hands one to me. Our fingers brush. I notice his hand is steady.

Mine is not.

"We're good," he says, gently, like he's trying to convince me. "Everything's in place. We leave by ten. We're just a married couple out for a Sunday hike," he adds. "I already sent both Sean and Aaron texts that you and I were going to go on a Sunday drive and hike to look for property to build a cabin retreat. Remember, we talked about that last year."

I do remember. The way he'd spun the fantasy back then, painting a picture of pine trees and mountain air, a cabin with wide windows and a stone fireplace. A place that sounded like freedom. Now it's just another alibi, another story to keep the world convinced we're perfect. His dream has turned into my cover.

He continues, "Everything is in place."

I nod, numb. Sean and Aaron are Matthew's colleagues. I

wonder what will happen to them. Did they know? Will their clients' collectors come after them too? I think of their wives and children.

My stomach lurches again.

God, this is so messed up.

"We'll cross the border tonight," he says, lowering his voice. "Once we're in Mexico, we'll switch plates and disappear."

He sounds almost excited. Energized.

Like this is an adventure. Like we're damn Bonnie and Clyde.

He sips his coffee, then lowers it slowly.

His eyes find mine.

"I love you," he says. "After this, everything is going to be better. We'll wake up every morning on a beach somewhere. No more debt. No more stress. Just us."

He leans in and kisses me, long and slow. I kiss him back.

It's the last time I will.

"I'm going to shower," I whisper.

"Okay. I'm headed down to the basement to grab the rest of the bags I packed last night. Text me if you need anything."

I walk down the hallway slowly. I can't even feel my legs.

When I reach the bedroom, I close the door and press my forehead against it, trying to breathe.

My pulse thunders in my ears.

For a moment I just stand there. Focusing on my breath. On the plan.

On *my* plan.

"You can do this," I murmur. "You *must* do this, Olivia."

I tiptoe to the closet. I reach up behind the shoeboxes on the top shelf and pull down the small black duffel bag I packed in the middle of the night. Inside is everything I've secretly scraped together: A few grand in cash I had in a savings account that Matthew didn't know about, clothes, toiletries, and the last remaining shards of my conscience.

While Matthew was busy crafting the perfect vanishing act, I was quietly planning my escape. My escape from him. From this marriage. From the damn corner he'd backed me into.

Matthew has always had a spell over me. He knows how to speak like he's bleeding from his soul. How to make you feel chosen and cherished—like you're part of him, and he's part of you.

But it took this for me to finally see him for the monster he truly is.

So if Matthew ends up dead, or rots in a prison cell for the lies he built his empire on, that's not my burden to carry. That's on him.

And damn him for ever making me believe it was my job to protect him.

I don't know what happens next or what my fate will be in the wreckage of all this. But I do know one thing with absolute clarity:

I will not live in exile with a man who can make me feel both in love and in danger in the same breath.

Am I betraying my husband?

Yes.

Do I give a shit?

Not. Even. A little.

I glance around the bedroom. The silk bedding. The perfume bottle on the dresser. The ring dish on the nightstand.

None of it feels like mine anymore.

Because it's not.

This is day one of my new life. Whatever that may be.

I open the curtain, glance over my shoulder. Then, as quietly as I can, I punch out the screen, catching it just before it goes tumbling. I gently lay it against the siding. The early morning air rushes in—cool and wet with dew. Birds chirp around me as if they're clapping, celebrating my escape.

I climb out, duffel in hand, my bare feet landing on the damp grass with a soft thud.

I don't look back.

SIXTY-ONE
OLIVIA

The storm rages outside, rattling the windows so hard I'm sure they'll shatter. A pop of lightning slices the room, and for a split second, Kyle looks inhuman—jaw clenched, eyes wild, face contorted into something that belongs in nightmares. His chest heaves, blood dripping from his knuckles onto the crumbled sheetrock. The gun in his other hand is still pointed directly between my eyes.

"Why?" I ask. "Why are you doing all this now?"

He snorts, like the question should be obvious. "Everyone thought I was dead; my picture was everywhere. I had no choice but to leave the country—unlike *you*. Imagine my surprise when I came back to find you here. New name, new home, new life, new boyfriend. Fooling *everyone* all over again, just like you did to me. You make me *sick*, Olivia."

His jaw twitches. "I want to know exactly what happened," he growls, low and controlled. "Start at the beginning. When you decided you were going to ruin my fucking life."

I realize then that Kyle has no idea how I got away from him that morning, where I went, or the aftermath even.

When I don't speak, he screams, spittle flying onto my face. "Talk!"

My mouth is dry. I can hardly speak. "I couldn't do it, Kyle. I couldn't go through with it. So, I made a plan to escape."

"*How*, Olivia?"

I take a deep breath. "Remember while we were packing our go-bags and I suggested you hide them in the basement in case anyone came over, saw them, and asked where we were going? I did that because I knew you couldn't hear a car leave the garage from down there. The next morning when I asked you to get the bags, I snuck out the window, into the side door of the garage, and just started driving. Eleven hours straight."

"Where?" His tone sharpens.

"A cheap motel off I-66," I admit. "A place I knew you would never look for me."

Lightning flashes again.

The storm is intensifying.

"Did you tell anyone? Did anyone help you?"

"Why, so you can go kill them next?"

He takes a step closer, the barrel of the gun closing in on my forehead.

I swallow hard. "No. No one else knew. I hid out for two days —I didn't know if you were looking for me, if you'd declared me a missing person. So I bought a burner phone and called our landline to check voicemails."

"Who had called?"

"There were eight voicemails." My voice cracks. "Worried colleagues, worried neighbors. All asking where *you* were—not me. Asking why *your* phone was off, why *you'd* missed meetings. No one was looking for me—they were looking for *you*."

The corner of Kyle's lip quirks.

God, I hate him *so much*.

"You didn't report me missing," I say, rage bubbling. "Instead, *you* left. You fled the country—*without* me. You became a missing person. You weren't worried or searching for me. No, instead, you carried out the plan—*without* me." I jab a finger into the air, fighting the urge to just leap forward and claw his eyes out. "After all our planning, all your bullshit whispered promises. After your 'we'll live like kings' fantasy, the new names, the new lives. You went through with it—and left me behind."

Kyle moves so fast he blurs. He spins, ripping the lamp from the socket, cord snapping against the wall like a whip before the lamp explodes against the wall next to me. I jump, a scream tearing from my throat before I can stop it. Shards of glass and metal ping against my exposed skin, my neck, my cheek, stinging like needle pricks. The crack of impact is deafening, drowning out even the thunder outside.

The storm outside roars in unison with what's happening inside.

The gun jerks back toward me, Kyle's chest rising and falling like he's been fueled by the destruction.

My hands are shaking, my voice gone. I can't control it anymore—my body, my fear, my fury. He's shredded every last nerve I had left to hold onto.

"Now you know exactly how I feel!" he screams. "Betrayed!"

I snap, screaming back, "Betrayed? I felt *relief*! Because I no longer had to worry about what a monster you'd become..." I curl my hands into fists, my nails biting into my skin. I'm so scared, so mad, so frustrated.

"But it didn't stop there, did it? You *knew* how suspicious it was going to look that I fled town the day my husband mysteriously 'went missing.' You planned on that, didn't you? You knew I'd bail at the last minute—didn't you?"

"Don't say that!" His manic eyes fill with tears. He's become completely unhinged. "That wasn't part of the plan, Liv! I'm *not* lying about this. I meant what I said—I wanted us to leave together."

He heaves a breath and drops his hand—dropping the gun from my face—and begins pacing like a madman.

"And then you go and find someone else. Like *I never existed*." He rakes a hand through his hair, tugging hard at the roots. "You didn't even wait, Liv. You didn't mourn me. You let him into your home, your bed—"

He stops mid-step, twisting toward me, eyes blazing. "You really think he loves you? He doesn't know the first thing about you. I do. I know how you breathe in your sleep, how you bite your lip when you lie, how you run when you're scared. He'll never know you like I do. Do you think you love him, Liv? Is that it? Do you love him the way you were supposed to love me? I bet you would run away with him, wouldn't you?"

The gun jerks back up as he snarls the question, though his hand trembles violently now.

It isn't love driving his rage. It never was. He's furious because I fooled him. Because after years of grooming me, molding me, bending me into something he thought he owned, I slipped through his fingers. I was supposed to be his masterpiece, the one thing he could control. Instead, I became the one thing he couldn't. And he'll never forgive me for it—and he wants me to pay.

Pinned in the corner, my gaze skitters across the room, desperate for anything—a weapon, an exit, a chance. But there's nothing. The walls press closer, the storm whips against the glass, and he's between me and every way out.

"You are still technically married, do you realize that?" He continues, "Your betrayal went far beyond sneaking out that day, it went even deeper when you allowed some random stranger to put his dick inside you."

"Stop it, Kyle." My voice is trembling now.

He loves it.

He steps closer, eyes wild. "I heard you the first night you two had sex, do you know that? I was right outside the window. I heard you moan as you climaxed."

I cover my ears with my hands and close my eyes.

"You know what it reminded me of, Liv? Not us when we were together, because you were always like fucking a limp, cold, dead fish. No, that moan reminded me of my brother's moan when he was choking on the sedative I'd put in his drink."

My eyes pop open. "Are we confessing now? Good. Because I've got one for you. Every night before I went to bed, I prayed you'd die just so I'd be free of you."

"See? You're no better than I am, Olivia. Who else thinks vile thoughts like that? What woman would wish evil things on the man who gave them the world? You thrived in our life together, don't even try to act like you didn't. You liked it. The cars, the dinners, the way people looked at you like you were untouchable. You wore the crown right beside me, Olivia. You were queen of the con. You're no better than me."

"You manipulated me and dragged me into this, just like everyone else in your world."

"You think I dragged you into this? Hell, no. You stayed. You kept the secrets. That makes you my partner, not my victim. You *chose* to stay—never forget that."

"I stayed alive, Kyle. That's what I did. You call it lying? I call it surviving. You destroyed everything you touched, and all I ever did was crawl out from under your wreckage." I take a step forward. "You're not even real. You're a parasite who stole someone else's life because you'd messed up your own so badly. You're *sick*, Kyle."

"And you're a *liar*, Olivia. You don't even go by your real name anymore. You've lied to everyone. The feds, your boyfriend. You made everyone believe that you had no idea what I was up to. But the truth is, you helped me plan it."

"What the hell was I supposed to do?" I yell, breaking under the weight of it all. "I panicked! I figured the only way I was going to get through it was to pretend I had no idea what was happening with your business. I'd go back home, play the part of a worried wife. Say I left for a few nights because you and I had an argument. And because we were fighting and not on speaking terms, of course I'd have no idea where you were."

Thunder booms like a shotgun through the air.

"But that plan didn't work, did it, Olivia?"

"No. Because of you," I seethe. "You faked your own damn

death like some insane lunatic. When I got home I saw the breaking news banner that said…" My voice cracks. "A body was found along Ridgeview Lake. Male. Blue dress shirt. Slacks."

I shake my head, shocked at the tears welling up. "Of course I thought it was you. I was completely gobsmacked. I thought: No, he didn't flee, he didn't vanish, he's dead. I thought maybe one of your clients killed you or something, but no, you dug the knife in deeper by making it look like a suicide. God you are truly, truly sick in the head, do you know that?"

His eyes have gone wild now.

"It could have ended there, Olivia. But no, you were too curious. You had to see for yourself. You picked up your keys and drove to the bridge, and that's where this story began…" His hand trembles as he inches closer. "See? It's *all* your fault."

SIXTY-TWO

OLIVIA

Tears stream down my face. Not because I know I'm about to die, but because of how it all came to this. How stupid I was for thinking I was safe. That I could outwit and escape my evil husband.

Right now, standing here with a gun between my eyes, reliving it all, a part of me does believe him. It was all my fault. I wish I had just gone along with the plan. I would be somewhere in South America—without a gun between my eyes. Rachel would still be alive. And Jake wouldn't have broken my heart, only to be sent away and have his job threatened.

Instead, I chose myself. I snuck out the damn window, to spare myself, and now this is where my story ends.

"Get on your knees," Kyle yells over the rain lashing against the windows.

Tears fill my eyes.

Thunder cracks like a gun shot.

It's so loud it's dizzying—the storm, the adrenaline pumping in my ears.

The lights flicker above me, followed another pop of lightning.

I slowly lower to my knees.

I close my eyes.

"Just do it," I whisper, voice shaking.

"Open your eyes."

When I don't, he screams—

"I said open your eyes!"

Spittle flies onto my face.

I blink, open.

Kyle looms over me, gun pointed to my forehead, execution style.

"I want you to be looking at me when you die. I want my face to be the last thing you see before your rot in hell, you fucking cunt."

The tears come, hot and silent and I lock onto his gaze.

My entire body begins shaking violently as he leans closer, the barrel inches from my forehead.

Looking into my husband's eyes right now, I am completely overwhelmed with such an extreme mixture of both fear and hatred that I think I'm going to pass out.

Then, I think of Jake. His hands. His voice. The way he looked at me.

I think of Rachel. Her beautiful smile. Her wasted bravery.

I think of the roses in the garden. Nora and Maurice. Still feuding.

And I whisper goodbye.

His finger tightens around the trigger.

His lips curl into a smirk.

"You were never good enough for me. I don't even know why I married you. What a disgusting, unfortunate waste of a human, you are. See you in hell, bitch."

CRASH.

The window beside me explodes. Shards of glass shatter across the floor. Wind and rain whip into the room.

I scream, cover my head, and fall to the ground, pulling my knees to my chest.

I'm vaguely aware of someone screaming my name—far away, muffled by the storm.

Then—

A body crashes to the floor beside me with a sickening, wet thud.

I open my eyes.

Kyle's face is inches from my foot. Eyes wide, unblinking. Staring straight at me. His mouth is open slightly, like he was just about to say something.

A bullet hole blooms like a black coin in the center of his temple. Blood trickles from it in a slow, syrupy line, curling down the side of his face. I can smell it.

For a second, I can't move. Can't scream. I'm frozen in his death stare.

Then, hysteria bubbles up and I lurch backward, thrashing, screaming, sobbing, trying to crawl away from his face, from that awful, still-smiling mouth.

My back hits the wall. I curl into myself.

He's still looking at me, blocking my exit. Backing me into a corner, *again*.

I hear the front door crashing open, boots pounding the floor, a rush of movement in the room.

Strong, solid arms wrap around me, lifting me from the floor like I weigh nothing. I gasp, the sudden shift jarring, but then I inhale—and I know.

Cedar. Soap. Gunpowder.

Jake.

My body collapses against his chest, every muscle giving out at once. I clutch his shirt with shaking fingers, bury my face in the space between his neck and shoulder, and begin screaming.

He holds me tighter. With one arm under my knees, the other around my back, he hurries me out of the room. His heart thuds hard against my cheek.

"I've got you," he murmurs into my hair, his voice raw. "You're safe. I've got you."

SIXTY-THREE

RACHEL

I awaken to an explosion of noise.

I startle so hard my body jostles the bed.

A burst of blinding light slices through the cracks in the curtain and the door, like someone has spotlights on the cabin. Rain *hammers* the roof and thunder rattles the walls. Outside, tires crunch over gravel. Boots hit the ground—hard, fast, dozens of them. Men's voices, sharp and commanding, shouting over the roar of the storm.

I can't make out the words. Everything sounds warped, underwater, like I'm trapped in a dream I can't wake from.

My mind spins. Is this a dream?

I clutch the sheets, trembling. The thunder, the yelling, the pounding footsteps—*it's too much.* Too loud. Too fast. My head lolls. I'm so confused. So *confused.*

A voice booms outside, distorted through a megaphone:

"Kyle Grayson—come out with your hands up! This is the FBI!"

But Kyle isn't here.

"This is your final warning, Mr. Grayson!"

Another voice outside, closer now:

"Stack up. Breach in five!"

Stack? Breach? That's what they say when they're about to storm a building. I know that from true crime shows. My breath stalls in my chest.

Then—

BOOM.

The door flies open with a crash like thunder. I scream behind the tape, the sound trapped in my throat.

Black-clad agents flood the cabin—helmets, guns, shields. Shouts everywhere.

Someone else, a woman, drops to their knees beside the edge of the bed. Her voice is calm but firm. "Rachel, my name is Agent Angela Winslow. We're here to rescue you. You're safe now. We've got you."

I nod furiously, tears already pouring down my cheeks. She peels the tape from my mouth gently, then cuts the cuffs from my wrists. I'm lifted to a seated position and handed a bottle of water.

Outside, I hear a voice shouting: "Get Ryland on the phone! We've got her!"

A second voice: "I've tried calling him five damn times. No answer."

"Where is he?"

"Last I heard, he was headed to Olivia's. That was a few hours ago."

"Get someone there, now! Go!"

SIXTY-FOUR
OLIVIA

When we reach the guest bedroom, Jake kicks open the closet door with his foot. My hiding place. My safe place.

He sinks down with me still in his arms, settling us onto the floor. He tucks me against his chest and begins to rock—slow, steady, grounding. His chin rests on top of my head.

"He's dead, Olivia," Jake whispers, voice rough with emotion. "He's gone. He can't ever hurt you again."

My whole body convulses with a sob. "But Ryland," I cry out. "He's on the porch—he was—he—"

Jake's arms tighten. "Yes, I know." His voice cracks. "I was hidden in the pines at the back of the property. I didn't have a clear view of the porch. Of Ryland. I didn't even know he was here. I didn't see Kyle until he was already in the house, in your room. I couldn't get a clean shot through the window—I couldn't risk hitting you so I had to wait. I'm so sorry—I'm so, so sorry."

"No, please—please don't. You saved my life."

I look up, grab his face, force him to look at me. "You weren't too late. You promised you'd keep me safe and you did. Keller would be proud."

The tough exterior cracks. Jake begins crying, and I sob into his chest, curling my fingers tighter around his shirt. "Rachel. He killed her," I whisper, the words hollow and raw.

Jake pulls back just enough to cup my face, his eyes shining fierce and tender. "No, sweetheart," he says. "Not ten minutes ago they raided a cabin across town. She's alive. She's safe."

The relief knocks the breath out of me. I gasp then begin sobbing harder than I have in years. Rachel's alive.

Oh God, she's alive.

Jake rocks me again, murmuring soft words against my forehead.

"I love you," he says suddenly, his voice hoarse with emotion. "I never left, Olivia. Even when Ryland told me to. I've been right outside this house every night, watching over you. Waiting. I knew something was going to happen."

I pull back, searching his face through blurry vision. "You didn't leave? You've been here? All this time?"

He nods, brushing the hair back from my damp face. "I never left—and I never will again. You don't have to be alone anymore."

"Jake, I need to tell you something," I wipe the tears from my eyes. "I... I was going to help Kyle. In the beginning. I agreed to disappear with him. He'd confessed everything to—I knew. But, at the last minute, I couldn't go through with it and I bailed on the plan. I'm so sorry I didn't tell you. I knew—and I lied to the feds. I didn't leave because of an argument, I left because I didn't want to sneak away and spend the rest of my life in hiding. So I snuck out the window and ran."

Instead of surprise or even anger or disappointment, he smiles —soft, sad, proud. "Smart girl."

I blink. "Smart?"

He pulls me closer. "If you hadn't been brave enough to sneak out that window, we never would've met."

He kisses my forehead, gentle and lingering.

And just as I feel myself start to breathe again, the sound of sirens cuts through the air, growing louder, faster, racing up the driveway.

SIXTY-FIVE

OLIVIA

The fluorescent lights hum overhead, the unrelenting white light fueling the stabbing headache between my temples. The air smells of burned coffee and damp rain, like every police station I've ever imagined while watching cop shows. Plastic chairs scrape against linoleum, phones ring somewhere behind a glass partition, and a printer spits page after page into the void.

I sit hunched forward on one of the hard blue chairs, my hands twisted together in my lap. My statement is done, signed and dated, but my mind feels anything but settled. My clothes are damp from the storm, my hair frizzy against my cheeks.

My nerves? Shot.

Across the room, a uniformed officer opens a door.

I look up.

Rachel steps out.

I'm momentarily frozen. She's exactly like the social media pictures, but also so far removed it's jarring. Her face is ghostly pale, her hair greasy and pulled back messily, her eyes rimmed in red. She looks like she hasn't slept in days. And still, there she is. The woman the real Matthew once loved. The woman who lost him.

She hesitates when she sees me, clutching a crumpled tissue in her hand. For a moment, I think she'll turn away. But then, slowly, she crosses the room.

"You're Olivia, right?" she asks, her voice thin, frayed.

I nod. "And you're Rachel."

Her throat works in a deep swallow. "I don't even know what to say. It feels wrong to meet like this."

"I wanted to say..." Tears sting my eyes before I can stop them. "Thank you."

She blinks, surprised. "For what?"

"For looking for Matthew. For not giving up. For being the reason the truth finally came out."

Her lips tremble, and she whispers, "Thank you for saying that."

"Will you sit?"

Rachel lowers herself into the chair beside me, her tissue twisting tighter in her fingers. For a long time, neither of us speaks. The station buzzes with noise around us, but we sit in our own silence, suspended in grief.

"I loved Matthew—Kyle." I say finally. "Or... I thought I did. I clung to him, even through all the lies and manipulation. I wanted to believe there was something real beneath it all." My voice shakes. "And you—you loved him too, in a weird way. *Your* Matthew. The real one. It almost feels like the we lost the same man, just in different ways."

"Right?" Her eyes glisten. "God, I miss him. He was so kind. We were going to get married some day."

I press my fist to my mouth, holding back a sob. "Meanwhile, I was married to his shadow and too weak to leave. To the monster who stole his name. I can't imagine how much worse it feels for you."

"It feels really, really hard," she admits, tears slipping down her cheeks.

We sit in that truth, letting it hurt.

"I keep thinking," I say, my voice barely above a whisper, "I feel like I owe you an apology. If I had done things differently... if I had just ran away with him, maybe none of this would've happened."

Rachel shakes her head, her own tears falling faster. "I think that too. Every day. If I hadn't gone looking, if I'd just stayed quiet—"

"No." I reach for her hand, clasping it tight. "You did the *right* thing."

"And so did you." She looks at me, eyes wet with tears. "You got away from him."

We turn toward each other, knees touching, clasping hands.

"We can't blame ourselves," I say. "Kyle would have wanted this. He would have wanted us sitting here, questioning ourselves, feeling guilty for how we acted—or reacted—when we were just trying to do the right thing. But we're here. We survived. That has to mean something."

Her lip trembles. "I don't know how I'm supposed to go home. To explain any of this. To live with it."

"Then don't do it alone." My voice steadies as I squeeze her hand. "I'll be there. Whatever you need—someone to call in the middle of the night, someone to sit with you when it feels unbearable—I'll be there."

She stares at me, stunned, then whispers, "Thank you."

We lapse into quiet again, only the hum of the vending machine filling the space. After a long while, Rachel lets out a breath that sounds half like a laugh, half like a sob.

"Funny," she says. "I feel like we should hate each other."

I manage a small, broken smile through the tears. "Right? We both thought the other was in love with the same man—our man."

She snorts, shakes her head. "I thought Matt had an entire other family in the States that he'd been keeping from me."

Rachel leans her head against the wall, her tissue crushed to nothing in her fist. I sit beside her, our hands still clasped, the storm outside finally fading.

SIXTY-SIX

OLIVIA

One year later...

Every Saturday morning, we make coffee at the same time.

It doesn't matter that she's in Ontario and I'm on the coast, or that our lives are full and loud and bursting with things we never used to have. Rachel and I still meet—10 a.m. her time, 7 a.m. mine —with oversized mugs and messy buns and zero pretense.

She appears on my screen now, framed by rising sunlight and kitchen chaos. One of the twins behind her is dancing to something on the TV, the other is trying to balance a piece of toast on his head.

"Sorry," Rachel laughs, adjusting her earbuds. "They're feral this morning."

"Mine too," I say, nodding toward the garden window, where Jake is chasing a squirrel out of the tomato bed with a broom. "It's the moon or something."

Rachel grins and warmth blooms across my chest. I love that grin. I love her. I had acquaintances, lunch partners, people who smiled wide but meant none of it. She's the friend I never knew I needed. And now, I can't imagine my life without her.

Rachel texts me daily. Sometimes it's deep—grief over losing

Matt, healing, therapy, PTSD triggers. Other times it's memes, screenshots, pictures of her dinner disasters. We send voice notes, birthday gifts, inside jokes.

"How's Paul?" I ask as I sip.

"He's great," she says. "We actually had dinner with the kids last night, here at my house. He made homemade pizza, and I didn't even yell when he put pineapple on half of it. That's growth, right?"

"Good! And... the date?" I raise an eyebrow.

She blushes. "Fine. Nice, even. No conspiracy theories, no pyramid schemes, and he didn't mansplain the wine list. He has a dog. And all his teeth. Which is apparently the bar now."

We both laugh, but I see it in her eyes — she's trying. She still misses Matt, but she's also moving forward. She'll never go back to the woman she was before. Neither will I.

"I still talk to him, sometimes," she says quietly. "Out loud. Usually in the car."

I nod.

I don't talk to Kyle. Not ever. The moment he left my life, it felt like a thousand pounds had been lifted from my shoulders. I was free—free of my past, my guilt, but also free to become the woman I hadn't realized was waiting to emerge. The real me. And I like her.

I do think of Ryland, though. I carry the pink rock he gave me in my pocket, and every time my fingers brush against it, I smile, knowing he and his wife are together again. I just hope they have Starlight mints in heaven.

For a moment, we sit like that—both of us holding mugs, and memories, and the weight of a past that we didn't choose but lived anyway.

Then Rachel brightens. "Oh! Did I tell you? I got the tickets!"

"For the show?"

"Yes! We got front row balcony. Best seats in the theater. You're going to cry. I'm going to cry. The kids are going to pretend they're too cool and cry anyway."

My heart lifts.

"I can't wait to see you," I say.

She smiles. "You're going to love Ontario in the fall."

There's a pause. Soft, warm. Then, together—

"See you soon, sister."

I rinse out my mug and step barefoot onto the back porch, where the garden hums with early light. Lavender sways in the breeze. Bees drift lazily between the blooms.

The roses are blooming again.

Not just blooming—*thriving*. Nora and Maurice, once twisted in opposite directions, have finally grown toward each other, their stems now tangled in a quiet, perfect knot. As if all that resistance, all that turning away, was just part of the dance that led them here.

It wasn't force that brought them together. It was surrender. The kind that breaks you open.

And now, they bloom—not despite it, but *because* of it.

Like me and Jake.

He's with them now, sleeves rolled up, coaxing a trellis into place with the same gentle precision he once used to stitch a gash in my leg. He doesn't know I'm watching. Jake hums when he works, low and off-key, and talks to the plants. He doesn't know I know that, though.

There are muddy boot prints on the back porch and a sunhat on the hook by the door. The couch has a permanent dent from where he reads at night, and his computer now sits on his desk in the sunroom. I didn't ask him to move in. He didn't ask either. He just never left. And one morning, I realized I didn't want him to.

So we live here now. Together. In this place I once thought I would have to abandon in order to survive.

But this time, I didn't run.

A quote I read recently runs through my head:

Healing doesn't come from fleeing. It comes from reclaiming the space where pain once lived.

I step off the patio and pause at the new garden gate. Jake built it. Cedar, with wrought iron detailing. I thought he was just fixing the hinges, but he came in one morning and handed me a small brass plaque.

"What's this?" I asked.

"Just something I was thinking."

He didn't elaborate. He never does.

Together, we mounted it on the gate. It reads:

THIS IS WHERE WE BEGIN.

There are still nights when I wake up drenched in sweat, heart pounding like it's trying to claw its way out. There are still shadows I can't quite make peace with. But when I walk barefoot through the garden in the morning, when I breathe in the lavender and rose and feel the cool earth between my toes, I remember that I survived.

That I *stayed*.

Jake meets me on the path now, dirt on his hands and a smudge across his cheek. He pulls me into his chest without a word, and kisses me.

We don't need new beginnings.

We just needed the courage to return to what remained.

And grow something new.

A LETTER FROM THE AUTHOR

Dear Readers – let's stay in touch!

Sign up here to hear about my new releases with Storm:

www.stormpublishing.co/amanda-mckinney

Sign up here to be included in my personal newsletter:

www.amandamckinneyauthor.com/contact

If you enjoyed *The Stranger in My Bed* and could spare a few moments to leave a review that would be hugely appreciated. Even a short review can make all the difference in encouraging a reader to discover my books for the first time. Thank you so much!

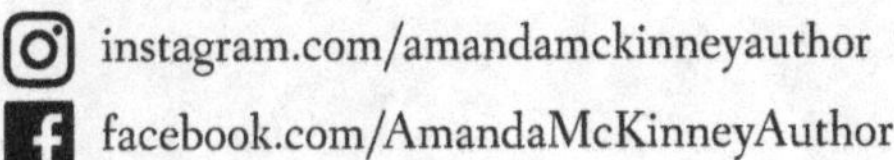

instagram.com/amandamckinneyauthor

facebook.com/AmandaMcKinneyAuthor